BUCK FEVER

For my mother, Helen Fanick, an inspiration

BUCK FEVER

A BLANCO COUNTY MYSTERY

BEN REHDER

ACKNOWLEDGMENTS

Many people contributed their time and effort to this book, and deserve thanks.

Several friends and family members read drafts and offered valuable criticism, including Helen Fanick, James Haught, Martin Grantham, Kate Donaho, and Jacob Winters. Thanks also to Christine Aebi for her sharp copyediting skills. A huge debt of gratitude to Mary Summerall, my friend and mentor, for teaching me how to write. I owe you many lunches. Thanks to Trey Carpenter, David Sinclair, and Jim Lindeman—all with the Texas Parks and Wildlife Department—for their input on everything from wildlife biology to game law, as well as some darn good anecdotes. Health-care and nursing insight was provided by Jill Rodriguez; Spanish-language assistance came courtesy of Joe Brummer; police language and procedural guidance was given by Tommy Blackwell. Thanks, too, to my lifelong buddy Phil Hughes for helping me tweak the plot. A note of appreciation to Jan Reid, a man who inspires writers across Texas, for his assistance. Special thanks to Tim Dorsey for generously aiding a newcomer.

I'd also like to thank the kind people of Blanco County, including Bob and Mary Anne Daughdril, for making a weekender feel at home. Very special thanks to my agent, Nancy Love, and my editor, Ben Sevier, for their wisdom and guidance, and for giving a new guy a chance. And lastly, I'd like to thank my wife, Becky Rehder, for her unending support and encouragement.

All errors, omissions, and distortions of reality are my own.

BUCK FEVER

CHAPTER ONE

BY THE TIME Red O'Brien finished his thirteenth beer, he could hardly see through his rifle scope. Worse yet, his partner, Billy Don Craddock, was doing a lousy job with the spotlight.

"Dammit, Billy Don, we ain't hunting raccoons," Red barked. "Get that light out of the trees and shine it out in the pastures where it will do me some good."

Billy Don mumbled something unintelligible, kicked some empty beer cans around on the floorboard of Red's old Ford truck, and then belched loudly from way down deep in his three-hundred-pound frame. That was his standard rebuttal anytime Red got a little short with him. The spotlight, meanwhile, continued to illuminate the canopy of a forty-foot Spanish oak.

Red cussed him again and pulled the rifle back in the window. Every time they went on one of these poaching excursions, Red had no idea how he managed to get a clean shot. After all, poaching white-tailed deer was serious business. It called for stealth and grace, wits and guile. It had been apparent to Red for years that Billy Don came up short in all of these departments.

"Turn that friggin' light off and hand me a beer," Red said.

"Don't know what we're doing out here on a night like this anyhow," Billy Don replied as he dug into the ice chest for two fresh Keystones. "Moon ain't up yet. All the big ones will be bedded down till it rises. Any moron knows that."

Red started to say that Billy Don was an excellent reference for gauging what a moron may or may not know. But he thought better of it, being that Billy Don weighed roughly twice what Red did. Not to mention that Billy Don had quite a quick temper after his first twelve-pack.

"Billy Don, let me ask you something. Someone walked into your bedroom shining a light as bright as the sun in your face, what's the first thing you'd do?"

"Guess I'd wag my pecker at 'em," Billy Don said, smiling. He considered himself quite glib.

"Okay," Red said patiently, "then what's the second thing you'd do?"

"I'd get up and see what the hell's going on."

"Damn right!" Red said triumphantly. "Don't matter if the bucks are bedded down or not. Just roust 'em with that light and we'll get a shot. But remember, we won't find any deer up in the treetops."

Billy Don gave a short snort in reply.

Red popped the top on his new beer, revved the Ford, and started on a slow crawl down the quiet county road. Billy Don grabbed the spotlight and leaned out the window, putting some serious strain on the buttons of his overalls, as he shined the light back over the hood of the Ford to Red's left. They had gone about half a mile when Billy Don stirred.

"Over there!"

Red stomped the brakes, causing his Keystone to spill and run down into his crotch. He didn't even notice. Billy Don was spotlighting an oat field a hundred yards away, where two dozen deer grazed. Among them, one of the largest white-tailed bucks either of them had ever seen. "Fuck me nekkid," Red whispered.

"Jesus, Red! Look at that monster."

Red clumsily stuck the .270 Winchester out the window, banging the door frame and the rearview mirror in the process. The deer didn't even look their way. Red raised the rifle and tried to sight in on the trophy buck, but the deer had other things in mind.

While all the other deer were grazing in place, the buck was loping around the oat field in fits and starts, running in circles. He bounced, he jumped, he spun. Red and Billy Don had never seen such peculiar behavior.

"Somethin's wrong with that deer," Billy Don said, using his keen knowledge of animal behavioral patterns.

"Bastard won't hold still! Keep the light on him!" Red said.

"I've got him. Just shoot. Shoot!"

Red was about to risk a wild shot when the buck finally seemed to calm down. Rather than skipping around, it was now walking fast, with its nose low to the ground. The buck approached a large doe partially obscured behind a small cedar tree and, with little ceremony, began to mount her.

Billy Don giggled, the kind of laugh you'd expect from a schoolgirl, not a flannel-clad six-foot-six cedar-chopper. "Why, I do believe it's true love."

Red sensed his chance, took a deep breath, and squeezed the trigger. The rifle bellowed as orange flame leapt out of the muzzle and licked the night, and then all was quiet.

The buck, and the doe of his affections, crumpled to the ground while the other deer scattered into the brush. Seconds passed. And then, to the chagrin of the drunken poachers, the huge buck climbed to his hooves, snorted twice, and took off. The doe remained on the ground.

"Dammit, Red! You missed."

"No way! It was a lung shot. I bet it went all the way through. Grab your wirecutters."

Knowing that a wounded deer can run several hundred yards or more, both men staggered out of the truck, cut their way through the eight-foot deerproof fence, and proceeded over to the oat field.

Each man had a flashlight and was looking feverishly for traces of blood, when they heard a noise.

"What the hell was that?" Billy Don asked.

"Shhh."

Then another sound. A moaning, from the wounded doe lying on the ground. Billy Don was spooked. "That's weird, Red. Let's get outta here."

Red shined his light on the wounded animal twenty yards away. "Hold on a second. What the hell's wrong with its hide? It looks all loose and ..." He was about to approach the deer when they both heard something they'd never forget.

The doe clearly said, "Help me."

Without saying a word, both men scrambled back toward the fence. For the first time in his life, Billy Don Craddock actually outran somebody.

Seconds later, the man in the crudely tailored deer costume could hear the tires squealing as the truck sped away.

Just as Red and Billy Don were sprinting like boot-clad track stars, a powerful man was in the middle of a phone call. Unfortunately for the man, Roy Swank, it was hard to judge his importance by looking at him. In fact, he looked a lot like your average pond frog. Round, squat body. Large, glassy eyes. Bulbous lips in front of a thick tongue. And, of course, the neck— or rather, the lack of one. It was as if his head sat directly on his sloping shoulders. His voice was his best feature, deep and charismatic.

Roy Swank had relocated to a large ranch southwest of Johnson City, Texas, five years ago, after a successful (although intentionally anonymous) career lobbying legislators in Austin. The locals who knew or cared what a lobbyist was never really figured out what Swank lobbied for. Few people ever had, because Swank was the type of lobbyist who always conducted business in the shadows of a back room, rarely putting anything down on paper. But he and the entities he represented had the kind of resources and resourcefulness that could sway votes or help introduce new legislation. So when the rumors spread about Swank's retirement, the entire state political system took notice— although there were as many people relieved as disappointed.

After lengthy consideration (his past had to be weighed carefully—life in a county full of political enemies might be rather difficult), Swank purchased a ten-thousand-acre ranch one hour west of Austin. Swank was actually planning on semi-retirement; the ranch was a successful cattle operation and he intended to maintain its sizable herd of Red Brangus. He had even kept the former owner on as foreman for a time.

But without the busy schedule of his previous career, Swank became restless. That is, until he rediscovered one of the great passions he enjoyed as a young adult: deer hunting. The hunting bug bit, and it bit hard. He spent the first summer on his new ranch building deer blinds, clearing brush in prime hunting areas, distributing automatic corn and protein feeders, and planting food plots such as oats and rye. It paid off the following season, as Swank harvested a beautiful twelve-point buck with a twenty-two-inch spread that tallied 133 Boone & Crockett points, the scoring standard for judging trophy bucks. Not nearly as large as the world-renowned bucks in South Texas, but a very respectable deer for the Hill Country. Several of his closest associates joined him on the ranch and had comparable success.

Swank, never one to do anything in moderation, decided that his ranch could become one of the most successful hunting operations in Texas. By importing some key breeding stock from South Texas and Mexico, and then following proper game-management techniques, Swank set out to develop a herd of whitetails as large and robust—and with the same jaw-dropping trophy antlers—as their southern brethren.

He had phenomenal success. After all, money was no object, and the laws and restrictions that regulated game importation and relocation melted away under Swank's political clout. After four seasons, not only was his ranch (the Circle S) known throughout the state for trophy deer, he had actually started a lucrative business exporting deer to other ranches around the nation.

Swank was tucked away obliviously in his four-thousand-square-foot ranch house, on the phone to one of his most valued customers, at the same moment Red O'Brien blasted unsuccessfully at a large buck in Swank's remote southern pasture.

"They went out on the trailer today," Swank said in his rich timbre. He was sitting at a large mahogany desk in an immense den. A fire burned in the huge limestone fireplace, despite the warm weather. He cradled the phone with his shoulder as he reached across the desk, grabbed a bottle of expensive scotch and poured himself another glass. "Four of them. But the one you'll be especially interested in is the ten-pointer," Swank said as he went on to describe the "magnificent beast."

Swank grunted a few times, nodding. "Good. Yes, good." Then he hung up. Swank had a habit of never saying good-bye.

By the time he finished his conversation, a man who sounded just like Red O'Brien had already made an anonymous call to 911.

CHAPTER TWO

JOHN MARLIN, BLANCO County's game warden for nineteen years, thought he had seen and heard it all.

There was the hapless roadside poacher who shot an artificial deer eight times before Marlin stepped from his hiding spot and arrested him. The man claimed he thought it was a mountain lion.

There was the boatload of fraternity boys who unsuccessfully tried dynamiting fish in a small lake. They sank their boat and one young Delta Sig lost three fingers. Even after all that, one of the drunk frat boys took a swing at Marlin when he confiscated the illegal fish.

And, of course, there was the granddaddy of all his strange encounters. The hunter who shot a doe one night out of season. That wasn't strange in itself—but when Marlin found the doe on the ground, it was wearing a garter belt and stiletto heels. The poacher had seen Marlin's flashlight and took off, but he left behind a video camera mounted on a tripod, set to catch all of the action.

Even so, when Marlin took this evening's call from Jean, the dispatcher, he had a little trouble believing what he heard. "A deer suit? You've got to be kidding."

"That's what the caller said," Jean replied. "The ambulance is already on the way. And Sheriff Mackey."

"Six miles down Miller Creek Loop?" Marlin was making a mental note.

"Right. Look for the hole in the fence."

Marlin hung up and started to roll out of bed. Louise, still under the sheets, grabbed his arm. "You're not going to leave me hanging, are you?" She pushed out her lower lip in a mock pout.

"'Fraid so. Duty calls."

Louise was a tall, blonde waitress at the Kountry Kitchen in Blanco. For six months, she and Marlin had enjoyed a series of passionate trysts. No strings attached—an arrangement that suited them both.

Marlin pulled on his khaki pants and his short-sleeved warden's shirt. It was late October, but the evening temperatures still averaged in the low seventies. As he looked for his boots, he told Louise what the dispatcher had reported.

She was equally intrigued. "That's over by the Circle S, right?"

"Yep. Miller Creek Loop is the southern border of the ranch, all the way out to the Pedernales River. From what Jean said, the guy's lying in one of Roy Swank's pastures."

Louise could pick up a trace of sadness in John Marlin's voice. Setting foot on that ranch, even at night, would bring back some bittersweet memories.

"You think Roy will be out there?" Louise asked.

"No idea. Don't really care." Marlin said as he strapped on his holster. Even without his revolver, Marlin was an imposing figure. Just over six foot two, with a broad chest and thick arms. Getting a little thick through the middle in the last few years, but he could still feel the hard muscles underneath. He had short black hair, a square jaw, and eyes that could make a veteran poacher drop a stringer of fish and run.

Marlin bent down to kiss Louise, who let the sheet fall to her waist. She grabbed one of his hands and playfully placed it on her breast. "Hey, that's not fair," Marlin said softly.

"It's your choice. Roam around in the woods playing lawman, or stay here and write me up for some kind of violation." She put special emphasis on the word "violation."

Marlin smiled. "You know you can stay here if you want." He always offered. She always passed. Just the way they both wanted it.

Louise told him to be careful. Then John Marlin went outside, climbed in his state-issued Dodge Ram pickup, and headed out for the Circle S Ranch.

Ten minutes after John Marlin left, Louise let herself out, locking the door behind her. She got into her ten-year-old Toyota hatchback, checked herself in the mirror, and drove away.

Five minutes after that, a small, wiry man with a handlebar mustache slithered out from the crawl space underneath Marlin's small frame house. Marlin had a pair of floodlights at every corner of his house, so a passerby could have easily spotted the intruder. But the quiet country lane Marlin lived on was sparsely populated, so nobody saw the man.

He started at the front of the house, checking the doors and windows. Finding them all locked, he circled around the house and climbed the four steps to the back door. Standing on the small porch, he turned the knob and gently shoved the door with his shoulder, trying to force it open. No luck. He tried a little harder. The door wouldn't give. Pretty soon, the man began throwing himself against the door.

He stopped and took a breath, hands on his knees. After a minute, he faced the door again. He raised his right Wolverine workboot to waist level and began to kick the door with the bottom of his foot. The wooden porch shook with each blow.

With each kick, the man was backing up a little farther to get maximum force. On what was to be his last effort (whether he intended it that way or not), the man accidentally stepped backward off the porch, windmilling his arms wildly as he tumbled down the stairs. He landed hard, his head bouncing smartly on a large limestone rock in Marlin's rustic backyard. Anyone listening would have said the impact sounded like a shopper thumping a ripe melon.

At ten-fifteen P.M. on Thursday, October 28, Barney Weaver, Louise's ex-husband, lay unconscious at John Marlin's back door.

The first thing John Marlin saw after winding his way down the familiar county road was a gauntlet of deputies' cars, volunteer firefighters' trucks, and two ambulances, one on each side of the road. Pulling through the chain of vehicles, he saw Sheriff Herbert Mackey leaning over the hood of his cruiser, leveling a rifle at the oat field on the Circle S Ranch. A deputy was training a spotlight on a massive white-tailed buck, not fifty yards away, prancing around in the field.

Marlin parked his truck and climbed out. As he approached the crowd surrounding the sheriff, he heard Mackey say, "Gentlemen, you're about to learn something about the fine art of marksmanship." Several of the men murmured their approval.

"What's up?" Marlin said to the crowd in general.

Bill Tatum, one of the sheriff's deputies, answered. "Got a crazy buck on our hands, John. Wounded, too."

Marlin looked out at the buck. The animal seemed to know that a rifle was being aimed at it. The big deer would run quickly back and forth across the field and then come to an abrupt stop. Then it would bound on all four legs like a kid on a pogo stick. Marlin could occasionally glimpse a thin trail of dark-red blood running down one of the animals forelegs.

"Looks like a flesh wound to me," Marlin said to nobody in particular. When no one responded, Marlin walked over and stood next to Sheriff Mackey. "Do you really think this is necessary, Herb?"

Marlin knew it bothered Sheriff Mackey when he called him by his abbreviated first name rather than his official title.

Mackey raised his large belly off the hood of his Chevy, spit a stream of tobacco juice at Marlin's feet and said, "Don't see as how I got a choice. Damn buck's gone nuts. Nearly gored us all when we were fetching Trey."

"Trey Sweeney?" Marlin wished someone would tell him the full story.

Bill Tatum spoke up again. "You know about the nine-one-one caller, right? Well, Trey's the one in the deer costume." Tatum nodded toward one of the ambulances just departing. "He took a pretty good hit across the ribs, but he should be all right."

Marlin shook his head and grinned. Trey Sweeney was a state wildlife biologist and Blanco County native. Known for his eccentric behavior, Sweeney had gained national attention when he traveled to Yellowstone Park and holed up for three days with a hibernating black bear. His intention was to prove that the bears are not territorial and will attack only when their cubs or their food supply is threatened. After three days, Trey was certain that his theory was correct. Then the bear, apparently unaware of Trey's presence for the first seventy-two hours, awoke with a yawn, scratched his privates, and tore Trey's right ear off. (The chief reason Trey wore his hair long nowadays.) Trey still counted the whole episode as a victory, maintaining that the bear was only exhibiting post-hibernation playfulness. Nationally recognized wildlife authorities disagreed.

"So what's the story on the buck?" Marlin asked.

"Trey told us it was one of his test deer," Tatum said, referring to the small radio collars Trey had fitted on several deer on the ranch years earlier. The biologist had been conducting an ongoing study on the nocturnal movements of whitetails. "That's all he said. Except for asking us not to shoot it."

The crowd turned toward Sheriff Mackey, still holding his rifle. "That deer is obviously a danger to the community," Mackey said, feeling a little foolish as he looked around the isolated pasture.

Yeah, and he'd look damn good on your living-room wall, Marlin thought.

The sheriff shifted uneasily as the crowd remained silent. Most of the men were hunters and couldn't stand to see a deer killed in such an unsporting manner.

Finally the sheriff asked bitterly, "All right, then. Anyone else got any brilliant ideas?"

"I say we tranquilize him." Marlin said.

"You gotta be kidding. Then what? You gonna play like Sigman Fraud and ask him what's troubling him?" Several of the men smiled.

Marlin started to reply when one of the deputies spoke up. "Sheriff, I got Roy Swank on my cellular."

The sheriff opened his mouth as if to say something, then shuffled over to the deputy's car and grabbed the phone. The men could not hear the ensuing conversation, but Mackey gestured wildly several times. After a couple of moments, the sheriff returned with a tense look on his face.

"You win, smart boy," he said to Marlin. "That's one of Swank's trophies and he don't want it killed."

Marlin tried not to gloat, but he felt a sense of relief. Just being around Sheriff Mackey made him a little edgy. The man was obstinate, obnoxious, and downright rude. More than once they had butted heads over the finer letters of the hunting laws, chiefly because Mackey was one of the county's biggest poachers.

Wordlessly, Marlin walked over to his vehicle and reached into the backseat of the extended cab. He took out a hard-sided gun case and removed the tranquilizer rifle inside. After loading it properly, he walked up to the fence, took aim, and made a perfect shot.

CHAPTER THREE

THE POACHERS WERE holed up in Red's mobile home. Billy Don was sprawled on the couch underneath the velvet Willie Nelson painting as Red bent over him, using pliers to pull cactus thorns out of his left hand.

"What'd you have to go and push me for?" Billy Don glowered at Red.

"Because you couldn't get your fat ass back through that fence. Somebody needs a little help from Jenny Craig," Red said as he plucked at a particularly stubborn thorn.

"Damn, that hurts! Take it easy, will ya?"

"Hold on. You need a little medicine." Red stumbled into the kitchen and came back with a bottle of tequila. He unscrewed the cap and took a gulp. Then he shuddered from head to toe, like a dog shaking water off its back. He passed the bottle to Billy Don. "Take a few swigs of that."

Billy Don tipped the bottle to his lips and took a mouthful. "What is this shit, Clorox?" He took another big drink.

Red sat down on the coffee table, which used to be a packing crate, and stared hard at Billy Don. He knew he'd have to spell things out for him. "Now, I don't know exactly what happened out there tonight. But I do know we could be in deep shit for it."

Billy Don said nothing as he tipped the bottle again.

Red watched him closely. "You and me known each other for a long time,

Billy Don. I wanna know, can I trust you?"

" 'Course you can. What're you talking about?"

"If word gets around what we done, we could both be in trouble. But especially me, since I did the shootin'.'"

Billy Don nodded at him with liquor-moistened eyes.

"But you're in it, too, 'cause you was there and you helped me," Red continued. "So both our asses are on the line."

"How we gonna get caught? Wasn't nobody around to see us."

"But still, we should have a good story. Just in case anything comes up. You follow me?"

"My momma didn't raise no dummies."

"All right, then here's the plan." Red leaned back and smiled, like he'd just authored the theory of relativity. "We was here all night watchin' 'rasslin' on the TV."

Billy Don shook his head. "Shit no. Everybody knows that's all fake."

"What're you talkin' about?"

"That pro 'rasslin's a buncha crap."

"Is not."

"Is too."

"The hell are you, some kind of expert?"

"They punch like a bunch of faggots and that ain't blood, that's Karo syrup with food coloring in it."

"The hell it is, I seen the Big Bomber versus Iron Man down at the Coliseum and they punch harder'n hell and goddamn, Billy Don, what in the hell are we talkin' about? Just listen to me. We gotta have a story. You back me up, I back you up."

"I ain't gonna tell no story about watchin' 'rasslin' 'cause everybody knows that shit's all fake. People will think I'm some kinda dullard. Plus they'll know we're lying."

Red took a deep breath. Sometimes talking to Billy Don could be as taxing as talking to the foreigners who ran the convenience stores in Austin. As far as Red was concerned, if you can't speak the language, you shouldn't be let in the country. He often thought all of the immigrants should be tested on their communication capabilities, and if they couldn't understand such basic terms as "I need a pack of Red Man, Pedro," or "Give me some Marlboro Lights, Habib," then they should be deported.

But this was his friend, so he paused for a minute and then smiled at Billy Don and said, "Okay, no 'rasslin'. What do you think we oughta say?"

"How about the Nashville Network? We just say we was watchin' music videos all night." Billy Don lifted the bottle once again. "I like that Shania Twain."

Red thought it over. He had to admit, it was a good idea. There wasn't a single video they hadn't seen, so they could easily describe several of them if asked. Of course, Red wasn't a fan of Shania Twain because she was Canadian. Talk about fake. Red shuddered to think about the future of our great country when something as sacred as country music was being taken over by foreigners.

"That's perfect." Red clapped Billy Don on the shoulder. "Just you and me and Shania all night long."

But Billy Don had already passed out on the couch, still clutching the bottle of tequila in his uninjured right hand.

John Marlin pulled into his winding gravel driveway and proceeded up to the house. He cut the engine, jumped out of the truck, and walked around to the rear of the vehicle. The deer was lying peacefully, with its head up, in the bed of the truck. Marlin smiled as he looked up at the sky full of stars that seemed to wink back at him. *What a night,* he thought. *Sometimes things just seem to turn out your way.* He couldn't wait to spread the good news in the morning.

He turned back to the deer. "Easy, boy," he spoke reassuringly as he lowered the tailgate. The deer struggled to its feet, still wobbly from the tranquilizer. Its head hung low like a vulture's. Marlin spent a few minutes just stroking the deer's coat, talking to it in soft tones. After a time, the deer seemed to become more alert and regain some of its coordination. Slowly, like a nurse assisting a patient, Marlin helped the drugged buck out of the back of the truck and onto the ground.

Marlin prodded the deer gently toward the fenced side yard of his house. "Come on, big fella. You remember this place, don't you? We'll get you all set up with some water and corn. Might even have a little alfalfa in the barn."

Man and deer proceeded to walk tentatively toward the gate, with the buck occasionally wavering like a boxer who's gone too many rounds.

Behind the house, Barney Weaver was staggering off just as unsurely into the night.

Sixty-eight-year-old Junior Barstow was the proud sole proprietor of the Snake Farm and Indian Artifact Showplace on Highway 281 just south of

Johnson City, a town with about nine hundred residents. Highway 281 ran a north-south course through Blanco County, dissecting Johnson City, which was in the center of the county, and Blanco, another small town fifteen miles to the south. Barstow took advantage of the traffic between the two communities by placing small billboards two hundred yards from the Showplace on both sides of the highway. Hand-painted by Junior himself, the nearly legible signs read:

LIVE SNAKES! INDAIN ARROWHEADS!
Directly ahead!
Thrill the kids! Its a scientific
and historic wonderland!
(Visa excepted)

As promising as the name sounds, visitors were often disappointed when they first saw the Showplace, which consisted of three dilapidated structures: a drooping double-wide mobile home, a garishly colored former fireworks stand, and a Blue Bell ice-cream truck with no wheels. (The truck provided cold storage for deer carcasses. Barstow was also in the business of deer processing and taxidermy.)

Appearances aside, the Showplace was actually a legitimate attraction. Barstow had collected more than two hundred indigenous and exotic snakes, from common Western rattlers and hog snakes to exotic cobras and pythons.

And Barstow's display of Indian artifacts was in fact one of the most interesting and valuable collections in the Southwest. He had a wide variety of weapons and tools, from common Pedernales point arrowheads to rare Clovis points he had traded and bartered for over the years. Reputable archaeologists and anthropologists from around the country were always amazed that Barstow housed part of his collection in a fireworks stand fortified with a cheap padlock. That is, until Barstow revealed that he placed two of his meanest rattlesnakes in the stand every night.

Through the years, Barstow had been bitten by a variety of venomous snakes and had suffered some nerve damage. While he could easily maintain his snake and artifact collections, the butchering and taxidermy operations were becoming more and more difficult. After some urging from John Marlin, Barstow had hired Phil Colby to help.

On the morning of Friday, October 29, Marlin pulled into the gravel parking lot of the Snake Farm and Indian Artifact Showplace.

Colby had already walked out to meet him. "You ready to grab some breakfast?" he called as he went to shake his best friend's hand.

Marlin slipped past Colby's hand and gave him a hug instead. Then he gave his friend a mysterious smile. "Guess where I went last night." Standing in the parking lot, Marlin proceeded to tell Colby about the previous night's events.

The conversation flowed easily, as it always does between old friends. Marlin and Colby had known each other since boyhood. The Colby family had been in Blanco County for six generations, and at one point they had owned more than thirty thousand acres of prime ranchland. Some of the land was lost in the Depression. Over the years, various family members had moved away and tracts of the Colby property had been sold. By the time Phil Colby was born, the Colby family lived on what remained of the original homestead—four thousand acres of some of the prettiest acreage in Texas, with over a mile of Pedernales River frontage. Rolling hills thick with live oak, Spanish oak, cedar, elm, and madrone trees. John Marlin and Phil Colby had grown up on that ranch—hunting, fishing, and looking for arrowheads. They knew every square inch of it as well as they knew each other.

Unfortunately, the remainder of the Colby property was now owned by Roy Swank, as part of the Circle S Ranch. A drought a few years earlier had been particularly hard on ranchers throughout Texas. Colby had fallen desperately behind on his property taxes and was nearing bankruptcy. The county had finally set a date in stone, essentially telling Colby to pay up or lose his ranch. As the final due date neared, Colby had thought he had it all figured out. He was going to consolidate all his debt with one large loan from First County Bank in Blanco. The day before the taxes were due, Colby went to the bank to pick up a certified cashier's check. Claude Rundell, the bank president, squirmed in his chair and told Colby that he was sorry, but the loan had been turned down.

"By who?"

"Well, many people provide input on these decisions."

Colby, struggling to control his well-known temper, stood up and placed both hands flat on the desk in front of him. "Just tell me who makes the final decision."

Rundell looked down nervously at his desk. "That would be me."

Colby spoke through clenched teeth. "You just told me yesterday that I was approved."

"I'm sorry."

"You gave me your word."

"I know, but I'm sorry, it's really not a risk we're prepared to take." Rundell went on to say that he couldn't afford the possibility of a default, and that the bank didn't want to end up owning a ranch in these tough economic times.

Colby did not take the news well. When the deputy arrived, Colby was force-feeding Rundell his own toupee. In the end, though, Rundell declined to press charges.

Losing the ranch had put Phil Colby in a deep depression for many months. He lived for a while with Marlin, who was nearly as devastated by the loss. Now, as Marlin neared the end of his story, he hoped he had a small bit of news that could lift his friend's spirits a little.

"You're all excited because Trey got himself shot?" Colby asked.

"No, let me finish: So Sheriff Mackey wanted to shoot this buck. And I have to admit, it was acting pretty weird. But Swank called and didn't want it shot. So I tranquilized it." Marlin paused and grinned.

"What in the hell are you gettin' at?"

"It wasn't just any buck, Phil. It was *Buck*. I got him penned up in my yard."

A look of wonderment crossed Colby's face as his mouth fell open. Then he stepped forward and returned the hug Marlin had given him earlier.

CHAPTER FOUR

THE DOMINOES BEGAN to fall on the afternoon of Friday, October 29.

Paul and Vicky Cromwell, co-owners of a small ad agency in Austin, were enjoying the sunshine along the shores of the Pedernales River west of Johnson City. He was lazily casting a fishing lure, hoping he wouldn't ruin the peaceful afternoon by actually catching a fish. She was lying in a lawn chair, engrossed in a romance novel..

I'm no expert, Cromwell thought, *but that doesn't look like county-approved paving material.* He had spied a tuft of blue tarpaulin protruding from a makeshift low-water crossing that spanned the shallow, gravelly river.

"Hey, Vick. What do you make of that?"

"Hmmm?"

"See that blue stuff sticking out of the dam?"

Vicky didn't answer. *Swell,* thought Paul. *She's to the part where the muscular young hero embraces the heroine with rugged passion, yet sensitivity.* You could hit her with a crowbar and she wouldn't look up from the book.

Paul laid down his fishing pole and began walking down the shoreline.

Two years earlier, the Cromwells had purchased a small cabin on a ten-acre tract in a rural subdivision named Mucho Loco. The local real estate agent had assured them that most of the residents were weekenders only, as the Cromwells planned to be.

"City folks like yourself, just looking for a little peace and quiet," he lied.

The Cromwells agreed with the agent—the countryside seemed quaint and serene, with small cabins barely visible behind cedar trees. They puttered along the dirt roads of the subdivision in the agent's Ford Explorer. Paul and Vicky spied an armadillo, a possum, and a family of raccoons in the late-afternoon light. By the time they reached the advertised property, they had spotted a dozen white-tailed deer bounding through the trees and were eager to spend their weekends in such a pastoral Shangri-la. As Paul signed the dotted line, the real estate agent smiled and thought: *Nothing like a few Bambis to close the deal.*

The Cromwells soon discovered, however, that the populace of Mucho Loco consisted primarily of ex-bikers, white separatists, and trailer-park refugees. Weekends were anything but relaxing as frequent gunshots split the night. Stereos blared from neighboring cabins as teenagers threw wild parties. One spring afternoon, the Cromwells pulled on their swimsuits, slathered each other with Coppertone, and strolled down to the common area on the river. There they interrupted what appeared to be an orgy of Woodstock alumni. A dozen people lounged in the shallow water, all long-haired and nude. At least one couple was openly engaged in sex. Women with hairy armpits and free-swinging breasts cackled in merriment as Lynyrd Skynyrd played from a boombox. Empty cans of Lone Star littered the riverbank, and the smell of marijuana hung in the air like dirty gym socks. The Cromwells politely declined an invitation to join the festivities.

All of this was more than enough to motivate Paul and Vicky to put their cabin back on the market. (*For Sale by Owner* this time; Paul couldn't stand the thought of giving the deceptive real estate agent another commission.) But bad luck follows the lower middle class like a loyal hunting dog, and the Cromwells were unfortunate enough to be caught in the middle. Early that summer, torrential rains had annihilated a portion of the low-water bridge on the only road into Mucho Loco. Unless you had a rowboat and Schwarzenegger-sized arms, you were effectively stranded in or out of the subdivision. Most of the full-time residents were grateful for the crisis, which was, in essence, a reprieve from work.

As it happened, that summer continued to produce record rainfall, and the county postponed repairs to the bridge. The residents finally found some relief by way of a rancher who let them cut through his property on horses and four-wheelers. Nothing else could manage the rugged terrain. But for the Cromwells, the restricted access to Mucho Loco was a major setback. Nobody will want to buy the place now, Paul said, except maybe a swimmer with a death wish.

Finally, after the rains, the county roads department sprang into action. That is, they patched the missing segment of the bridge with a questionable mixture of cement, rock, and clay. Even an untrained eye such as Paul's could tell that the repair was no more than a Band-Aid, sure to wash out with the next big storm. *Better than nothing,* thought Paul. *We'd better sell this place while the selling is good.*

Paul placed an ad in the *Austin American-Statesman* and the *San Antonio Express-News* the following week:

```
Rustic cabin on ten acres. Friendly neighbors. Seclusion
courtesy of Mother Nature. 512-551-1649.
```

Paul considered it the best ad he had written all year. *But it better pay off soon,* Paul was thinking as he approached the dam. He walked out onto the low-water crossing with the cool water rushing past his ankles. The surface of the original dam was slick with algae in some places, but he picked his footing carefully. As he got closer to the repaired portion, he could see the small flap of blue tarp just inches underwater.

Paul walked out onto the rough new segment of the dam. He could see where the patchwork was already eroding from the current; that was the only reason the previously buried tarp was visible at all. He thought: *What the hell, my shoes are already soaked. Might as well check it out.*

He leaned over the side of the dam, reached into the water and took hold of the tarp. The water was clear and cold. The tarp was rolled up like a carpet. Paul pulled the tarp back like one pulls up a shirtsleeve.

Meanwhile Vicky had finally realized that Paul had wandered off, and she was watching from fifty yards away. She saw Paul walk out onto the dam. She saw him lean over and reach into the water. She saw him jerk back and then scramble, slipping and sliding, back to the riverbank.

"Jesus H. Christ!" Paul yelled. "There's a fucking human hand in there!"

Tim Gray was in dire need of narcotics but the goddamn Pekingese on the exam table wouldn't hold still. Taking a stool sample was, without a doubt, the worst part of being a veterinarian—especially for a man with a squeamish stomach, like Tim Gray. Growing up, Gray had thought being a veterinarian meant delivering cuddly puppies and mending horses' lame legs. *Yeah, right,* he thought. *Nobody told me I'd spend half the day mining for crap in dogs' butts.* Unfortunately, Gray's occupation offered all types of intestinally challenging tasks, such as cleaning up cat piss and emptying canine anal glands. Though he still loved animals, Gray had come to hate caring for them.

As a fresh-faced graduate of Texas A&M a decade earlier, Gray had set up practice in Blanco, his hometown. His clientele had grown quickly. Dogs and cats, horses, cows, sheep, pigs and poultry—even llamas, emus, and ostriches— they all needed attention. Dealing with such a broad range of species also meant Dr. Gray handled a variety of animal medications. Over the years, Gray had developed a taste for some of the rather potent pharmaceuticals he dispensed to his furry and feathered patients.

His first experimentation had been with acepromazine, a tranquilizer commonly used for dogs frightened by thunderstorms or fireworks. He had packed a light lunch, a six-pack of Heineken, and three hundred milligrams of "Ace." Then he went sailing on Lake Buchanan. Under an enormous blue sky, he ate a sandwich and washed the tranquilizers down with three beers. He had wonderful, vivid hallucinations for about thirty minutes, and then he passed out.

When he woke up thirty-six hours later, every inch of exposed skin was blistered by the unforgiving August sun. He was suffering from heart palpitations, double vision, and a severe case of dehydration. And he couldn't wait to explore other possibilities from his medicine cabinet.

Next he had tried phenylbutazone, a horse medication commonly used for arthritis. He swallowed a hundred-milligram tablet at six P.M. on a Saturday night. The next thing he knew, he was waking up in a seedy motel room in Houston at three P.M. on Sunday. The TV blared a rerun of *M*A*S*H.* He was surrounded by empty beer cans. Two soiled condoms lay on the carpet. The lingering smell of cheap perfume assaulted his nostrils. He quickly pulled on his clothes and left. Later the next week, snippets of the evening came back to him. Something about being escorted out of a Wal-Mart because he was found nude lying in a canoe in the sporting-goods section. Vague recollections of ordering a dozen supertacos at a Jack-in-the-Box. One freeze-frame memory of riding down Loop 610 in a limousine with his head out the moonroof, singing an AC/DC tune. Other than that, he didn't have a clue.

After these "lost time" episodes, Gray was more prudent with his experiments, starting with a small amount and working up to a pleasant and "safe" dosage. He was hopelessly hooked, though he had yet to admit it to himself. Throughout the day, as he dealt with dogs, cats, snakes, and ferrets, his center of concentration remained on the illicit substances waiting in his office.

As he wrestled with the Pekingese on the exam table, he could feel the raw hunger for drugs beginning to eat at his belly.

"Agnes, give me a hand," Gray hollered to his assistant in the adjoining room. She was bathing an Australian shepherd, a popular breed with local ranchers. "Flopsie is being a real bitch today." Flopsie looked up at Gray and bared her tiny white teeth with a pitiful growl.

"You just have to give her a little loving," Agnes said as she walked in. Flopsie immediately began wagging her tail. Agnes petted her shaggy head. "Hold still, sugar, and let nice Dr. Gray get a little sample."

With Agnes distracting Flopsie, Gray quickly inserted the instrument and completed the task, while his mouth filled with pre-regurgitation saliva. Finally, all done.

While Agnes put Flopsie back in her kennel, Tim Gray slipped quietly into his office and closed the door. He sat at his desk and opened the bottom left-hand drawer. "Come to Papa," Gray said as his heart began to race and beads of sweat broke on his forehead. As he fumbled with the small zippered bag that contained his stash, the phone rang. He could hear Agnes answering it outside.

"Dr. Gray, it's Roy Swank on the phone."

"Tell him I'll call him right back."

"He says it's urgent."

"All right, all right." Gray unscrewed the top of a small vial, dipped a tiny spoon into the snow-white powder and sucked it into his left nostril. He did the same with the right nostril. Then he grabbed the phone.

Two minutes later, Agnes watched as Tim Gray bolted from his office, ran outside to his Honda Accord, and squealed out of the parking lot.

Agnes turned to Flopsie in the small wire kennel: "Somebody's having a bad day."

Flopsie wagged her tail in reply.

CHAPTER FIVE

THREE YEARS AGO, one of the most despised and unethical men in Blanco County was voted in as sheriff. Herbert Mackey had won the election by the slimmest margin in county history—thirteen votes, to be exact.

Mackey's greasy supporters knew it would be a tough race, but they had anticipated a somewhat wider victory. After all, they had been bolstered by a late development that should have made Mackey a shoo-in. His opponent, Ed Calhoun, had committed suicide one week before the election.

Many county residents were appalled that Mackey had managed to secure a victory, since nobody seemed to know anybody who had actually voted for him. Not since Lyndon Johnson's run for the U.S. Senate in 1948 had so many rumors of ballot-stuffing buzzed through the sparsely populated county. Officials resisted calls for a recount. *Let's all be realistic,* they said. *What will we do if a dead man actually wins the race?*

Prior to the election, Mackey ran a used-car lot in Blanco, where he had a penchant for selling to immigrant workers and people living below the poverty line. He had a knack for devising financing contracts that allowed him to accept personal property as collateral for late payments. A deer rifle here, a microwave oven there. Sometimes the odd satellite dish or lawn tractor. Coincidentally, Mackey also owned the only pawn shop in all of Blanco County. In effect, property was redistributed among many of Mackey's less-fortunate future constituents— and Mackey stood shamelessly in the middle profiting from it all.

Not surprisingly, Mackey developed a reputation as a shyster and a mercenary. This reputation followed him into the sheriff's office, where he was known to greedily extend his palm and close his eyes.

The high point of Mackey's larcenous career came in the spring of his second year as sheriff. The well-known television evangelist and alleged tax evader, the Reverend Tommy Clyde, was conducting a fifty-city Southern tour, themed "What We Owe the Lord"; *60 Minutes* ran a segment on the tour, calling the story "What We Owe the IRS."

After drawing large crowds in towns like Amarillo and Abilene, Reverend Clyde headed south to save sinners in the Texas Rio Grande Valley. On the way, his caravan stopped overnight in Johnson City. His large tour bus, a restored Greyhound with a rendition of *The Last Supper* on the side, drew curious stares from bystanders all along Main Street. The bus came to a stop in front of the twenty-unit Phelps Motel, where Reverend Clyde's entourage had reserved every room for the evening.

Apparently the reverend liked to sample the Communion wine on occasion, and things got a little rowdy down at the Phelps place. After receiving a few complaints about the noise, Mackey drove over to the motel. He knocked on Reverend Clyde's door, which was answered by a RuPaul look-alike. Mackey scrambled back to his cruiser, grabbed a Polaroid camera, and burst into the motel room. He managed to fire off a dozen shots of the reverend and the prostitute before they barricaded themselves in the bathroom.

Three days later, an unidentified man delivered a briefcase containing fifty thousand dollars cash to the home of Herbert J. Mackey. Mackey reciprocated with a small envelope containing the twelve snapshots. *Praise the Lord.*

Friday afternoon, Sheriff Mackey pulled on his brown Stetson, loaded himself into his cruiser, and drove out to see John Marlin.

Marlin heard Mackey pull into the driveway and stepped out to meet him. They exchanged a stiff handshake. Around each other, they had always been about as comfortable as two tomcats sharing the same alley.

"'Morning, John," Mackey said, with an uncharacteristic grin.

Marlin did not return the smile. "What brings you out here, Herb?"

"I really think we need to talk about that deer you hauled off the other night. I got a call from Roy Swank and he was asking for that deer back."

"Now, Herb, we've been through all of this before. You know as well as I do that native whitetails belong to the state of Texas. Swank doesn't own that deer any more than he owns the sky."

"Sure, I know that. But let's think this through. Roy Swank has done a lot for Blanco County. He donated all that money to rebuild the courthouse. He gave us that two hundred acres for a county park. Not to mention all the things he's done for the Parks and Wildlife Department. The man paid for that new truck you're driving, Marlin. You ever stop to think of that?"

Marlin noticed that Mackey didn't mention the contributions Swank had made to the Sheriff's Department over the years—funds to buy new cruisers, Kevlar vests, and dash-mounted video cameras. Rumor had it that Swank had also bankrolled Mackey's election campaign for the sheriff's office, making Mackey one of Swank's biggest fans.

Marlin said, "I don't really want to sit here and argue Roy Swank's finer points with you. It's no use anyway."

Mackey smiled again. "Well, sure it is. I know we can work something out. After all, it's just one deer."

"Yeah, but that one deer is gone."

"What? When? Who has it?"

"I had him penned up in my yard, and this morning he was gone."

Mackey's face tensed. "Goddamn it to hell. That's just great."

"I thought his injury would keep him from jumping, but I was wrong. Tell you what, I'll call Swank and let him know," Marlin said. *And then I'll call Phil*, he thought, *and tell him to keep Buck out of sight.*

"That sounds like a real problem," Tim Gray said.

"You're damn right it's a problem, and thanks ever so much for your concern," replied Roy Swank, sitting behind his desk. "But what I need to know from you is how big a problem it is."

Gray wrung his hands. "You know, it could just be the effects of the rut."

Gray was referring to the yearly breeding season for white-tailed deer, when the doe is in estrus. It is then that the bucks are most active and the most combative with each other, trying to win the favor of receptive females.

Swank smiled a menacing grin. "Gray, are you a hunter?"

"No."

"Then shut the fuck up. It ain't like any rut I've ever seen, and I've seen plenty. So what say we begin to deal in reality?"

Gray was fumbling in his mind for a reply, but his verbal skills were hampered by the drugs coursing through his veins. Finally: "All I can do is make an educated guess, and my guess is that it won't die. It will exhibit some rather unusual behavior for a while, then it will be okay."

Swank didn't look convinced.

"Deer are very hardy animals, you know," Gray continued, trying to sound confident. "No sir, my guess is it will be just fine."

"It better be." Swank took a long drag on his cigar. "Because if it dies, guess who gets to go looking for the carcass?"

As John Marlin drove to San Antonio on Saturday to see Trey Sweeney, the biologist, in the hospital, he laughed to himself. Buck wasn't any more inclined to jump a fence than Herbert Mackey himself was. After all, Buck was thoroughly domesticated. Phil Colby had raised Buck from a fawn, after finding him bedded beside a dead doe on his ranch five years ago.

Back then, Trey had advised Colby as to the proper methods of feeding and caring for the fragile fawn, scarcely a few weeks old. Colby had risen at all hours of the night to bottle-feed Buck with a colostrum-replacement formula to help build the fawn's immune system. Colby kept the deer tucked away in the barn at night, away from the cold and safe from foxes, coyotes, dogs, and other predators. He even immunized Buck against common deer ailments.

When he was two weeks old, the deer was ready for solid food. Colby would put Buck on a leash and walk him down to the Pedernales River, where forage and browse were plentiful.

As the deer grew strong and healthy, the bond between Colby and Buck flourished. Buck was more like a dog than a deer, following Colby around as he completed his chores. Buck even slept inside on occasion, and seemed to prefer it.

It always pained Colby to think of releasing Buck back onto the ranch, but Marlin assured him it was the right thing to do. Finally, the day after deer season ended, Colby and Marlin drove out to the north pasture with Buck in the back of Marlin's truck.

"You made your first mistake when you named him, you know that," Marlin said to his unusually quiet friend.

Colby nodded.

"He'll be all right. Doubt he'll ever even leave the ranch. And you've run all the coyotes out of here."

Colby stared out the window.

Finally Marlin reached the location they had agreed on—a grove of towering sycamore and cypress trees near a flat, wide creek that fed into the river. Their favorite campsite when they were boys. Both men considered it the most beautiful place on the ranch.

Marlin stayed in the cab while Colby coaxed Buck out of the bed of the pickup. He watched sadly as his best friend helped the deer down to the ground and then walked him into the trees. Marlin thought: *Don't know why I'm getting choked up, it's only a deer.* But he had to compose himself before Colby returned.

Afterward, the men drove wordlessly back toward the ranch house. Marlin headed up a hill and past the high bluff overlooking the creek. He eased his way through some cattle who had heard the truck and thought it was feeding time, then he bounced along a rutted stretch of dirt road ravaged by recent rains. Finally they navigated around an oak grove and the house came into view.

There in the yard was Buck, waiting for Colby.

The men laughed and shook their heads. For four years after that, Buck rarely strayed more than a quarter-mile from the house.

These were sweet memories for Marlin, but they brought back some ugly ones as well. When Colby lost the ranch—after Roy Swank had bought it from the county—Colby had stayed on as Swank's ranch foreman. But one day last spring, when Colby found himself a new place out in the country—a nice rock home on twenty acres—he tried to take Buck home with him. As he began to load Buck into his truck, Swank pulled up alongside and protested, saying that he owned the deer.

"When I bought the place, that gave me all rights to the animals as well," Swank said.

"Come on, Roy. It's just one deer. And it's *my* deer."

"I can see why you want him. He's a great trophy," Swank said, hinting at his future plans.

"I'm afraid they don't enter any live deer in the record books."

Swank just nodded and let a pause say it all. Finally he said, "I know that."

In an instant Colby realized that Swank was planning on letting Buck be slaughtered by paying hunters. But this would be no hunt; it would be like shooting a dog on your front porch.

Ever since Swank had taken ownership of the ranch, Colby had been struggling with a fierce resentment. He had come to despise not just Swank's affluence, but his smug attitude and cold demeanor. Now his brain went into vapor-lock as his anger boiled over. He grabbed a tire iron out of his truck bed and began slamming creases into the hood of Swank's new Chevy Suburban.

Swank fumbled for the ignition. Next, Colby shattered the windshield. Swank locked the doors. Colby was kicking serious dents into the passenger side when Swank finally got the vehicle started and roared away.

Colby had taken the deer home that day, but later he came out the loser. A judge informed both men that native wildlife is, from a legal standpoint, property of the state. In short, Colby had broken the law by transporting wildlife without a permit. He was fined one hundred dollars and ordered to return the deer to the Circle S Ranch. If he refused, he would be jailed for contempt of court and Marlin, as game warden, would have to return the deer for him. Colby didn't want to put his best friend in that position, so he had returned the deer himself. And he and Marlin had been dreading the opening of this year's deer season ever since. Until two days ago.

Deer season is one week away now, Marlin thought as he pulled into the hospital parking lot. Ol' Buck wouldn't have lived through opening weekend.

CHAPTER SIX

"I WOULD PREFER you didn't handle that," Roy Swank said rather curtly to one of his visitors.

They were in Swank's expansive den, where the walls were adorned with the heads of elk, buffalo, deer, warthogs, and antelope. Gold-trimmed display cases contained African tribal weaponry, relics, and artifacts. The smaller, slender visitor had opened one of the cases and was examining one of Swank's prize possessions.

"What in tarnation is it, anyway?" he asked, reluctant to put it down.

"That," Swank responded, "is a dried rhinoceros penis."

The object practically leapt from Red O'Brien's hands back to its rightful place in the case.

Red's faced turned bright red. "That's just sick, is what it is."

Billy Don was laughing heartily. "I guess you're not used to handling a dick that long, are you, Red?"

Red was about to fire off a comeback when he noticed that Swank was staring at them sternly and drumming his fingers on the desk. "Quit horsing around, Billy Don," Red said. "The man called us here for a reason. Let's hear what it is."

Swank motioned the men to two upholstered chairs in front of his desk while he took a seat behind it. He did not offer them a drink. "I'm not sure what you gentlemen know about me, but I run a fairly successful hunting operation out here."

Both men nodded. Red thought: *We saw one of your best bucks up close and personal three nights ago. But I missed it.*

Swank continued. "I have a lot of great deer out here, some for harvesting, some for breeding. It takes a long time to build a healthy trophy herd, you know. And now, one of my trophies is missing." Swank briefly told them about the situation with Marlin and Buck.

"John Marlin told Sheriff Mackey that the buck jumped the fence," Swank said. "But I'm not so sure that's what happened. I'm inclined to believe that he has it stashed away somewhere, or that he gave the deer back to Phil Colby. Colby used to own the deer. Of course, he used to own this ranch, too, but look who's stoking the home fires now." Swank laughed merrily, and Red and Billy Don joined in, although they had no idea what was so humorous.

Swank finally regained his composure and stared intently at Red, who was the clear leader of the two. "I understand Sheriff Mackey is your cousin?"

"Yessir, second cousin twice removed on my daddy's side."

Swank nodded. "Well, Sheriff Mackey and I have gotten to be good friends in the last few years. I called him about a problem I'm having, and he told me something interesting. He said you and Billy Don know this county inside and out—all the people, all the back roads—and that y'all might be able to help me get my deer back. I'm willing to pay a fair price, of course."

Red could sense the sweet smell of opportunity in the air. After all, if a trophy buck's antlers were sometimes worth thousands of dollars, imagine what the whole critter was worth! Play this guy right, and there could be some serious money on the line. Of course, ol' cousin Herb would want a finder's fee, but that was fine with Red.

"Sheriff Mackey was right," Red said. "Me and my associate here are awful good at that sort of thing. But it's gonna be expensive."

"How much?"

Red started adding up some of his past-due bills in his head. Which meant the men could all be sitting there till Christmas.

"Don't be bashful, Mr. O'Brien. I'll be honest—it means a lot to me to get that deer back immediately. I'm having a large hunt here on opening weekend. You know, with Skip Farrell, the hunting columnist, and some other media types. It will mean a lot of great publicity for the ranch, so I'm willing to pay a fair price."

"Ten thousand bucks. Cash."

"Done."

"Apiece," Billy Don spoke up.

"No problem. I'll give you half now and half when the job is complete." Swank opened a desk drawer and withdrew a stack of crisp hundreds. Before he handed the cash over, he said, "Anytime, day or night—when you find that deer, call me."

The men rose and Swank showed them back to the front door, where he handed them each a business card with half a dozen phone numbers on it. "I am never completely out of touch. Just keep trying those numbers and you'll find me."

Red said, "Mr. Swank, it's a pleasure to be working with you. You won't be disappointed."

"I'm sure that I won't. Oh, and gentlemen, do me a favor. Don't do any more poaching on my property."

"Oh shit. How did he know it was us?" Billy Don asked when they were back in the truck.

"Hell if I know. But I say we keep our traps shut and earn some easy money."

"Aren't you nervous, Red? I mean, how come if Swank knows it was us, Mackey hasn't figured it out? He may be your kinfolk, but you *shot* a guy!"

"*We* shot a guy, you ingrate. But I think Swank was just taking a wild guess anyway. Besides, all he seems to care about is that damn deer. That must be a awful special buck."

Red pulled into a convenience store on the edge of Johnson City. He was ready to start spending some of his newfound money. "Billy Don, run in there and get us a twelve-pack of Busch. Wait a minute. Hell, get us a case of Corona. We can afford it."

Billy Don climbed out of the truck.

"And get me a handful of Slim Jims," Red called after him. "And some Moon Pies. And a pack of Red Man."

After Billy Don went inside, Red wasn't thinking about Trey Sweeney lying in a hospital. He wasn't thinking about last week's poaching disaster. All he was thinking about was where John Marlin and Phil Colby might have hidden the trophy buck.

* * *

Trey Sweeney was in room 312 according to the front desk. Marlin knocked gently, but didn't receive an answer. The door was slightly ajar, so he eased it open and saw that Trey was sleeping.

Marlin entered and took a seat in one of two chairs for visitors. *Not bad,* he thought. *A private room.* One of the benefits of state health insurance.

Marlin noticed several magazines on a small end table. *Zoologists' Monthly. Fauna World.* Definitely Trey's. Marlin was thumbing through *Wildlife Weekly* when a nurse came into the room.

"Oh, hello. I didn't know Mr. Sweeney had a visitor."

"Yeah, I was just waiting to see if Trey would wake up."

"He's still on some pretty heavy pain medication."

Marlin stood. "I'm John Marlin, game warden in Blanco County."

The nurse took his outstretched hand. "Becky Cameron. Pleased to meet you. You're a friend of Mr. Sweeney's?"

"Well, we work together on some things. But yeah, I'd say we're friends, too."

Becky smoothly removed an IV bag from its holder and replaced it with another.

Marlin said, "What can you tell me about his condition?"

"Actually, since you're not family, I really can't tell you a lot." She gave him a smile. "Unless you're conducting an investigation of some sort...."

Marlin got the hint. "On an informal basis, yes, that's exactly what I'm doing."

Becky sat down in the empty chair. "As the cliché goes, your friend is lucky to be alive. The bullet broke several ribs, but it passed almost parallel to his chest, so his internal organs were untouched. It really was pretty miraculous."

"Did they have to do surgery?"

She nodded. "We had to remove one of his ribs completely, since it was too shattered to mend properly. But that's fairly common and shouldn't be a problem. Two other ribs were broken, but they should heal on their own. Overall, he should be just fine."

"That's easy for you to say." Trey spoke from his bed.

"Well, look who's awake." Marlin rose and stood at the bedside. "How you doing, Trey?"

"Oh, not so bad, I guess, other than comin' damn close to being a ten-point buck's love slave." Trey was slurring, clearly medicated.

Becky Cameron said, "Mr. Sweeney, I just replaced your IV and your pain medication isn't due for another two hours. So just call me if you need anything." She started toward the door.

"Hold on, Nurse Cameron. Have you met ol' Johnny here? John, I don't know if you've noticed, but Nurse Cameron bears quite a resemblance to Julia Roberts."

Marlin had noticed. The nurse was quite attractive, with flowing reddish-brown hair, dark-green eyes, and a knockout figure.

"That's enough out of you, Mr. Sweeney," Becky said, stifling a smile. "Don't embarrass me in front of your friend. Now, I'll leave you two alone."

After she left, Marlin pulled a chair up next to the bed. Nobody had been to see Trey, so Marlin told him of the events with Buck, starting with the tranquilizing and ending with the visit from Sheriff Mackey.

"So where is Buck now?" Trey asked.

"Let's just say the last time I saw him, he was in my yard."

Trey was starting to seem a little more alert. "You wanna be careful with that deer, John. He's been acting real strange lately."

"Tell me about it."

"He's one of my test deer, you know that. And I've been doing a little research, getting ready for the breeding season. You know how active the males get during the rut, but Buck has been an aberration lately. He doesn't sleep. He never quits moving. I don't think he even eats. He just keeps wandering, day and night."

"Maybe some of the does are already in heat," Marlin said.

"Believe me, even if they are, this is like nothing I've ever seen. Two solid weeks of activity. I mean, it got to the point where I was thinking it was something neurological."

"So you thought you'd go wandering around a pasture in the middle of the night looking like some kind of circus performer. Real clever, Trey." Marlin felt obligated to give him a little grief.

"You know as well as I do that I could have just walked right up to him and examined him. But I wanted to see how he was behaving in his natural habitat. Only, I got shot first," he said sheepishly.

"I was concerned, too," Marlin said, "when I saw how he was acting that night at the Circle S. But by yesterday, he seemed fine. Like the same old Buck."

"I'll be honest with you. I'd much rather see Buck back with you or Phil instead of with Swank. Just promise me you'll be careful."

"You're telling *me* to be careful?" Marlin said, gesturing around the hospital room.

"I'm serious, John. Just keep an eye on him. You never know what he's going to do."

"Relax. You don't have to worry about Phil and me."

Trey smiled and shook his head. "I'm not concerned about you. Just don't hurt the damn deer."

CHAPTER SEVEN

SUNDAY MORNING, BARNEY Weaver watched television and wished it was Monday, when his food stamps would come by mail. They always arrived on the first of the month, and Barney was anxious. His pantry was running low.

Barney soon lost interest in the tube and decided to write in his journal instead, a practice he had begun during the Unabomber hearings. The idea of keeping a journal appealed to Barney—something about it seemed mysterious and intelligent. It also implied that he had something to say, something worth putting down on paper. So he wrote.

Sunday, October 31
Tried to brake into Marlin's the other day. No luck. Had a minor mishap. Can't find the proof I need but I will sooner or later. Louise ain't doing me like that. If I can proove it I'll be rich and she won't have the last lauhg. She never did lauhg though. And I kind of like Marlin ever since he caught me with too many doves but didn't write me a ticket so maybe I won't hurt them. I just want my share of the money and I think that's right There's plenty to go around. My lawyer's telling me to find something that will show she was fooling around before the divorce. Have to keep trying.

Barney was happy with the entry: concise and well-written. Someday his heirs would read the journal and realize what a wise man he was, and appreciate how he had struggled to deliver their portion of the American dream. They would respect him for his persistence in the face of adversity and admire his determination. But right now, it was time for a cold beer and some pork rinds.

As an officer of the law, Blanco County deputy Bobby Garza was everything that his boss, Herbert Mackey, was not. Honest. Respectable. Concerned. Intelligent. He lived by a code of honor born of a family history rich in law enforcement.

Garza was born in Marble Falls, about thirty minutes north of Johnson City in Burnet County, but his family had moved into Blanco County when he was three. His father had been sheriff of Blanco County in the 1970s, a firm but fair public servant respected by citizens countywide. Bobby's master plan—and he was a meticulous planner—-included holding the same office himself. Several friends and neighbors had already encouraged him to run for sheriff, even at the age of thirty-four, but he was biding his time. His father always told him that if he didn't win the first election, he wouldn't win a second.

Being a precise man, Garza was one minute early for his ten o'clock meeting with Lem Tucker, the county coroner. Garza parked his cruiser and waited outside the tiny county morgue, which used to be a Dairy Queen. The windows were painted black and the signage had been removed, but the festive red-and-white exterior seemed much too lively for its purposes. There was even a sticker on the inside of the front door that said, Y'ALL COME BACK. Garza often chuckled about the irony, though nobody else seemed to notice.

Lem Tucker pulled in at five minutes past ten, driving his huge old Chevy Suburban instead of his county car. He climbed out wearing work clothes—old jeans, muddy boots, and a faded shirt. He was a few years older than Bobby Garza, but just as trim. The men had know each other for years, as most residents did in the area. They had a friendly relationship and were occasional hunting partners.

"You didn't have to get all dressed up on my account," Garza teased, leaning against the fender of his car.

"Sorry. I was just out fixing up a few blinds. You ready for deer season?"

"Just sighted in the thirty-thirty last week."

"You still using that old brush gun? You'd think a lawman like you would know a little something about firearms."

The men exchanged a little more small talk as they made their way to the front door. Once they stepped inside, the bantering stopped, as it usually did. Tucker flipped on the lights, revealing the standard floor plan familiar to Dairy Queen customers the nation over. The large main room was sparsely furnished with a few filing cabinets and battered desks. A smaller adjoining room led to the walk-in freezer, the chief reason the old building had been selected as the new morgue site. Lem pulled the handle on the freezer and both men walked in.

"I'm afraid I don't have a lot to tell you at this point," Lem said as he pulled back the sheet that covered the body. The blue tarp the body had been wrapped in was safely tucked away at the sheriff's office as evidence, along with the man's clothing. There was no jewelry or identification.

"There's no obvious cause of death," Lem said, "but we're hoping the autopsy will tell us something."

"Any wild guesses?"

"Actually, no. I'll admit I'm stumped. Appears to be a healthy male in his early twenties. Body's in pretty good shape considering where it was buried. The materials they used to build that low-water bridge helped preserve it. The exposed right hand is the only part with any significant decomposition."

"But no sign of trauma?"

"Nothing. Not even any bruises. So it's gotta be something internal. That's what I'll find out tomorrow. How's things on your end?"

Garza shook his head. "I talked to the contractor, a guy out of Blanco, and he was absolutely no help. Says they laid the bridge materials down in layers over several days. Somebody could have snuck in overnight and dug a pit for the body. Next morning, the workers would have paved right over it."

"You buying it?"

"No reason not to. I talked to his whole crew and they all backed him up. Truthfully, anyone looking for a good spot to stash a body could have put it there. It would have taken a few hours of shovel work, that's all."

"And no ID yet, I guess?"

"Nobody seems to know him, so I don't think he's local. We're running the Polaroids in the paper on Tuesday, so we're crossing our fingers. After that, I guess we'll have to put word out in Austin and San Antone."

Lem grabbed a small flashlight off a shelf and raised the dead man's left arm. "Here's what I wanted to show you." He shined the light on the palm of the rigid left hand, revealing faint writing from a ballpoint pen.

"Looks like a phone number," Garza said. "What is that, 555-1508?"

"That's what it looks like to me. Another month and that writing would have been gone."

Garza took a small notebook out of his shirt pocket and wrote the number down. "This could be what we need, Lem. Good eye."

"Just call me Quincy."

"We sure are jumping into this awful fast," Billy Don said. It was Sunday evening and the two men were sitting in Red's truck at the Sonic Drive-In. Two bags filled with deep-fried favorites sat between them.

Red responded while munching on a handful of Tater Tots: "No sense in waiting around when ten thousand bucks is on the line. You know how long it would take us to earn that in the construction business?"

"How long?"

Red paused for a moment. "A good long while, that's for sure. And another thing—what if someone else finds the deer first? Or what if something happens to it? Marlin or Colby could have already hauled it off a hundred miles away."

Billy Don nodded. Red always had a good answer for everything. But the idea of using a gun on Colby scared him. Even if it was a pellet gun.

Red sensed his nervousness. "Now, don't worry. All we do is stick this in Colby's face like this." He pointed the gun at Billy Don. "'Give me the damn deer,'" he practiced between clenched teeth.

"Red, don't point that thing at me." Billy Don slid toward the door.

"Don't be a baby."

"I mean it. Aim that somewhere else."

"Hell, it ain't even loaded." Red pointed the gun toward the unopened passenger window, just inches in front of Billy Don's face, and pulled the trigger.

The corn dog sticking out from Billy Don's mouth exploded as a loud pop filled the cab of the truck. The window immediately became a weblike network of cracks surrounding a small, neat hole.

Billy Don cursed while opening the door and climbing out of the truck. "Dammit to hell, Red! That thing missed my head by about an inch."

Red looked around the drive-in diner to see if they were drawing attention. Nobody seemed to notice. "Get back in here, Billy Don."

"Go to hell."

"Nobody even heard it, so get back in here before everybody hears your hollerin'."

"Put that damn gun down. First you miss that deer the other night, and now you almost take my head off. And you ruin a perfectly good corn dog. Shit."

Remaining inconspicuous was more important than maintaining his pride at the moment, so Red laid the gun on the seat. "Billy Don. I'm sorry. Now get back in here. Please."

Billy Don slowly eased himself back into the truck. He grabbed the pellet gun and put it on the floorboard at his feet.

"Okay, good," Red said. "Now, here's the plan."

Roy Swank sat at his desk in his den Sunday evening and contemplated the whole debacle with the trophy deer named Buck. Damn, what a mess it all was! Swank always felt confident, even when things weren't going his way. His years at the state capitol had forged nerves of steel. But for the first time, he was beginning to feel a little antsy. Maybe he was in over his head this time.

Part of his nervousness had to do with being in a new line of business—and dealing with an entirely different breed of clientele. Oscar, for one, was a threatening figure. How do you gauge a man like that? Who knows how he would react if he knew about this current situation?

No, he was definitely getting too old for this type of stress. He would clear this mess up and then retire for good. Isn't that what he had in mind when he originally moved out here? Maybe lease a few pastures to deer hunters during the season and run a few cattle the rest of the year, but that was it. Just sit back and enjoy life in the hills.

But first things first. He stared at the phone, wishing Red O'Brien would call. *Oh man,* he thought. *What have I done, putting my future in the hands of those two bumpkins?*

CHAPTER EIGHT

PHIL COLBY WASN'T expecting a busy evening at the Snake Farm and Indian Artifact Showplace. Visitors rarely showed up this late, even though he stayed open till eight in the summer and fall. Colby was dropping live rats into the snake cages while Junior Barstow, his boss, did some paperwork. (They were ordering a new king cobra now that Fang had finally passed away. Junior had named him Fang because he had only one.)

"I'm all done here, Phil, so I'm gonna head to the house," Junior said. "Lock up for me."

"No problem."

"Tomorrow we'll get all the butchering equipment out of the back room and start setting up for deer season."

"Sounds good."

Junior walked toward the front door. "Oh, and don't forget to put Maggie in with the Clovis points when you leave." Maggie was a fat, five-foot-long Western diamondback rattlesnake who guarded the most valuable items in the arrowhead collection.

Phil finished feeding the snakes and then called John Marlin at home. Marlin told Colby about his conversation with Trey Sweeney in the hospital and asked how Buck was doing.

"He seems perfectly normal now," Colby said. "Nice and calm. Maybe it really was the rut."

"Could be, but it might be that he's finally turning wild." It was an old discussion between the two men, one that neither wanted to contemplate. Marlin had always warned Colby that there would come a day when Buck would no longer come to his call or eat from his hand. When Colby first let Buck roam the old ranch, Marlin emphasized that deer rarely, if ever, remain tame when given a taste of freedom.

"I've been watching Buck all these years, waiting for the signs, Phil. And now that Swank's had him for so long …"

"I guess we'll have to wait and see," Colby said. "But right now, he's been sleeping in my barn acting as tame as a newborn calf."

"I think that's a good idea, keeping him penned up. Swank's dying to get him back. He sure is getting uptight about one trophy deer. Did I tell you Mackey came by to see me?"

"What did that jerk want?"

"He asked about Buck, and he almost came unglued when I said he had run off."

The men agreed that they would have to keep Buck out of sight, at least until deer season was over. They hung up, promising to touch base again in a few days.

Colby turned on the small desk lamp they left burning at night, and then grabbed a snake hook from a rack on the wall. He went to Maggie's cage, opened the top, and gently lifted the docile snake by the midsection while holding her tail.

Just as he was lifting her out, there was a knock on the door. Colby carried Maggie over to the desk and placed her in the bottom drawer with a metal lockbox that contained the Clovis points. Then he went to the window and looked out. Two men were standing outside wearing masks, one dressed as Moe and the other as Curly. Colby had almost forgotten: It was Halloween.

"Little old for trick-or-treating, ain't you, boys?" Colby said as he opened the door, wondering who was playing a joke on him.

Then Moe stepped forward and aimed a gun at Phil Colby's head.

John Marlin liked the pecan pie at the Kountry Kitchen almost as much as he enjoyed the long legs of the waitress who served it. That's what had attracted Marlin to Louise in the first place. So he ordered some pie with vanilla ice cream as he waited for her shift to end Sunday night.

Louise was a sweet, smart, and sexy woman. Definitely the kind of woman Marlin had always imagined himself spending a lifetime with. But for some reason, the feelings just weren't there. He loved her humor, her intelligence, her beauty. But he didn't love *her*. And it made him feel guilty to not return the love he thought Louise was feeling for him.

Finally, a month ago, Marlin had sat Louise down and spoken from his heart. He tried to tell her delicately that he wasn't in love with her and didn't think he ever would be. He expected a slap or some tears of heartbreak. Instead, a look of relief passed over Louise's face, and then she started to giggle.

"What's so funny?" Marlin asked, a little uncomfortably.

"I was all worried, thinking you were gonna tell me you loved me. And here you were all worried because you had to tell me you don't." She took a long breath and placed her hand on Marlin's shoulder. "John, believe me. I am not ready for anyone to love me. The divorce was hell, and I'm having the time of my life as a single gal. Why would I want to ruin that?"

So they agreed to keep it casual. But they also promised to let the other person know if one of them began seeing someone else. Since then, Marlin and Louise had been free to enjoy the pleasure of each other's company, without complications or guilt.

"Here's the *piece* you've been waiting for," Louise said with a wink, setting the pie in front of Marlin.

"What if I'm still hungry after this?" Marlin asked, grinning. He loved flirtatious women.

"Oh, I bet we could arrange for something a little more satisfying," Louise replied. Then she got serious. "John, are we going over to your place tonight? There's something I want to talk to you about."

"Sure. You about ready?"

Marlin wolfed down his pie while Louise gathered her things, then she followed Marlin out to his place in her Toyota. As usual, they proceeded directly to the bedroom.

Afterward, Louise flicked on the nightstand light and turned to Marlin. "There's something really funny—-and a little weird—that I need to tell you."

Marlin sat up in bed and gave her a quizzical look.

"No, don't worry," Louise said. "I still don't love you."

After they finished laughing, she continued. "As you know, I've been married twice. Neither of them were what you'd call catches. I don't know how I ever got mixed up with either of them. Live and learn, I guess. You've seen my second ex, Barney, around town, so you've probably figured out that he's sort of a head case. When I married him three years ago, I had just moved here from California. I wanted to get away from my first ex-husband, Bill, and Blanco was perfect for me, because my hometown was just as small, just as friendly." Louise paused and reached over to the nightstand for a cigarette. "So while I was married to Barney, I found out what a strange guy he is."

"How so?"

"Kinda paranoid and, I don't know, out of touch with reality. He was always asking me about my first husband. At first, I thought it was jealousy, but then one night he got drunk and told me that he knew my first husband was rich. I told him he was crazy, but he wouldn't give in. He demanded to see a picture of him but I didn't have one. He asked me where I kept all the money I must have gotten in my first divorce. Don't I wish! Even during our divorce, Barney was hounding me constantly, and he even hired a private investigator to track down Bill. No luck."

"He definitely sounds a little goofy," Marlin said. "But why are you telling me all this now? You've been divorced for a while now."

"He's been calling and leaving messages on my answering machine, saying that he wants his share. He told me that his lawyer said he should try to get it before I get married again and—quote—'really cause a cluster-fuck.'" She stared Marlin in the eye.

"Oh, now I get it. You're thinking that ol' Barney might try to keep us from getting married." Once again they burst into laughter. When they stopped, Louise spoke again.

"Actually, I have to admit that I've worried about it a little more than that. I'm afraid that he might try to hurt you."

Oh, perfect, Marlin thought. *A jealous ex-husband. A mentally confused ex-husband.* "What the hell's wrong with this guy, anyway? Why's he think you're rich?"

"I told you, it's my first husband, Bill."

"What about him?"

"His last name is Gates."

Phil Colby stepped slowly backward as Moe and Curly came through the door.

"Sit down over there," Moe barked, gesturing toward a chair next to the desk. He was using a fake voice—-a silly rumble that sounded like a combination of Darth Vader and the bass singer from the Statler Brothers.

Colby sat down slowly. "What the hell is going on? This some kind of dumb joke?"

"No joke, boy."

Colby immediately thought of the Clovis points. "You can take all the arrowheads you want, but it won't do you any good. They've been microscopically inscribed and you'll never be able to sell them."

"Now, what would we want with a bunch of rocks? No sir, we're looking for something a lot more valuable." Moe paused for dramatic effect—a trick he'd learned from *Matlock*—and stared at Colby. Colby stared back.

"What we want is the deer you've been hiding. And if you just tell us where it is, we won't have any trouble."

"I assume you're talking about the buck from the Circle S."

Moe nodded.

"Last I knew, John Marlin had him. Then he jumped the fence."

Moe shook his head. "Bullshit. We know all about that pet deer of yours. He didn't run off, you've got him hidden somewhere. Now, I'm gonna count to five, and you better tell me where it is so I won't have to get nasty."

"You really think you can do it?" Colby asked.

"Find the deer?"

"No, count to five."

Curly tried to stifle a laugh but a giggle squeaked out. Moe fixed him with a baleful glare, then turned his attention back to Colby. "Very funny, smart guy. But you won't think it's funny if I have to use this gun."

"I think there's something you need to know," Colby said.

"What's that?"

"That's a pellet gun."

Red clenched his teeth. This was not going at all the way he had planned. Why did things always have to be so complicated? He decided to try another tack. "Listen up, Colby. You and I both know the rack on that deer is worth a lot of money. But the thing is, he's worth even more alive. You do this nice and easy and that buck of yours just might not end up hanging on my wall." He could tell from Colby's face that he was having some effect. "All I'm trying to do is return it to the rightful owner. But if you give us trouble, I just may have to keep that deer for myself."

Colby opened his mouth to speak and then paused. He looked over at the desk. "In the bottom drawer you'll find a ring with the key to my barn. That's where he is."

Red smiled like a sailor in a whorehouse. Finally! Now all they'd have to do is tie Colby up while they collected the buck. And then the money. Yes, life was good for Red O'Brien. "You heard him, Billy Don … uh, I mean Curly. Grab that key and let's get out of here."

Billy Don Craddock lumbered over to the desk, bent low, and yanked the bottom drawer open.

CHAPTER NINE

THE BRAIN OF Maggie the snake functioned on a very basic level. Her single goal in life was to survive. Thus Maggie looked forward to her weekly feedings of live mice, generously dropped into her cage by Phil Colby and Junior Barstow. Like an unintentional Skinnerian experiment, Maggie had begun to equate each man's unique scent to the delivery of food.

Unfortunately for Billy Don Craddock, he smelled nothing like Colby or Barstow. So, mere milliseconds after Billy Don opened the drawer and began rummaging around for the nonexistent key ring, Maggie decided to plant her fangs firmly into Billy Don's forearm without so much as a warning rattle.

Red was surprised to hear Billy Don let out a shriek as he was reaching into the desk drawer. He was even more surprised to see Billy Don jump backward with a rather large rattlesnake attached to his arm.

"Red, git this thing offa me!" Billy Don bellowed as he started swinging his arm in circles.

Colby took a chance and bolted for the door, but Red stuck a foot out and tripped him. Colby's head slammed solidly against the door frame.

"Let's get outta here," Red yelled. Billy Don was now holding his bloody arm and the snake was nowhere to be seen. Both men stepped over Colby and ran out the open door into the night.

Five minutes later, Maggie emerged from under the desk and curled up beside the familiar man unconscious on the floor.

"Hello?" Marlin said in gruff voice. It was six A.M. Monday morning and he wasn't too fond of receiving early-morning phone calls. It usually meant someone was reporting a poacher or a wounded animal that he would have to deal with. Not this time.

"John, it's Junior."

Marlin sat up quickly in bed. He couldn't remember ever receiving a call from Barstow. "What's up, Junior?"

"Bad news. I came in early this morning to get ready for deer season and I found Phil in the office unconscious."

Marlin's heart thudded. "What? Is he all right?"

"The chopper just took him away. They're flying him down to San Antone."

"What happened?"

"That's what the deputies are wondering. There's no sign of intruders— nothin's missing—but he thumped his head pretty good. He coulda slipped, but …"

Marlin was way ahead of him. This was not an accident, and pangs of guilt turned Marlin's stomach queasy. He never should have given Buck back to Colby. Roy Swank was a man who was used to getting his way and he didn't care how he did it. They'd all known that ever since he moved to Blanco County.

"Listen, John. I know all about the deer. I figure I better go over to Phil's place and tend to him."

"No, sir. Swank's tied into all this somehow, and whoever has that deer could be in for trouble."

"Ain't never been any trouble that Junior Barstow couldn't handle. Now just you relax and leave it to me."

"Junior, I really appreciate that, and I'm sure Phil would, too. But it's me who has to deal with it. I promise to call you if I need anything, all right?"

Barstow sighed and agreed. "I never was one to argue with a game warden."

Bobby Garza tried the phone number early Monday morning. He wasn't exactly sure what he was going to say if anyone answered. Certainly not: *Oh, good morning. I just wanted to let you know that I found your phone number on a dead man's hand.*

But there was no answer after ten rings. Garza hung up and then dialed the operator, identifying himself as a Blanco County deputy. "I've been trying a number and getting no answer. Maybe you could give me some information on it?"

"What's the number, sir?"

Garza recited it and could hear the operator punching it into a keyboard. After a few seconds, the operator said, "I'm afraid that's a pay phone, sir."

Damn! Just the kind of thing he was dreading. "Okay, thanks anyway." Garza was prepared to give up on the number when he had a brainstorm. The exchange for Johnson City was 555, and he had immediately assumed that the phone number on the corpse's hand was a 555 number. But the exchange for nearby Dripping Springs, east of Johnson City in Hays County, was 556. A six could certainly be mistaken for a five, especially when you consider the writing surface in this case. So he tried the number again using the 556 prefix.

A young man answered on the third ring.

Garza responded: "This is Deputy Bobby Garza with the Blanco County Sheriff's Department. Who am I speaking to?"

"Uh, Willie Combes. You must have the wrong number." Combes sounded like a misplaced surfer from the beaches of Malibu. A regular Jeff Spiccoli from *Fast Times at Ridgemont High.*

"Actually, Willie, I need to ask you a few questions. Do you mind if I come by for a minute?"

"Like, what's this all about?"

"Just routine stuff." Garza didn't want to show his hand just yet. "You live in Dripping Springs, right?"

"Dude, you're really on the wrong track here."

"I probably am, Willie. But if so, we can get this cleared up and I'll be out of your hair." Garza was sure Willie had plenty of hair. Probably a dark tan and sandals, too.

"Can't you even tell me what's going on?"

"I'd prefer to do that in person. Now, if you'll just give me your address, I can come over and we'll straighten this out."

"No warrants, right?"

Garza thought, *This kid definitely knows something. That's the kind of question only a guilty person would ask.* "No, Willie, I promise. No warrants." Not yet, anyway.

* * *

Tim Gray, the veterinarian, was accustomed to working on animals. Humans were another matter. Especially for something as serious as a snake bite. But Swank had called Gray first thing Monday morning and ordered him to get over to Red O'Brien's mobile home pronto.

"Doc, it hurts real bad," Billy Don moaned.

Gray surveyed Billy Don's arm, which was now the size of a watermelon. "Well, why the hell did you wait so long to get medical attention? You could be dead by now."

"We had to go get the deer outta the barn at Colby's place. And Red told me tequila would take care of it anyhow." He glared at Red, who was sprawled on the sofa, still recovering from their impromptu celebration the night before.

"Just hold still and I'll fix you up."

Gray scanned the bottle of antivenin. The first thing he saw was a warning that said: FOR VETERINARY USE ONLY. Oh well. He himself had tried plenty of pharmaceuticals that had that same warning.

The bottle listed a recommended dose for dogs up to one hundred pounds. Gray wondered: *How much do you use for an animal that weighs about the same as a grand piano?* He decided to triple the amount on the label.

Gray expected a moan from Billy Don when he inserted the needle—this big man was proving to be quite a complainer—but Billy Don didn't even wince. Bad sign. Billy Don had lost feeling in his arm.

"All right," Gray said, "That should help with the swelling and prevent heart failure."

Billy Don's face immediately turned an ashen color. "What are you talking about?"

"That's what snake venom does. First, you get necrosing tissue. That means it pretty much rots and falls off. Then you go into shock, which causes respiratory failure and heart failure. Your ticker just plain gives out."

Billy Don's eyes got as big as pool balls. Gray figured that if Billy Don was going to die, he would already be gone by now. But he was actually enjoying tormenting him. It was kind of fun dealing with a patient who could talk.

Gray packed all his things back into his bag and turned to the two men. "All right, boys. Now let's have a look at that deer."

John Marlin had plenty of time to think while he drove to the hospital in San Antonio. Obviously something was going on with Buck. Something important enough to land two men in the hospital in a matter of days. But this time, it was his best friend. Marlin decided it was time to quit playing hide-and-seek with the deer and confront Swank directly. Or he might have a face-to-face chat with Sheriff Mackey, try to rattle his cage a little. The sheriff had close ties to Swank, and he had seemed awfully intent on getting the deer back for him. Could be that Mackey knew what was going on.

By the time Marlin arrived at the hospital, a light drizzle had begun to fall. He pulled into the parking garage and found a spot marked FOR EMERGENCY VEHICLES ONLY. One of the perks of the job.

Marlin crossed the elevated walkway to the hospital and proceeded to the front desk. An employee told him Colby was in room 211. Intensive Care. Right away, Marlin's sense of guilt came back. His best friend was in serious condition with a closed head wound, and he couldn't help but feel responsible.

He tapped lightly on the door, expecting no response, but a gentle female voice told him to come in. Marlin swung the door open and met familiar eyes. Becky Cameron, the nurse who had taken care of Trey Sweeney, was in the room tending to Phil Colby. She did a double take when she saw who the visitor was. "Hello again, Mr. Marlin."

Marlin noticed that she had remembered his name. He nodded to her. "Miss Cameron, please call me John."

"If you'll call me Becky. What brings you here today?" Becky asked. Then her eyes got wide. "Don't tell me this is a friend of yours, too?"

Marlin nodded. "It hasn't been a good week."

Marlin walked over to the bed and was shocked at what he saw. Phil lay motionless, eyes closed. He looked pale and much too thin. A small machine that monitored Colby's vital signs beeped and blinked at the bedside. Marlin decided to take a seat in a chair next to the bed before his knees gave out on him.

Moments passed, and Marlin had all but forgotten about the nurse, when she spoke again.

"John, I'm really sorry to see you here again, in these circumstances." She stepped closer to the chair. "If there's anything I can do ..."

Marlin smiled at her and nodded. "Thank you."

"Do you know him well?"

"He's my best friend. Has been since kindergarten."

Becky wrapped herself with her arms, as if she was suddenly cold. Marlin could even see tears in her eyes. "I'm so sorry. Please, just let me know what I can do," she said. "I can get you extended visiting hours if you like. I could probably even get another bed in here if you want to stay."

Marlin nodded and turned back toward Phil.

"I'll leave you alone," Becky said as she turned toward the door.

"There is one thing you could do for me," Marlin called after her.

"What's that?"

"Have lunch with me."

The room was dimly lit, but Marlin thought he saw Becky blush. She glanced at her watch and looked up with a small smile. "You have perfect timing. My lunch hour just began. I'll grab my purse and be right back."

Alone, Marlin stood and looked down at Phil. He reached out and grabbed his hand. It was warm, just like it should be, but there was no life to it. No response at all.

All this for a fucking deer, Marlin thought. *Hell, we shoot deer just like Buck every year, Phil. So why did you have to get so attached to this one? Was he worth this much trouble?*

Marlin gave Phil's hand a squeeze and then went to wait for Becky Cameron in the hall.

CHAPTER TEN

"IT'S BASICALLY A light coma," Becky said while waiting for her enchilada plate to arrive. "What that means is, Phil doesn't need any life-support devices. He can breathe just fine on his own. Brain activity is normal. It's just that his brain had too much pressure on it from cerebral hemorrhage. But everything is stable and we're monitoring him very carefully. As soon as the body reabsorbs the blood, he should come out of it just fine." She gave Marlin a smile meant to comfort. The man was obviously concerned over his friend's condition—he almost acted as if he was responsible.

Marlin nodded and took a big drink of iced tea. But he didn't smile or act relieved.

"John, do you know how long the average coma patient remains unconscious?"

Marlin looked a little startled, and Becky wondered if she was being a little too matter-of-fact. Life as a nurse sometimes left you a little less than sensitive in situations such as this. Health emergencies become an everyday circumstance, and one begins to talk about them in the same manner as describing a trip to the mall.

Marlin paused for a minute and then said, "I don't know—six months?"

Becky shook her head. "A couple of days, that's all. But everybody sees the movies and soap operas where a person will lie in a coma for months or years.

That rarely happens. I've seen people in far worse shape than your friend come out of a coma one day and walk out of the hospital the next."

Marlin reached across the table and grabbed Becky's hand. She hadn't expected it, and she immediately felt nervous. But it was a good kind of nervous.

"I appreciate your support, Becky. I really do. If something was to happen … I don't know what I'd do."

Marlin looked Becky straight in the eyes and she was struck by the sincerity she saw in his face. *Here's a man who knows what honesty is about,* she thought. *He seems so vulnerable, but so powerful at the same time. None of the typical macho crap.*

Marlin opened his mouth to speak again, when the waiter arrived with their lunches. "Enchiladas for the lady and the taco plate for you, sir."

As they dug in, Becky said, "You were about to say something…."

Marlin looked down at his plate and smiled. "Just wanted to say thank you again. For taking care of Phil. And for going to lunch with me."

For Nurse Becky Cameron, enchiladas had never tasted so good.

Bobby Garza followed McGregor Road one mile north of Highway 290, then turned left on the dirt driveway like Willie Combes had told him. At the head of the driveway, a rusty mailbox proudly announced COMBES to anyone who was interested.

As he approached the house, a mobile home sitting on twenty or thirty cedar-covered acres, Garza thought maybe Willie was a local after all. Not many newcomers live out in the sticks like this, and the ones that do are Californians who pay three hundred grand or more for beautiful hilltop homes.

Garza swung his cruiser up next to an old Buick and climbed out. Four dogs immediately began barking in a pen next to the mobile home.

Garza had seen homes like this plenty of times, both in Blanco County and here, to the east, in Hays County.

A satellite dish sat atop the mobile home. Two old refrigerators sat on the front porch next to a plaid sofa. No fewer than six rusting vehicles were clustered together in high grass a hundred feet away.

As the dogs continued to bark, three geese approached Garza and began to make a racket. Garza knew from experience to keep an eye on them. They were quick to take a snap at your ankles and could easily draw blood.

Behind a nearby fence, Garza could see seven or eight goats and several hogs lying in the shade next to a small sheet-metal shed.

Out from the shed came a hefty, older woman in a floral print dress. She was carrying a galvanized bucket and waved at Garza with her free hand. "Hello! Be right with you."

The woman exited through a small gate and walked up to Garza. The dogs and geese fell silent as she approached. "Lordy, it sure is a hot one today."

"Yes ma'am, it sure is." Garza removed his Stetson and said, "Ma'am, I'm Bobby Garza from the Blanco County Sheriff's Department."

"Thelma Combes, glad to meet you." She extended a pudgy hand, warm and soft, like her voice. She must have been about seventy-five, everyone's idea of the perfect grandmother. Large and robust, her weight tested the seams of her dress. Bobby's dad used to spot a woman like that and say she was smuggling grapefruits.

Garza said, "I was looking for Willie...."

Thelma Combes' face got a worried look. "Uh-oh, is that boy in trouble again?"

"I don't know at this point. I just need to ask him a few questions. Has he been in trouble before?"

"Ever since he started smoking that pot weed, he hasn't been quite the same. My daughter sent him out to me to see if I could straighten him out. As you can see, I'm the one doing his chores, so I haven't had a lot of luck."

"You're his grandmother?"

"Yeah, but it ain't easy."

Garza smiled. "No, ma'am, I'm sure it's not. Is Willie somewhere around?"

"He's in the house. Willie!" She shrieked loudly enough to startle Garza and quiet all the birds in nearby trees. "Willie! You got a gentleman out here that needs to talk to you."

They both stared at the trailer door. After a moment, a scraggly teenager emerged.

"Willie, I'm gonna get right to it." Garza and Willie Combes were sitting on a picnic table under some oak trees near the trailer. Garza had already asked Willie about his record. *Coupla misdemeanors is all,* Willie had said. Both for possession of marijuana. No big deal. Garza could sense that he wasn't dealing with a bad kid. Just your average confused youth. The kind who was slow to answer questions, but not clever enough to lie his way out of trouble. Garza continued: "We found a dead body buried in a bridge over at Mucho Loco. You know where that is?"

Willie nodded.

"So far, we're not sure what the cause of death is—but we don't think there was any foul play."

Willie nodded again.

Garza looked Willie straight in the eye. "The dead man had your phone number written on his hand."

Willie looked at the ground. If he wasn't involved, he'd be smiling by now, knowing he was free and clear.

"Willie, before you answer my next question, let me tell you a little something about the way the judicial system works." Garza paused and took a drink of the iced tea Thelma had brought him. A very kind woman, bless her heart.

"Sometimes folks get involved with stuff they don't want to be involved in. Their first inclination is to cover it up, get out of it somehow. You know what happens? They end up in way more trouble than they would have gotten into in the first place. Now, my guess is that this guy somehow died—through nobody's fault—and someone got nervous and did something a little stupid with the body. If that's the case, I really don't see where anybody would get into any trouble at all."

Willie looked back at the trailer anxiously. "I really, really don't want to get screwed around on this deal. I didn't do anything wrong, too much."

Garza nodded, thinking: *Sure, Willie, nothing wrong at all. Other than illegally disposing of a corpse and failing to report a death.* "Tell me what happened, Willie, and I think everything's gonna work out just fine."

Willie took a deep breath. "The guy you found—his name's Michael. I worked with him on the surveying crew."

"Was he from around here?"

"No, Austin."

That would explain why Garza hadn't heard about a missing person.

"He came over one night and we were drinking…"

"And getting high?"

"Yeah. See, Michael had asthma that would bother him some when we were out in the field. He'd have to sit for a while and catch his breath. And he had an inhaler that he used sometimes. But he'd still get high, saying that it actually made it easier to breathe. So we smoked a joint and I noticed that it tasted a little funny at first. Michael did, too. But by the time we were done, we didn't even notice it anymore. Then we smoked another one later. Michael used his inhaler a few times, and it seemed like he was getting a little sick … out of breath … but he said pot never did this to him, so it must be something in the air. We were smoking our last joint when he really started gasping. I went inside to get him a glass of water, and when I came back, he was just laying there. His eyes were open, but I couldn't tell if he was breathing or not."

"What'd you do?"

Willie looked embarrassed. "I felt for a heartbeat. I didn't find one, so I tried CPR on him."

"Are you trained in CPR?"

Willie shook his head no.

"Then what?"

"I started to go inside and get Grandma, but she was asleep. And you got to understand that I was really smashed ... between the pot and the beer. So I just went to bed, hoping everything would be cool when I woke up. But in the morning, Michael was still behind the barn, in the same position."

Garza resisted a strong urge to grab the kid and shake him like a rag doll. Why on earth hadn't he even called 911?

Willie saw the look on Garza's face. "Man, I was really freakin'. I didn't do anything wrong, but I just knew I'd get in trouble for somethin'. It had to be something wrong with the weed. So I knew I had to do something with Michael."

"And that's where the bridge at Mucho Loco comes in?"

Willie nodded.

"You buried him and just forgot about it all?" Garza asked incredulously.

"What was I supposed to do?"

"Call for an ambulance, that's what!" Garza stared at Combes, but the kid wouldn't meet his eyes. "All right, Willie, last question: Where did you get the pot?"

"Aw, man ..."

"I'm not kidding about this. Tell me where you got it or I'll take you in right now."

Willie sighed and finally said, "His name is Charles Walznick."

CHAPTER ELEVEN

THE COLOMBIAN MAN had been in Texas several times, but he had never been to Johnson City.

And from what he had seen so far, he had already made a vow not to come back. Nothing but pickup trucks and rednecks, as far as he could determine. Couple of mom-and-pop restaurants, nothing that looked too promising. The obligatory Dairy Queen. Even a couple of small hotels on the main strip. Every building in town could use a coat of paint, except for the courthouse. It was made of stone. Just like other small towns in Texas, hardly more than a wide spot in the road.

The man pulled into Big Joe's Restaurant, hoping the crowded parking lot was a sign of good food. He hated the thought of having to sit down and eat in the midst of a bunch of yokels, but he was getting hungry and couldn't wait any longer.

He squeezed his rented Cadillac between a rusty Ford truck and a Chevy Suburban. Tight spot. He was already picturing how he'd have to fuck up some hick if he came out and found a scratch on this nice car.

He walked through the door and a cute brunet girl was waiting for him, asking if it would be just him for dinner. She sat him down at a small table and gave him a big smile. He smiled back. Maybe this wouldn't be all that bad. He felt pretty sure she was impressed by his linen jacket, which was imported from

France. Nice Italian shoes, too. Slicked-back hair with two-hundred-dollar shades perched on his head. Impeccably groomed mustache. Sure, there was plenty for a girl to smile about.

Scanning the menu, the man started to groan inside. *Christ, don't they have anything here that isn't fried in fat?* Chicken-fried steak. Chicken-fried chicken. Deep-fried okra. He imagined they'd fry the pecan pie if they could find a way. When the brunet girl came back, he ordered the chicken-salad sandwich.

"Thass not fried, ees it?" he asked, flirting a little, thinking the girl might like his accent. He was a regular Ricardo Montalban.

She didn't catch the sarcasm. "No, sir. But you might want to try the chicken-fried steak. Best in town."

He told her he'd stick with the sandwich and a glass of iced tea.

The man glanced around the dining room and observed the crowd. Lots of guys in jeans and boots, colorful pullover shirts and cowboy hats. Plenty of women and young girls, too, dressed for a night on the town, it looked like.

The brunet brought his iced tea and he asked if something was going on in town.

"Big volleyball game tonight against Marble Falls. If we win, we take district."

"Don' you play volleyball?"

"I did, but I graduated last year."

"Bet you were the star player, with long legs like that." The man looked her up and down and the girl gave him an embarrassed smile.

She was about to reply when a young man, barely drinking age, caught her eye from a few tables over. He was shaking an empty beer bottle at her, asking for another round. She excused herself and went into a back room.

The man glanced over at the impatient customer's table. Four local men—boys, really—were hunched over plates hidden by enormous slabs of chicken-fried steak. They all wore workshirts and boots. About a dozen beer bottles were assembled into a pyramid in the center of the table.

The girl came back with another round for the young men. The one who had shaken his bottle at her—Mr. Impatient—said something to her. The Colombian man couldn't hear it, but he could sense tension between the waitress and the young punk. The customer said something else and then glared over at the Colombian.

As the man ate his sandwich, the crowd thinned. Nearly eight o'clock, time for the game. By the time he was done, he was alone in the room with the beer drinkers and a few older couples.

The waitress brought his check and the man gestured toward Mr. Impatient. "You know that guy?"

The waitress looked embarrassed. "Ex-boyfriend. Thank goodness."

The Colombian tried to flirt one last time. "Wass there to do in this town on a Monday night?"

"There's the River Ballroom, if you like two-steppin', but that won't really get going until after the game."

"Perhaps you and I could get together…. Maybe you teach me lessons to do this two-step…." The man gave her his best pickup smile.

She was clearly uneasy, glancing over at the locals. She said she couldn't make it tonight, thanks anyway, but she was in charge of cleanup.

Well, it was worth a shot. Time to find out which hotel was the least objectionable and get a room for the evening.

He laid a twenty on the table to cover his twelve-dollar tab and drained the last of his iced tea. Then he heard a voice.

"Mister, is that your Cadillac out there?"

The man looked up to see Mr. Impatient standing to his left. He had apparently just come in from outside, and he was folding up a Buck knife, inserting it into a sheath on his belt. The man didn't reply.

"Comprende inglés, amigo?" Mr. Impatient said. He smiled over at his friends, still at the table. They were all grinning back at him.

"I hate to tell you, but it looks like you picked up a nail out on the highway. Got yourself a flat tire. *El flatto tiro."*

Mr. Impatient stood there a moment while the man dabbed at his mouth with his napkin.

He stood without saying a word, nodded to the three locals at the table, and went outside. He could hear laughter as he went out the door.

The left rear tire was slashed. There was a gaping slit on the sidewall, clearly not the result of a nail. One word had been traced in the dust on the back window: SPICK.

Five minutes later, the young men came outside to find the Hispanic man leaning against the only truck left in the parking lot. Mr. Impatient spoke first: "I think you're a little confused, amigo. Those are my wheels. That's your Caddy right over there. The one low on air."

The man was standing with his arms crossed, so none of the locals noticed the brass knuckles on his right hand. And his hands moved so quickly, they probably never saw them at all. One quick shot to Mr. Impatient's forehead and it split open like an aging dashboard. He fell to the ground with a yelp as the blood enveloped his face.

The largest boy in the group took a swing, but the man ducked it and cracked his ribs, feeling the bone give. He, too, dropped like a sack of feed. The two remaining locals took off behind the restaurant.

The Colombian man slowly took off the brass knuckles and slipped them into his pocket. He reached over and grabbed Mr. Impatient by the hair and pulled hard.

He said, "My name ees not 'amigo,' it ees Oscar. Now which one of you sheetkickers is gonna change my tire?"

Early Tuesday morning, John Marlin received a call from Thomas Stovall, one of the best rock masons in Central Texas, a hell of a poker player, and a frequent poacher. Marlin knew him quite well, and had written him up for minor infractions several times over the years. But Marlin had to admit, he liked Stovall—he was quick with a joke and entirely honest when he wasn't hunting.

"This is a switch, Thomas. You calling me," Marlin joked. "Usually it's me trying to track you down."

Stovall gave it right back to him. "You know how I like to avoid the law, especially when they've got a hard-on for poor country folks like myself."

Marlin smiled while Stovall continued. "John, I need to talk to you about something. Actually, I need to show you something."

"What you got?"

"I'd rather show you if I can. Can you swing by my place this morning?" Stovall's voice sounded urgent.

"I imagine I could," Marlin replied. He wasn't used to Stovall being so serious. "I'll see you in about thirty minutes."

Marlin got dressed, grabbed a traveler's mug of coffee, and headed out the door. It wasn't until he was halfway to Stovall's small ranch that he remembered who Stovall's neighbor was: Roy Swank. Maybe this would be the right time to pay Swank a visit and have a talk about Buck. But first things first.

Minutes later, Marlin swung through Stovall's front gate, which had a sign that said, PEDDLERS AND MEDDLERS NOT WELCOME. Beneath that, someone had painted a crude rifle and written, WE DON'T CALL 911.

He parked by the beautiful rock home and saw Stovall come out the front door. The men greeted each other and Stovall got right to the point. "John, you and me have had a few run-ins, ain't we?"

Marlin agreed that they had.

"But I've always thought you were a straight-shootin' type … a good man," Stovall said.

Marlin thanked him for those kind words. He was patient—he knew the redneck rock mason had something to tell him. It was best to let him do it at his own pace.

"Now, I'm wondering if I can tell you something … and keep it just between us. Sorta man-to-man."

Marlin smiled. "Well, that all depends on what we're talking about, Thomas. But I imagine you could probably tell me what you want to tell me without it getting out."

"I'm not so worried about it getting out as I am about … getting in trouble."

"For another game violation?"

"Possibly. But that's not what you're gonna be interested in." Stovall took a deep breath. "Let's say that I was out doing a little hunting—maybe a few days before the season was open—but I came across something darn peculiar … something you should know about   "

Marlin was finally beginning to get a little impatient. "Thomas, I'm guessing you shot a deer out of season. So what else is new? Let's hear what all this is leading up to."

Stovall looked Marlin in the eye for a few seconds, making a decision. Finally he said, "Climb in my truck. Let me show you something."

"It's the damnedest thing I ever saw," Stovall said. The two men were walking through thick woods near Stovall's westernmost property line. The cedar trees were so dense, the atrophied lower branches raked the men's skin as they passed by. Finally they broke through into an opening along an eight-foot gameproof fence. "I was watching the fenceline.…Right there's where the deer come through. You can see where there's a hole in Roy Swank's fence." Thomas winked at Marlin.

Cutting holes was a poacher tradition, a way of keeping animals moving through high fences. Since cutting fences is illegal, some poachers applied battery acid to the fence—and when it would deteriorate a year later, it looked like natural rusting. It was a unique trick introduced to the innovative poaching community by none other than Thomas Stovall.

"It was a big ol' buck, a real wall-hanger," Stovall said. "I think Swank keeps some of his best bucks in this pasture"— pointing to the gently rolling hills across the fenceline. "I was just setting under one of them cedars over there, using my thirty-thirty. It was only a sixty-yard shot."

Stovall walked about ten yards and stood next to a heavily traveled deer path. "They wander onto my place at night, and then go back early morning."

"I would, too, if I was fed the high-dollar stuff Swank buys," Marlin joked.

Stovall smiled. "I mean to tell ya. His bill at the feed store beats my annual income. Anyway, he was heading back to Swank's ranch right at sunup. I took a lung shot, but I think I popped him in the gut. He fell down for a second, then jumped up and ran back onto Swank's place. I walked over here to check for blood," Stovall said as he approached the deer path.

Marlin could see several deep deer tracks where the buck had accelerated out of the soft dirt. He also saw a few specks of blood, some semidigested grass, and a curious white patch.

Marlin knelt down and took a closer look. About two tablespoons of snow-white powder lay sprinkled on the ground.

Stovall said, "I got to tell you, John, in forty years of hunting, I've never seen anything like that. What do you think it is?"

Buck's behavior all makes sense now, Marlin thought. *If my hunches are right.* "I'm not sure exactly what it is," Marlin said. "But I have a pretty good idea."

CHAPTER TWELVE

BACK IN THE cruiser, Marlin's adrenaline kicked in as he thought about nailing Roy Swank for good. And now he thought he had what he needed to get the job done. But first, he needed to find someone to test the white powder for him and see if his suspicions were correct. He couldn't go to Sheriff Mackey—if he was involved, he'd make the evidence disappear faster than a cheeseburger at lunchtime.

Then Marlin thought of Bobby Garza, a good deputy and a man he knew he could trust. He'd have to set up a meeting with Garza and get his input. In any case, now was not the time to confront Swank, not till Marlin figured a few things out. So he went directly from Stovall's ranch to Phil Colby's house.

He pulled into the driveway, expecting to see Buck's head pop up somewhere in the high grass. After all, nobody had been here in a few days, and the deer loved company.

But he didn't see Buck.

Maybe he's in the barn, Marlin thought. Colby always left the back door open a little so the deer could come and go. He also left high-protein feed in a bucket, away from other deer and varmints.

Marlin swung the barn's front door open. Still no Buck.

He checked the bucket of feed. It hadn't been touched.

* * *

Roy Swank was nervous. Just talking to Oscar on the phone made his palms sweat. Having the crazy Colombian right here in his den just about made him pee his pants. Nobody—from senators to presidents—had ever made Swank feel this uptight. Even in his discomfort, Swank couldn't help but admire the man. He would have made a hell of a lobbyist.

Right now, Swank was squirming in an uneasy silence. Oscar's last words had been: "What do you think we ought to do?" He said it as if he already knew the answer.

Seconds passed as Oscar's eyes bore a hole through the back of Swank's skull. Finally, Swank gave a weak shrug.

"I tell you, then," Oscar said. "When you have a problem, you fine a way to eliminate that problem."

Swank nodded. "But I don't see as how we have a problem anymore." He tried to sound confident. "We got the deer back, and Colby is in the hospital out cold. He probably won't even remember the whole episode."

Oscar had been sitting placidly in Swank's chair, fingers steepled in front of him. Now he exploded to his feet and swept several items off the desktop. "You fool! Probably ees not good enough. What if he does remember? What then? Having the deer back means nothing if we have the DEA, the ATF, and the FBI on our asses!"

Oscar walked slowly around behind Swank. He paused in front of a large mirror and ran one hand over his slicked hair. Moments passed in silence.

Then Swank jumped involuntarily as he felt Oscar's hands on his shoulders. Oscar leaned close to Swank's right ear and whispered: "You and I are not so different. We both have beeg dreams. But there ees one thing that sets us apart, like day and night." He squeezed Swank's shoulders. "You will go to almost any length to attain your dream. But when you strip away your *Americano* boldness, the truth ees, the thought of blood scares you, deep in your heart." Oscar stood straight again. Swank was still staring straight ahead. Oscar leaned down again. "But it excites me."

Oscar came around the desk and sat back down in the chair.

Swank knew he had to speak—try to contain things before they got out of hand. "I've got an idea—one so simple I can't believe I didn't think of it earlier." Swank chuckled and waited for Oscar to urge him on. Oscar simply stared at him.

Swank said, "Here's what we should do. I'll get Tim Gray—you haven't met him, but he's my vet—I'll get him to open up the buck and remove the heroin he musta missed last time." Swank couldn't remember the last time he had said that word. Normally he referred to it as "goods" or "merchandise," somehow giving himself a sense of comfort by not directly mentioning the wares he was now peddling.

Oscar nodded. "Go on."

"Then we give the deer back to Colby. It's that simple. He wants the damn animal anyway. And once he has it—bingo—nobody's breathing down our necks anymore."

"What do we say about the scar on hees belly?"

"Hell, we just say it had a tumor or kidney stones or some such shit. Who's to know better?"

Swank smiled broadly, revealing smoke-stained teeth, while Oscar sat in silence.

"It'll be worth losing a trophy buck just so we can get back to business as usual," Swank added.

Oscar placed his fingertips on either temple and closed his eyes, as if searching the recesses of his mind for divine inspiration. Swank listened to the ticking of the antique clock on the mantle. Funny, he had never noticed how loud it was before. Sounded like a miner deep in a tunnel, rhythmically picking away at hard rock walls.

Finally Oscar looked up. "Do eet tonight."

"I've been wanting to talk to you for a long time, Barney," John Marlin said. The two men were seated at Cisco's Bar-B-Q in beautiful downtown Blanco, south of Johnson City. "Downtown" meant being within spitting distance of the only traffic light in town.

Barney Weaver was meticulously adding Sweet 'n Low to his second glass of iced tea. He had already explained how he liked exactly two-thirds of a packet. Anything more made the whole glass "fouler than a boar hog's armpits."

Marlin sat across from him, learning more and more about this peculiar man by the minute. He had been surprised by how readily Barney had agreed to lunch. When Weaver entered the restaurant, wearing a backpack and looking like an escapee from the nuthouse in Big Spring, Marlin knew he should have arranged the meeting sooner. The man was wearing a camouflage jacket and red pants. That wasn't too bad in itself, but they didn't go too well with the foil hat. Barney said it was great for rainy days. In other words, he was the kind of character you needed to keep tabs on.

"There are a coupla things I want to discuss with you," Marlin said, trying to catch Barney's eye. He continued to stir his iced tea, as if the dissolved sweetener might convert back to solid form if he let his guard down for even a minute. "Barney?"

Marlin was a little embarrassed to do it, but he finally held his hand out over the table and snapped his fingers. Barney looked up.

"I know you and Louise had a good thing when you were together…."

"Did she say that?"

Marlin paused. "Well, not in so many words…."

Barney fidgeted with his teaspoon.

"But the thing is, she's on her own now. To do whatever she pleases."

Barney looked up at Marlin and nodded his head.

Marlin continued: "If she decides to get married again someday, that's really not anybody's business except her own."

"Hell, I couldn't agree more."

"I also don't mind telling you that she and I don't have any plans of that kind…."

Barney smiled and looked Marlin straight in the eye. "Good for you, bud. I shoulda done the same thing."

"What's that?"

"Hey, it's like the old saying—why buy the cow when the milk's free?"

Marlin wasn't thrilled with the remark, but he let it pass.

"There's another thing … Louise's ex-husband … he's not the Bill Gates that you think he is."

"Oh, I done figured that out."

"You did?"

"Yep, but a man's gotta be sure, ain't he? Can't pass up a gravy train like that."

Okay, Marlin thought, we're done here. Maybe ol' Barney is off the deep end, but he seems pretty harmless. Only problem, now he'd have to sit through dinner with him. Marlin cursed himself for not ordering just coffee.

Barney continued: "A man's gotta have an angle, know what I mean?"

"Not really," Marlin said, groaning inside.

"Take a guy like me, out there every day, pouring concrete. Hell, it ain't a bad livin', but it ain't gonna make me rich, is it?"

"I guess not, but there are other things…"

Barney interrupted: "So I got to keep an eye out for anything that might better my position, as they say." Weaver smiled like he had just learned his stock had doubled.

He reached for the backpack next to him and began digging around in it. "Let me show you something…."

Marlin started to get a little nervous and realized that he had placed his hand on his pistol.

Barney pulled a Polaroid camera out of the bag. "This here could be just the ticket. Picked it up the other day at Wal-Mart in Marble Falls. Thirty-two bucks. See, I'm gonna take some pictures of a certain celebrity who I been seein' around town." Barney glanced around the restaurant furtively. "Did you know some of those newspapers like the *National Enquirer* and even *People* magazine will pay top dollar for a good photo?"

Marlin wasn't sure what to say, so he just nodded.

"You know who I saw?" Barney leaned closer. "Antonio Banderas. You know, that Meskin or Cuban guy from *Zorro?* Good flick. I don't really know what all the ladies see in that string-bean, but there's somethin'. So what I plan to do is, foller him around, and if I can pop one or two good shots of him without his britches, I could make a small fortune. Maybe I could make a name for myself, move out to California, do it full-time."

The idea of Barney relocating certainly appealed to Marlin.

Barney got quiet as the waitress approached with the men's suppers. Large platters of beef ribs and sliced brisket, with sides of potato salad and pinto beans. Barney pointed to his glass. "Could you bring another glass of tea? I fouled that one all up."

"You what?" The waitress looked confused.

"I fouled it up. Wrong balance of sweetner."

The waitress looked at Barney and then at Marlin, who could only smile.

Antonio Banderas. *Give me a break.*

When Marlin got home, he had two messages on his answering machine. He punched the button….

"Marlin, this is Roy Swank. Listen, that ol' buck showed back up over at my place somehow. Maybe with the rut coming on, he just wandered back to his home territory. But I'll tell ya, he sure is a lot of trouble…and I feel kinda bad with Colby in the hospital and all. So I'm figuring on just giving him back when Colby gets back on his feet. I'll just haul him over in one of my trailers later this week and let him go out there around Colby's place again. Put an end to all this bad blood between us. That's where he belongs anyways. So I guess

I'll talk to one a y'all later."

Marlin was elated and pissed off at the same time. Just what in the hell was Swank up to? At least he knew where Buck was now, though. Then the machine played the second message....

"Hi John, this is Becky, uh, Nurse Cameron, at the hospital. Just wanted to call and tell you some great news. Your friend Phil came out of his coma this evening....Didn't I tell you it wouldn't be long? He ate about ten pounds of our nasty hospital food, so you know he must be doing pretty well....Anyway, he's asleep now, but I'm sure he'll be ready for visitors in the next day or two.... Tomorrow's my day off, so I won't be here...but maybe I'll see you again sometime....I'd like that. By the way, my home phone number is 559-0091, in case you have any questions...or anything. 'Bye."

Marlin almost tripped going to get a pencil off the bar.

CHAPTER THIRTEEN

RED AND BILLY Don hadn't been to Austin in several months. Sure, they made a weekly trip to the western outskirts of the growing city to pick up lumber or other supplies they couldn't find in Johnson City or Blanco. But they usually stayed away from downtown.

Tonight was different. Now they each had ten thousand bucks in cash to play with.

They had gone east from Johnson City on Highway 290, through Oak Hill and all the way to Austin, then began a slow northward cruise up Lamar Boulevard. They were in Red's 1972 Ford pickup, a vehicle that would have been right at home in Austin twenty years ago, but now was greatly outnumbered by shiny Mercedes sedans, BMWs, sport utility vehicles, and other late-model foreign cars.

"Damn, this town has changed," Red said. " 'Member when we used to cruise into the Soap Creek Saloon over in Westlake? And the Armadilla over on Barton Springs?"

Billy Don nodded as he drained the last drops from a Lone Star longneck. He had noticed that a couple of six-packs helped numb the pain of the snakebite he had received two days earlier. Plus, the swelling had gone down considerably. The horse-doctor had given him a sling, but Billy Don had discarded that after Red called him a sissy.

"Now there ain't nothing here but Yankees and for'ners," Red continued. "Sucked the life right out of this town. I been to Houston, and I'm tellin' ya, this ain't much different no more."

Billy Don belched in agreement.

Red pulled from his own beer. "Buncha high-tech geeks everywhere come over from California, all going on and on about the Innernet....hell, I don't see the value in it. You wanna talk to someone, why not just call 'em on the phone?"

"There's porn," Billy Don said.

"Wazzat?"

"From what I hear, you can dial up pitchers of naked ladies right there in your living room. Even *Playboy* magazine."

"Well, hell," Red said. He'd have to think that over.

Moments later, Red tapped on the brakes. "Hey, lookee there, McLeod's Guns is open late," he said as he swung into the parking lot. A banner hung over the double front doors that said: HUNTERS, START THE SEASON WITH A BANG! "What say we go inside and have a look around?"

As Red climbed from the truck, he patted his camouflage jacket for the hundredth time that night, smiling at the deck of hundred-dollar bills tucked away safely in the pocket. He'd always wanted a high-quality firearm—maybe a Colt or a Smith & Wesson—but none of that foreign stuff. Keep the money right here in the U.S. But he had to admit, those Glocks and Rugers were well-made, he had to give 'em that.

Inside, McLeod's was crammed wall-to-wall with hunters preparing for deer season. Hundreds of pistols, deer rifles, and shotguns were on display, and Red headed straight for the handgun counter.

He elbowed himself between two burly men, who gave him hard looks he didn't catch, then caught the eye of the old guy working the counter.

"Can I help you this evening?"

"Yeah, I'd like to take a look at that Anaconda," Red said, pointing.

"That's a fine choice, one of Colt's finest products," the old guy said as he placed the revolver on the counter. "You hunt with a handgun?"

Red picked it up and gave a low, approving whistle, liking the way the weapon felt in his hand. Solid, but not too heavy. "I'm thinking about using one this year. What kind of range can this handle?"

"With open sights, about fifty yards. But you put a scope on that baby and you can make shots up to about a hundred yards. It all depends on the ammo—and the hunter. You look like a guy who can handle a pistol."

Red passed the gun to Billy Don. "What do you think, Billy Don? We could sure drop one in its tracks with that, couldn't we?"

"Damnation, Red. This sucker's huge. You gonna haul that cannon around on your hip?"

"Or I could just keep it in the truck."

"But we already got the two-seventy. What do you need a revolver for?"

"A man can't have too many guns, you oughtta know that." Red smiled at the salesman, who nodded back.

The old guy said, "Fill your Brady forms out and you can pick it up in plenty of time for opening day."

Red paused. "Brady forms?"

"You know, the five-day waiting period and all."

"I can't take it tonight?"

The man shrugged his shoulders. "Nothing I can do. Gotta wait five days before you can take possession, courtesy of Mrs. Sarah Brady. Federal law."

"Well, shit," Red said, cradling the gun again. "Just like the guv'mint to go and fuck up something as American as buying a gun."

After a few seconds, the old guy leaned forward and said quietly, "On the other hand, there is no waiting period when you buy from a private individual—and I happen to have a pretty good selection of handguns myself...."

Red perked up immediately.

They sat in the cavernous, smoke-filled room, listening to the driving beat of "Panama" by Van Halen. Red ordered another round of beer each time a new stripper came onstage. They were on their ninth or tenth dancer now; Red had lost track.

"What time did that geezer say to come back?" Billy Don yelled over the music.

"Ten o'clock. Hell, a few hours is a lot less than five days," Red replied.

"Than what?"

Red cupped his hands. "Five days!"

"I thought you said ten o'clock."

It was no use shouting.

"I still don't see why you want a handgun," Billy Don hollered. "You already manage to get yourself in plenty of trouble with a rifle."

Red wasn't ready to tell Billy Don what was brewing in his head, how he'd feel better having a little protection, so he ignored him and watched the redhead onstage. She was dancing just a few feet in front of him, giving him a big smile.

For good reason, too. He and Billy Don had been handing out ten-dollar bills like a Hare Krishna hands out fliers. *The way you do it,* Red had told Billy Don earlier, *is to kinda slide your hand along their thigh when you're putting the ten-spot in their G-string. Get a nice feel. Another trick, sometimes they put their hands on your shoulders when you're putting the money in. You do it just right, you can lean back a little and they fall right into you. You play like you're catching them, but you grab yourself a big handful of tit. Hell, they don't mind, long as you keep the money coming.*

After a few more dancers and a few more beers, Red thought Billy Don was in the right frame of mind. He could tell by the way Billy Don was hollering out occasional random sounds and clapping way off-beat to the music. So when a slow, quiet song came on, Red leaned in close and said, "How would you like to double the cash you got in your pocket?"

Billy Don looked at him with wet eyes that wouldn't quite focus properly. "Wat'you got in mind, pardner?"

"I been thinking about Roy Swank and that deer. And man, something just ain't right. I know them trophy deers are valuable, but twenty thousand bucks in cash? There's got to be more to it than that." Red took a long swig of beer and let that thought rattle around in Billy Don's head.

Billy Don had his eyes glued on the young lady on stage—a platinum-blonde, about five-nine, 34D. Jesus, those high heels did wonders for a girl's legs. Not to mention a red garter belt and stockings. But he was listening to Red at the same time. "What do you think's so special with that buck?" he asked.

"That don't really matter. All I know's that Swank wants to hold on to him."

"Yeah, well, he's got him."

"Use your noggin, big man. What if that deer was to disappear again? I 'magine Swank'd come right back to us to find it again. For the same price."

Billy Don hollered out at the dancer as she bent over backward and looked between her legs at him. Red shook his head. Man, this guy was dense as an oak stump. So Red waited until the song was over and the dancer left the stage. Then he leaned in again and said, "Let me spell it out for ya: We go over to Swank's place, grab the deer, and take off with it."

Billy Don turned and looked at him. Slowly a smile creased his face.

Red continued. "Best part is, hell, I don't know if that's even a crime. Can a man really *own* a deer?"

"You really think he'd pay us again?"

"I don't see why not. We did a hell of a job the first time."

Billy Don took a long pull from his beer and pondered it for a few minutes.

Then he said, "When do you wanna do it?"

"Well, Billy Don, my daddy always told me…there's no time like the present."

Red would look back on that night for many years to come and wish he'd done things a little differently.

For starters, he probably would have approached Swank's house a little more discreetly. They knew the deer was in the five-acre pen near the house—and rounding it up would be easy, as tame as it was—but to just go marching right up there at three in the morning was a bad idea.

He probably wouldn't have had so much to drink, and he definitely wouldn't have brought that bottle of Jack Daniel's along with him.

There was also the matter of Billy Don's singing. Bellowing a Hank Williams tune while you're sneaking up on someone wasn't something James Bond did on a regular basis.

And, oh yeah, he would have left the tit dancer in the truck. Sure, Crystal was a nice girl and all…a really nice girl…but what does a stripper know about stealing a deer? She was gorgeous and lean, with that nasty-girl look to her. And she could suck the hide off an alligator—she had proved that in the truck on the way over here for a hundred bucks each—but she wasn't exactly the animal-kidnapper type.

Red couldn't remember all of the crucial events very clearly. Too much booze, and it all happened so quickly. One minute they were approaching the pen, Red right on Crystal's behind in those tight leather pants. The next minute they were standing in the middle of a blinding spotlight. A Meskin-sounding voice yelled at them. Then a shot rang out and Billy Don fell like a sack of potatoes. Yeah, a sack that could hold every potato in Idaho.

CHAPTER FOURTEEN

WEDNESDAY MORNING AT seven A.M., John Marlin sat down with Blanco County deputy Bobby Garza at Big Joe's in Johnson City. The men saw each other often, both being law enforcement officers, and they socialized on an occasional basis. Each had a deep respect for the other, due to their mutual commitment to the law—and their contempt for Sheriff Herbert Mackey. Marlin knew that Garza was someone he could speak to in absolute confidence, and that was why he had arranged this meeting.

After shaking hands, they walked to a table in the back, away from the few other early-bird customers, where they could talk freely. They made small talk until the waitress brought coffee, and then Marlin dove right in.

He started at the beginning, telling Garza about Buck's strange behavior in the pasture after Trey Sweeney got shot. He mentioned that Sheriff Mackey wanted to shoot the deer, but a call from Roy Swank stopped him. He said that Buck had disappeared from Colby's barn. And now, apparently, Swank had Buck again—but he wanted to give him back. Then he told him about the trip out to Thomas Stovall's place, and the white powder the wounded deer had left behind. Marlin made a point of just stating the facts, without any of his own opinions, to see if Garza arrived at the same conclusion.

The deputy didn't say a word during the entire tale, just sat nodding his head and listening intently. When Marlin finished, Garza remained quiet for a moment, and then the questions began.

"Did you find the wounded deer?"

"No, he ran back onto Swank's place, and I thought it would be better to talk to you before I did anything."

"What did you do with the white powder?" Garza asked.

"I've got it all in an evidence bag in my glove compartment."

"Did you take photos of it on the ground?"

Marlin shook his head. He was kicking himself for the oversight, but he was a game warden, for Christ's sake, not a DEA agent. Marlin said, "I know I probably should have called Mackey instead of you, but…"

Garza shook his head and said, "No, you did the right thing. We both know he's pretty good buddies with Roy Swank. But the question is, is he tied up in all this?"

"For discussion's sake, Bobby, what do you think 'all this' is?"

Garza leaned closer and spoke quietly. "Sounds like we got some deer running around with contraband in 'em over at the Circle S. And we know Swank brings deer in from Mexico all the time. So that, to me, looks like a pretty good argument for drug smuggling."

Marlin smiled. That was one of the reasons he liked Garza: He was a straight shooter, with no bullshit, no what-ifs or maybes.

"Man, I'm glad you said that. I was worried you'd think I'm crazy."

"It does sound a little crazy…until you think about all the people who swallow condoms full of drugs and try to smuggle 'em that way. If it can be done with people, why not animals? So the first thing we need to do is test that powder and see what happens."

"And it if comes back dirty, what then?"

Garza paused for a moment. "To be honest, I really don't know, at this point. Let's just take this one step at a time. If we see any indication that Mackey is involved, we'll have to go around him. That may mean bringing in the DEA."

The thought of working with the feds made Marlin a little nervous, but there wasn't a way to avoid it. What if the powder tested positive, but then they couldn't find anything at Swank's place? He and Garza would look like fools, and Swank could even file a lawsuit. The men were discussing these possibilities as they left the restaurant and walked around to the back parking lot to Marlin's cruiser.

But even before Marlin unlocked his truck door, he could see, through the window, that his glove compartment was open. The powder was gone.

* * *

The mistake Thomas Stovall had made the night before was going to the Happy Trails Saloon, drinking a few too many beers, and then opening his mouth about the events on his property that morning.

"What the hell did Marlin think it was?" one of the regulars had asked.

"He wouldn't say," Stovall replied, "but it was obvious he thought it was cocaine, or heroin, or some such shit."

"What'd he do with it?"

"He scooped it into a baggie and put it in his truck."

The men were stunned. Could Swank be a dealer? Nobody really knew him too well, and they sure didn't like him. If he was dealing, what could be more strange than loading up a whitetail with drugs? Many of the men got downright peeved, saying that kind of behavior would be a crime against nature. They were angry. They were indignant. They were thrilled to have such a wild saga unfolding in their quiet little community.

The men were so wrapped up by Stovall's story, nobody paid any attention to the stranger sitting quietly at the bar, watching basketball on ESPN. Even though he did look an awful lot like Antonio Banderas.

Oscar was furious with himself for letting things get this chaotic. He prided himself on many things—his looks, his intelligence, his fine sense of style, and yes, his ability to run a smooth ship. But now things were messier than an old jar of hair gel. Oscar had four basic rules for doing business: Number one, only work with people you trust. Two, make sure they trust you. Three, if things get sloppy, fuck them before they fuck you. And four....Damn! He could never remember that one. Something about guns or cops or something.

Another thing—Oscar didn't know the gringos who were tied up in the house right now, but these weren't the kind of men he was used to dealing with. Such impertinence. Such drunkenness. Such stupidity. Whereas Oscar's henchmen in Colombia kept their mouths shut and their eyes open, these men seemed to operate in reverse. Last night, they had claimed to be employees of Roy Swank. But could these idiots possibly be the same two men who had reclaimed the deer for Swank? Those men would have to have had bravado and courage. But these men were simpering buffoons. He would have to question Swank at length this morning.

Swank himself was nearly as incompetent. How could a man sleep peacefully while intruders were parading across his compound? Did he not hear the dogs barking, the shotgun blast? Perhaps he was spoiled by his years working with the government. Could it be that lobbyists typically operate outside the law, with little concern about getting caught? If so, they had far more power and clout than Oscar ever imagined. But it was far more likely that Oscar had made the one mistake that spelled certain death in Colombia: getting involved with amateurs.

Oscar was concerned, but no, not nervous. He had no plans to let this situation get away from him. If it was necessary, there would be a long line of corpses on the floor of the Swank mansion by this evening, while he was slipping back to Colombia, free and untraceable. It would be a major setback, having to completely abandon the operation. But that was sometimes the cost of doing business.

He waited patiently by the pool, enjoying a full breakfast. When Swank joined him, Oscar would know then what to do. Swank's words would reveal himself for what he was: a pro or an amateur. And amateurs always wound up dead.

At nine A.M. on Wednesday, November 3, Bobby Garza and three other deputies raided the secluded home of Charles W. Walznick. Actually, calling it a home was charitable. The only building on the forty-acre property was a sixteen-by-sixteen shack with running water, but no phone or electricity. Garza had seen barns that were more inviting. The property was located on an unpaved dead-end county road that Garza couldn't remember traveling for at least ten years. Looked like Willie Combes had been telling the truth, Garza thought, because this place was perfect for a pot farm.

Two days earlier, Garza had logged on to the Sheriff's Department computer and learned some interesting things about Charles Walznick: Twenty-eight years old, college dropout. Twelve arrests since the age of eighteen, three convictions. No violent crimes, just forgery, burglary, and—what appeared to be Mr. Walznick's favorite pastime—possession of marijuana. He had been arrested seven times for holding weed. But he had always had good legal representation, so he had never done state time, just a few months in county facilities. None of the incidents had taken place in Blanco County. Walznick was an Austin native and had purchased the forty acres about three years ago.

The question foremost in Garza's mind was where Walznick had gotten the money to buy the place. Garza could find no records of Walznick ever holding a job, filing a tax return, or even having a Social Security number. This was the kind of guy for whom the phrase "no visible means of support" was coined.

Walznick himself was not an impressive figure. When the deputies burst through the flimsy door of the shack, Walznick was asleep on a cot wearing ragged blue jeans and no shirt. He weighed about 135 and stood five-seven. He had stringy blond hair, three or four days' stubble. Garza quickly realized that he really didn't need all the manpower for this scrawny punk. He could have come out here alone—without a firearm, for that matter. Walznick was just a meek little guy with a case of arrested adolescence—an adult in a prolonged high-school party phase—not a hardened criminal. The only problem, Walznick had been growing a healthy crop of marijuana every year on his acreage. According to Willie Combes.

Walznick didn't look surprised when Garza and his men came barging in. At first, Garza figured he was stoned. But then he realized Walznick had been expecting something like this to happen.

After one of the deputies frisked Walznick and the other men searched the sparse shack for weapons, Garza sent all three of them out to search the property. He remained in the shack with Walznick, who sat dejectedly on the filthy cot.

Garza said, "I get the feeling you know exactly why we're here."

"Yeah, I been waiting on you, man," Walznick said somberly. "I heard that Willie got busted so I knew the heat was gonna come down."

"Okay, so tell me what's going on."

"Sir, I can't tell you anything until I talk to my lawyer." Polite, but reluctant.

This punk was no different than Willie Combes, just a few years older, with a little more experience with the law under his belt. Garza had prepared himself for this.

"Charles, you can get a lawyer if you want. And with your history, I can see why you want one. You're very likely looking at state time and the forfeiture of your acreage and cabin." He gestured out the door. "Unless I'm an idiot, I expect my men to find marijuana growing in plots on the back side of your property. Maybe not a huge amount…I don't think you're a major dealer or anything. I think you grow just enough to get by. Sell some to your friends, and your friends' friends. Maybe sell a few keys to other dealers once in a while. But that's not the biggest of your problems, Charles. It looks like Willie's friend Michael died from smoking your weed.

Walznick's head jerked up quickly. "He what?"

"That's right, you probably thought we were just out here to burn the weed and take you in. But it's a little more complicated than that. See, the guy was an asthmatic, and he died because of your pot. Now, I'm guessing you treated your crop with all kinds of pesticides and herbicides. And seeing as how you're not exactly a Rhodes scholar, you probably had no idea what you were doing. Your negligence adds up to involuntary manslaughter, at least."

Walznick was shaking his head back and forth. "Shit. Shit!"

Garza was taking his time, enjoying himself. "You could be looking at five to twenty years. Twenty years is a long time, when you think about it, isn't it? Remember when you were eight years old, playing war games and sneaking peeks at your daddy's nudie magazines? How would you like to have been in jail since way back then? That's how long of a stretch we're talking about."

Walznick was now breathing very heavily. Just about to talk, Garza thought.

"Charles, any second now, one of my men is gonna holler out. That will mean he's found the first of your plots. I'm sure you've got small ones all over the place. But I'll make you a deal. If you start talking before one of my men hollers, telling me the whole story about your little farm here—who you deal to, who helps you with the operation, how you got the money to buy this place—I promise you…" Garza paused. "Look at me, Charles."

Walznick's head came up out of his hands and he looked Garza in the eyes.

Garza continued. "I promise you, I'll do what I can to help you out. I mean, it seems obvious to me that you didn't intend for the guy to die. But if you don't talk, I'll make you a different promise. I will do everything in my power—everything—to fuck up your life. I'll make sure you get sent to Huntsville for a good, long time."

Walznick nodded his head just in time, as one of the men whistled loudly from a few hundred yards away.

CHAPTER FIFTEEN

ROY SWANK FINALLY joined Oscar by the pool at nine-thirty. The weather was still and cool, in the fifties, and it looked like it was going to be a beautiful Texas autumn day, with plenty of sunshine.

Roy said good morning to Oscar and sat down next to him. Oscar nodded, but did not look up from his newspaper. The Colombian had a portable radio on the table and was singing along with it…something about being "too sexy for his pants."

Roy was in a bathrobe and slippers, and began to feel a little self-conscious sitting there with no conversation. He sipped orange juice and waited, sensing that something was wrong. Maybe it wouldn't be such a great day after all.

Just as Roy was about to speak, Oscar turned the radio off and asked, "Who are Red and Billy Don?"

Swank was puzzled. How did Oscar know those names? For some reason, Swank always felt like he should lie to Oscar, thinking the less the Colombian knew, the better. But it seemed an innocent-enough question, so Swank told him that those were the two men who had helped him take the deer back from Phil Colby.

"And where are they now?" Oscar asked, still not looking up from the paper.

"Hell if I know. I'm done with those two. Like you say, you gotta deal with professionals only, and those guys are rank amateurs." Swank was making an effort to appease Oscar, his way of saying, *See, I've been listening to you, and I'm trying to do things your way.*

Oscar folded the paper neatly and placed it on the table. "What would you say if I tole you that they are locked up in your house right now?"

Swank smiled, and then his mouth fell open as he realized Oscar was telling the truth.

Oscar continued, his voice beginning to rise. "Yes, the two men you have trusted before, men who know things they should not know, came to your house lass night. I believe their intention was to steal back the deer, for whatever reason. Maybe to milk more money out of you. But they have too much whiskey and become clumsy and loud. I shoot one of them, and..."

"You shot one of them?" Swank echoed in amazement.

"Yes, but he ees fine. Just a small wound. Big man like that, ees no problem for him." Oscar paused and looked at the sun rising over the oak trees around the pool. "Also, who is Thomas Stovall?"

"He's one of my neighbors. Why?"

Oscar recounted Thomas Stovall's tale at the tavern the night before, and told about breaking into the game warden's vehicle to retrieve the white powder.

"Shit. This whole thing is coming unglued," Swank said.

"You are right, my frien'. These men, we cannot have them running around causing trouble. Now is the time for me to call in some of *mis amigos* from my country."

"What for?" Swank was getting wound-up, but he was determined not to let it show.

"Something must be done with all of these...what you call loose ends. This Red and Billy Don. The game warden and his frien'. We must find a way to convince them to leave us alone, to go about our business. My frien's, they are experts at convincing people in such matters."

The last thing Swank wanted was a bunch of swarthy thugs running around his property. So he tried a new approach with Oscar: brashness. "Fuck your friends," he said, pounding his fist on the table. "That damn game warden doesn't know a thing. I already told him we're giving the deer back, so he'll get off our backs after that. Like you said, he ain't got nothing on us without the powder. And Red and Billy Don, hell, we just pay 'em a few bucks and they'll go on their merry way. I don't see why we need any of your buddies up here."

Swank looked out of the corner of his eye to see how Oscar would react. Swank had never spoken that forcefully to Oscar before. The Colombian merely smiled. Then he spoke in a calm, collected manner. "Who is running thees operation?"

Swank hated to answer that one. It was always an unspoken understanding that Oscar was the boss, but Swank hated to admit it out loud. "You are," he said bitterly.

"Yes, I am," Oscar said. "And I am bringing in some help. Some men I can trust."

At that point, Swank truly didn't give a damn anymore. Frankly, he was tired, and he didn't want to deal with any of this mess. His mind was humming, thinking that if Oscar's men could find a way to end all these problems, then what the hell. "Fine," he said, still trying to sound like the decision was a mutual one. "Bring your boys on up. Let 'em help us out a little bit."

Oscar went inside to call his men, while Roy Swank sat on the patio, wishing he had some men of his own. He had an uneasy feeling that he might need some soon.

Oscar was surprised. Swank had reacted more bravely than he had anticipated. If Swank could show a little machismo, without panicking, maybe there was still a way to salvage the remaining merchandise. After all, the game warden named Marlin no longer had the drugs. Popping the truck door open was easy, and the glove box wasn't even locked. These Americans were far too trusting…but that was a fortunate thing in this case.

So all the game warden could really say was that he had found a white powder on the ground. The *federales* from the DEA would ask: *How do you know it came from the deer? How do you know the powder was drugs?* Marlin would not only be ridiculed, he wouldn't even be able to get a search warrant. Especially not with Swank's connections. So Oscar felt confident that Marlin would do nothing.

The thing to do now, Oscar decided, was to continue with business as usual, with one exception. Bring no more merchandise to the Circle S Ranch. Simply unload what's already here, and then abandon Swank for another wealthy American who was equally greedy. And if Swank objected to that, Oscar's men would be here to deal with him.

* * *

Marlin stuck his head into the hospital room, expecting Phil Colby to look pretty awful. He wasn't disappointed. But his best friend was awake, thank God, and that's what really mattered. Colby was lying back, hand on the remote control, watching a Spurs game on TV.

"Knock, knock," Marlin said, swinging the door open.

Colby looked in Marlin's direction. "John?"

"Who were you expecting, the Pope?" Marlin said. Maybe some light humor would keep him from getting choked up.

Marlin walked up to the bed and the two men clasped hands. "Goddamn, buddy, you look pretty lame. You'd think you've been in a coma or something."

"You don't know the half of it," Colby said, easing himself up a little straighter in bed. "My head feels like I been kicked by a mule. They say I still have a pretty good concussion. But they don't want to give me any painkillers until they know I'm gonna be conscious for a while."

Marlin eyed the heavy bandage across Colby's forehead. "I guess you got some stitches…."

"About twenty. Right behind the hairline, though, so it won't mess up my movie-star looks. Plus a little double vision, vertigo, and I get a little confused now and then and think I'm a Vegas showgirl."

Marlin grinned from ear to ear. It was the old Colby, cracking jokes and taking things in stride. Damn, what a nice thing to see.

Colby griped a little about the hospital food and the boredom that came with watching TV all day, but it didn't take him long to get around to the big question: "So where's Buck?"

Marlin had been contemplating just how much to tell Colby about the last few days. He didn't want to load Colby down with a bunch of worries when he should be concentrating on getting better and getting out of the hospital. So Marlin had made up his mind on the way to the hospital to keep the details to a minimum. At least he could tell him the truth about Buck. He told him about the message from Roy Swank, and added that he felt confident that Swank wasn't pulling a fast one. "When he returns Buck, believe me, I'll keep an eye on him personally until you get home. The only thing I'm wondering is how Buck got back over to Swank's place. He said that Buck just showed up one day…"

"We both know that's a load of shit," Colby said. "Whoever cracked my skull took him."

"Any idea who it was?"

"It's a real pisser. I can't hardly remember anything. All I know is that I was closing up shop and someone knocked on the door. I look out the window and there's two guys standing there in Moe and Curly masks."

"In what?"

"In masks like Moe and Curly…you know, from *The Three Stooges*. Next thing I know, I'm waking up here last night."

"You don't remember anything they said?"

"Nothing. I don't even know whether they came into the shop or not." Colby bit his lip. "I guess I might have told them where Buck was."

"Hey, don't worry about it. We're getting him back."

"John, what in the hell do you think is going on? Would Swank really resort to this kind of crap just to get Buck back? We're talking about a bunch of felonies here, right? I mean, to you and me, getting Buck back is a big deal. But Swank has dozens of deer just like him. What's so special about Buck all of a sudden?"

Marlin wanted to spill his guts, to say, *Oh, it's no big deal, I just think Swank is running some kind of drug ring out there, importing deer with narcotics surgically implanted inside them.* But he kept quiet. Now was not the time. Marlin just shook his head and said he was doing his best to find out. Then he changed the subject. "Any idea when you're getting out?"

"So far, all they're saying is that it will be at least a few days. But to tell you the truth, I don't really mind." Colby had a sly grin on his face.

"Man, I'd be climbing the walls," Marlin said.

"I would, too, except I think I'm falling in love with one of the nurses."

Marlin's stomach lurched.

"She's sweet and funny," Colby said. "And man, you gotta see her, John. She looks like Julia Roberts."

CHAPTER SIXTEEN

RED O'BRIEN COULDN'T decide whether he should be angry or afraid. After all, here they were, tied up in a room in Roy Swank's house. What kind of gratitude was that for the job they had done? And who was that Meskin man anyway? He sure didn't act like the wetbacks they had around Blanco County. Those boys knew their place. Sure, they might get to drinking sometimes and get a little big for their britches. But most the time, they kept quiet and did what they were told. Fear of deportation is what it was. But not this guy from last night. Hog-tied all three of them, including the stripper, and dumped them in this small room. And Billy Don was lying over there bleeding and moaning. Well, whimpering, really, because of the tape over his mouth.

There was only one chair in the room, a big leather recliner, and Red and Billy Don had let the stripper have it for the night. Right now, she was fast asleep, snoring like a bloodhound.

Red could feel the nylon ski rope around his wrists. He had been trying to loosen it all night, and he thought he was making headway. His skin was getting pretty raw, but he was getting used to it. He wasn't a crybaby like Billy Don. Man, he'd love to get himself free and go looking for that Meskin. Red had just started working on the rope again when the door opened and the man entered.

* * *

"Good morning, my frien's," the man said with a fake smile. "I trust that you sleep well." He walked over and looked down at Billy Don, as if making sure he was still alive. Then he stood over the stripper and put his hand on her cheek. She woke up with a gurgle from behind her taped mouth. The man eased the tape off the girl's mouth while holding a finger to his lips, telling her to keep quiet. Then he removed a pocketknife from his trousers, leaned behind her, and cut her free. "You just stay right there," the man said. She rubbed her wrists but remained seated quietly on the chair.

The man turned to face Red and Billy Don. "My name is Oscar. Mr. Swank confirm who you are…Red and Billy Don. I think maybe we both make mistakes lass night. You should not have been on the property…and perhaps I should not have shot at you. But I think maybe you meant no harm." He smiled as Billy Don began nodding rapidly. "So I come in here to find out why you were really here lass night. I think maybe you will tell me now."

The man walked over to where Billy Don was leaning against the wall. "Beeg man…you look honest to me." Billy Don nodded again, with wide eyes. The man bent down and peeled the tape off Billy Don's face. "Tell me…why were you here?"

Billy Don looked in Red's direction, so Oscar stepped in between them, blocking Billy Don's view. Billy Don stammered for a minute and then said, "Well, we just had a little too much to drink and wanted to show Crystal that big ol' deer we rescued."

Oscar's smile slowly faded. He knelt down beside Billy Don and unfolded the knife. "Let's have a look at the gunshot you received last night." Oscar then cut away a swatch from Billy Don's shirt to reveal a hole the size of a pencil eraser in Billy Don's flabby midsection.

"Mister, that buckshot you used on me last night shore tore me up," Billy Don whimpered. "I think I need to go to a hospital."

"You are lucky you were just hit one time. Tell me the truth and you will be free to go wherever you wish. Why were you here lass night?"

"I already told you. Hell, we was just having a little fun."

Oscar shook his head and stared at Billy Don. Then, without warning, he leaned down and worked his forefinger into the huge man's wound, tearing it open wider. Billy Don cried out in pain. Oscar got right in Billy Don's face. "You feel that? You feel me moving your intestines around? Yes, I believe you are right…you need a doctor. But first tell me the truth."

Tears ran down Billy Don's cheeks, but he shook his head in defiance. Oscar said, "I now have my finger around your intestines. Start talking…or I'll start pulling. You end up looking at your own guts lying on the floor." To the amazement of the other three people in the room, Billy Don remained quiet. His eyelids fluttered, as if he were about to faint. Oscar's finger came back out of the wound…and with it, a narrow, gray tube of intestine. "Look!" Oscar said, like a child spotting a butterfly. "I can see wha' you had for dinner lass night." He smiled at his own sick joke.

"Okay!" Billy Don yelled.

"Tell me the truth."

"Just quit pulling!"

"The truth," Oscar said, having fun with this little game.

"We was gonna steal the deer back from Mr. Swank and then sell it to him again," Billy Don couldn't talk fast enough. "It was wrong and stupid and we never should have done it." His eyes remained locked in fear on Oscar's finger and the protruding U-shaped portion of his own entrails that the finger was hooked around.

"All you wanted was the money?" Oscar asked.

"We figgered if he paid us once he'd pay us twice."

"Do you know why that deer ees so special?"

"No idear. Honest."

Oscar gently prodded Billy Don's intestines back into the cavernous belly. He stood and faced Red. "That deer is Mr. Swank's most productive stud. He values him most greatly." Oscar handed his knife to Crystal and said, "Cut them loose. And then all three of you…leave this property and do not come back."

Oscar turned on his Italian heels and left the room.

John Marlin struggled long and hard with the idea of calling Nurse Becky Cameron. He asked himself, *Am I really interested in this woman—I mean, really interested?* Then he realized, just by asking himself that question, he already knew the answer. What's more, he had a reason to call her, a matter of official business.

After his hospital visit, Marlin had remembered something crucial: He had taken a blood sample from Buck the same night he had tranquilized him. He had wanted to check for rabies, more as a precaution than anything else. Deer seldom get rabies, but it was possible. Marlin no longer thought rabies could be the problem, but at the time, it could have explained Buck's behavior. So he would ask Becky to discreetly check the blood sample for drugs. Frankly, he was a little too embarrassed to mention the blood sample to Bobby Garza now; the deputy had given him a questionable look after the powder was stolen from Marlin's cruiser. No, he'd rather wait until the sample was tested. If it came back positive, he'd have the evidence he needed to take to the DEA. Sure, they'd think he was a nut job at first, but with the sample, maybe they'd start to buy into his theory. Well, at least they'd listen without busting a gut.

As for his other reason for calling Becky…his attraction…hell, he didn't know what to do about that. Moving in on a woman your best friend was attracted to, now that was low. So he decided to just play it by ear, see where the conversation went.

He dialed her number and was just about to hang up when she answered on the seventh ring, sounding out of breath. "Oh, Officer Marlin. Sorry, I was in the bathtub," she said. For some reason, that comment made Marlin a little nervous. He could picture small beads of water dripping off various parts of her anatomy. "But I'm really glad you called," she said. "Did you go see Phil today?"

"I did, and it looks like he's doing great. Thanks for the message yesterday. Most nurses wouldn't bother calling…."

"I could tell how close you two are, so I thought you'd want to know. I mean, two people who've been friends since kindergarten…that's just about unheard-of. At least in a city the size of Dallas."

"That where you're from?"

"Born and raised."

"Nice town. I've been up there a few times. They obviously know how to grow some good-lookin' ladies." Somehow, Marlin managed to make that remark sound sweet instead of hokey.

"Why, thank you," Becky replied in an exaggerated voice of a Southern belle.

Marlin said, "I was born right here in Blanco County, so I've known just about everybody all my life. I still see most of my teachers from school. A lot of my old classmates and football teammates are still around. In high school, I dated the former sheriff's daughter for three years, and now she's the dispatcher." *Now, that was a stupid thing to say,* Marlin thought. *Why did I bring that up?*

Becky got a teasing tone in her voice. "What happened with you and her? Couldn't stand the heat from her old man?"

"Naw, we just wanted different things. When I went off to Southwest Texas State University, we decided it would be best just to end it." Marlin felt a little funny discussing his private life with a woman he barely knew. But somehow it seemed kind of right. Like the way he felt when he talked about personal things with Phil.

"And what did she do?"

"She stayed and got married—which is what she wanted in the first place. Has three kids now, one of them already in junior high."

"So you're one of the non-marrying types?" Becky asked. Marlin could tell she was trying hard to sound casual.

"I was then." *That should suffice,* Marlin thought. Frankly, he didn't know what "type" he was now. All he knew was that he was giddy inside, just because he was talking to this woman. Hell, she was really just a girl, probably ten years younger than he was. What was there to be nervous or anxious about? He'd dated lots of women, but had never felt so self-conscious with any of them. Marlin snapped out of his thoughts, realizing that Becky had just asked him something. "Excuse me?"

"I was wondering if you were going to see him again in the next few days. I'm working tomorrow and I, uh…" She sounded a little nervous herself. "And I just thought I might stop by and say hello. If you're going to be there."

"Actually, I've got a lot going on in the next few days. Deer season starts on Saturday and I've got a lot of things to take care of before then. Meetings with the Wildlife Commission all day tomorrow. Phil'll probably get out of the hospital before I can make it back up there."

"That's too bad. I mean, it's great that Phil will be going home soon, I just, uh …" The pretty nurse stammered a little, and Marlin could remember phone conversations in high school that had had the same wonderful uneasiness. There is a certain rush of excitement and awkward romance that sweeps over you when you're young. Somehow, those sensations, those emotions, lessen as you grow older. Or Marlin had always thought they did, anyway, until now.

"I know what you mean. I was thinking the same thing," Marlin said, taking her off the spot. "Listen, Becky, I was hoping we could get together sometime…" he said, wanting to arrange a meeting where they could talk about testing the blood sample.

"I'd love to. What did you have in mind?"

It happened that quick. She thought he was asking her out on a date. And he certainly wanted to, he just didn't know whether his conscience would allow it. But now it was out of his hands, so he just rolled with it. "The next few nights, I need to be on patrol. You wouldn't believe the number of hunters who go out spotlighting, hoping to get an early start on the season. So what I do, I park on a county road and wait to hear shots. It wouldn't be the most romantic date you've ever had, but I was thinking you could join me—"

"That sounds great!" she interjected. "I could bring along some sandwiches. I have an ice chest …"

"That's right, you have a very nice chest," Marlin said, unable to resist the pun.

Becky giggled and said, "Why, Mr. Marlin, I didn't think you had noticed."

CHAPTER SEVENTEEN

OSCAR WAS ANTSY. He hated waiting almost as much as he hated being rushed. But right now, all he could do was wait for his men, who would arrive later that evening. They had immediately made arrangements for the next flight out, because when Oscar called, you answered.

Just before noon, to battle his restlessness, Oscar decided to go into Johnson City and pick up some food and other provisions. Everything his American host ate was so bland and tasteless. Besides, he'd need to lay in a good supply for his troops.

He left the main house and went to the smaller of two guest houses—complete with hot tub, wide-screen television, and full bar—and grabbed the keys to his rented Cadillac.

As he exited the front door and walked to his car, Oscar paused. He had the distinct feeling that he was being watched. Had he seen movement out of the corner of his eye? He couldn't be sure. There was just something....

He strutted slowly along the cobblestone walkway and out onto the crushed-gravel driveway. The small stones crunched under his feet. Then he heard something move in the nearby hedges. Oscar turned quickly, but saw only a solid wall of red-tipped photinia, lush from autumn rains.

He shook his head, sure that he was letting his imagination run away from him. Then, when he was just two steps away from the car door, Oscar heard something like the slide being pulled on an automatic handgun.

In one fluid motion, and without even thinking, Oscar pulled the .38 out of his waistband, wheeled, and shot Barney Weaver directly through the heart.

The source of the noise, the Polaroid camera in Weaver's hands, dropped and clattered on the gravel. The photo he had just taken fluttered lifelessly to the ground. He slumped to his knees, and then fell face-first onto the driveway. Weaver's last thought was: *Damn, that Antonio Banderas is one mean son of a bitch.*

Tim Gray was sure the stuffed animal heads on Roy Swank's den wall were coming to life. That goatlike thing—what had Swank called it, an oryx?—it was staring directly at the strungout veterinarian. Hadn't it been looking in the other direction earlier? And what about that damn red elk? Gray could almost hear the breath sucking in and out of its large nostrils. Jesus, it was hard to concentrate on Swank's babbling with all this weird shit happening. *Got to concentrate,* he thought. *This is important stuff.*

"You did great with Colby's buck last night," Swank was blathering, "and now I need some more help from you. I wouldn't say we're in an emergency situation, but it could turn into one. So what we gotta do is remove all the merchandise as quickly as possible. And I mean pronto. We're looking at a total of thirty head…"

Gray shook his head and tried to ignore the huge white-tailed buck that was blinking its eyes and staring down at him from behind Roy Swank's massive leather chair. "Damn, that'll take more than just a few days. It's about two hours per procedure."

"Sixty hours….Lessee, that's means you can finish up by midnight Friday. Perfect."

"Are you kidding me? You want me to operate for sixty hours straight? Wouldn't it be easier just to shoot 'em all and be done with it?"

"Doc, you got any idea how much those deer are worth?" Swank smiled. He loved talking about money, specifically his money. "Five grand apiece, easy. Some of 'em, more like ten. If you think I'm taking a rifle to a quarter-million dollars' worth of animals, you're nuttier than a squirrel's morning crap. Besides, when have you ever had any trouble staying awake?" Swank said as he reached into a desk drawer. He came out with an amber vial filled with white powder and placed it on the desk in front of Gray. "Few snorts of that, you'll not only finish by Friday, you'll want to paint my barn afterwards. And if that's not enough…" He reached into the desk again and tossed a pack of hundred-dollar bills to Gray.

Gray caught the bills and was reaching for the drugs when a shot crackled through the air.

A week ago, Roy Swank would have been puzzled, even a little concerned, about hearing a gunshot on his property outside of hunting season. But the events of the last few days had worn him down, first pushing his nerves to the limit, then numbing him to almost any development. He shook his head in dismay, more like a father hearing rap music from his son's bedroom than a man whose fortunes rested on the crazy Colombian who was almost certainly the source of the shot. "Damn. What now?" Swank said, pulling his froglike body out of his plush chair. He walked over to the eastern windows, hoping to get a glimpse of the front driveway. No, the trees were still too full of leaves. So he proceeded over to the bar and poured himself a brandy, without extending the courtesy to Gray. Then he waited. He was sure that Oscar would be joining them shortly.

Twenty seconds later, as if on cue, Oscar walked through the den door. He said nothing, but instead walked to the bar and grabbed the same bottle of brandy. He poured himself a healthy glassful, as Swank watched. Gray sensed the tension and took the opportunity to slip out the door.

Oscar sauntered over by the fireplace and stood with his back to the hearth, as if warming himself in front of nonexistent flames. "We have a small problem," he announced coolly. "I just shoot a photographer, perhaps from the FBI, perhaps from the DEA…"

Swank was incredulous. "Here? You just shot a government man here? Right on my ranch?"

"Yes, of course," Oscar said casually, as if he was discussing what he had eaten for breakfast. "He is in my trunk. I will have my men dispose of the body when they arrive."

Swank put his hands palms-outward in front of him. "Oscar, I don't want to know. I didn't hear a word you just said, and whatever you've done, I want no part of it." Swank didn't think the dead man could actually be a federal agent because the ranch house would be surrounded by now. But whoever it was, Swank didn't want to be involved.

Oscar nodded, acting unusually rational. "I unnerstan'. You are only being wise. But you have to see how this affects all of us. Before, we had concern.

Now we have more. If they send a photographer here, what do they know? How do they know it? It must be the game warden. But as you say before, they cannot get a search warrant. That is not our problem now. The man outside is our problem."

"Shee-yit," Swank said, making it two syllables. He wanted nothing to do with the corpse in Oscar's trunk.

Now Oscar began to pace, his patience thinning. "Okay, you say you don' want to be involve. My men will arrive tonight. We take care of everything."

This thought actually made Swank more nervous than knowing exactly what was going on. "But…"

Oscar put his hands in front of him as Swank had earlier. "No. You leave it to me. In a few days, we will have no problems. Truss me."

Charles Walznick, the pot dealer, had provided Bobby Garza with a long list of regular customers, other dealers, and a few friends who helped him work the marijuana farm. He had also supplied Bobby Garza with the name of Virgil Talkington, Blanco County's one and only bookie. Garza knew Virgil, and knew that he could cover just about any bet you wanted to place on any of the major sports. He'd been at it for nearly twenty years and managed to make a decent living. He knew sports well enough to put Marv Albert to shame, and he rarely had to pay off any of the bets with his own money. After all, bookies simply act as brokers between bettors. Then they take a commission, called a "juice" or "vig," on the losing bets. So the trick was to always have the same amount of money on either side of a bet. For instance, if the Cowboys were playing the Redskins, Talkington wanted the same amount of money betting on both teams. If too many people were choosing the Cowboys, he'd just adjust the point spread to entice more people to pick the Redskins. Once he had it all evened out a day or two before the game, he'd close the books. Then, no matter what, he'd walk away with ten percent of the losing side. Standard bookie procedure.

Talkington dealt with a fairly small betting pool—most of the adult male population of Blanco County. He'd seen rich men lose tens of thousands of dollars without batting an eye. He'd watched in morbid curiosity as poor men placed bets equal to their yearly salaries. Sometimes they got lucky. More often, they were driven by a frantic desperation that caused them to place bets they wouldn't normally place.

Talkington was never concerned about the losers paying up, because he never extended credit. Everything was cash up front—the bet you wanted to place, plus ten percent in case it tanked. Conveniently, Talkington had a cousin, a vice president at the local bank, who would happily extend a line of credit to just about anyone who could sign a loan application. Sure, the cousin received a small kickback from Virgil, but on paper down at the bank, everything looked nice and legit. Virtually every betting man in Blanco County had taken out a "debt consolidation" loan with Talkington's cousin. The winners usually paid it off the next week. Losers usually took years.

Like most small-time bookies, Talkington went virtually unharassed by local law enforcement officials. In fact, Sheriff Herbert Mackey was of his most loyal customers. (Mackey had a weakness for the A&M Aggies, and would bitch until the next season if they didn't beat the spread against the Texas Longhorns.) So, Talkington had been curious but unconcerned when he had gotten a call from Blanco County Deputy Bobby Garza earlier that day. Garza had been cordial but friendly, asking to stop by Talkington's house that evening. Maybe, after all these years, Garza was coming by to place his first bet with Talkington. Mackey had done well on the pro games last weekend. Maybe word had spread.

Garza arrived at seven and Talkington greeted him at the door. Garza took a beer that Talkington offered and followed him to his garage office, Talkington's customary place of business for drop-in customers.

"So what can I do you for?" Talkington said, gesturing for Garza to have a seat in a chair next to his desk.

"I wanted to talk to you about Charles Walznick," Garza said casually, and watched as Talkington's eyes widened a little. "We busted him this morning… growing pot on his place off Sandy Road."

"That right?"

"Had a pretty healthy crop, with all the rain we've been getting. Thing is, he told me he never could have afforded the place except he won a few bets a couple years back. What can you tell me about that?"

"Well, Bobby, you know I don't really like to talk about my clients…."

"I understand that, Virgil, and to be honest, I don't have much of a problem with you running a book. Doesn't seem that much different than the lottery to me. If people want to spend their money, hey, who am I to tell 'em how to spend it?" Garza took a long swig of his beer. "But when the money they win gives them the capital to start a small drug operation, that's when I have a problem."

Virgil scowled and adjusted the cap on his head. DRIPPING SPRINGS RANCH & FEED, it said above the bill, complete with a gaudy red-and-green logo. "Damn, Bobby, how'm I supposed to control what they do with their winnings?"

Both men sat in silence for a minute. Finally Garza spoke again. "I'm not trying to put you out of business. I just need you to cool it for a while. Shut down the books for maybe six months. Because when the bust makes the papers, people are gonna wonder where a lowlife like Walznick got the money for the land. Sure enough, it's gonna come back to you. Virgil, I don't need to tell you what kind of conservative population we got in this county. When they hear about drugs and gambling, they're gonna want some answers. I need to be able to tell 'em we shut you down."

Talkington stood and began to pace the concrete floor. "You gotta understand, this is my busiest time of year, right in the middle of football season. Hell, the playoffs and the Super Bowl account for half my annual business. If I skip them, I'll plain go broke." Talkington swung his arm and gestured around him. "You can see that I'm not exactly making a fortune anyway. Same three-bedroom house for twenty-two years."

"I know, I know. But the pressure's gonna be on me and the rest of the department to put an end to the gambling." Garza truly felt bad, asking a man to give up his livelihood.

Talkington plopped back down into his chair. Then his head lifted and a smile crossed his face. "What if I could tell you about something else that would be bigger than this Walznick thing, something that would blow it off the front page?"

Bobby Garza took another drink of beer, then said, "Let's hear it."

CHAPTER EIGHTEEN

THAT NIGHT, JOHN Marlin sat down at his desk and booted up his computer. It buzzed and clicked as it warmed up, then it asked him for his password. The security procedure—even for his home computer—was a Parks and Wildlife Department mandate. Game wardens often kept their own records of game violations, complete with offenders' names and addresses. Marlin typed his password, then opened his word processing program and began to type....

TO: Mark Russell, Texas Attorney General
FROM: John Marlin, Blanco County Game Warden
DATE: Wednesday, November 3

Mr. Russell:
    I'm sending you this note in confidentiality
because I'm not sure where else to turn at the
moment. I have a situation developing here in
Blanco County and, frankly, I don't know how to
handle it. It goes well beyond the laws that
encompass game and fish codes, and I thought it

best to present my thoughts to the state's top
law enforcement official. But a warning: What I
have to say might be a little hard to believe....

Marlin laid out all the details in a concise, factual manner. Even so, rereading it himself, it sounded ludicrous. Roy Swank, one of the state's most powerful men, a man from the inner circles of political power, a drug dealer?

In any case, it helped Marlin clear his head just by putting everything down on paper. He had no intention of mailing the letter right now; he couldn't really do anything until he had the blood sample tested.

Red O'Brien had led a disappointing life, even by Central Texas trailer-park standards.

For starters, there was his father. A kind and gentle man, Matt O'Brien had been one of the country's most beloved rodeo clowns. Sure, younger kids loved clowns, but by the time Red reached junior high—and his dad was still working the circuit—the other kids teased Red mercilessly about his father's profession. Red ended up with the nickname "Bozo Junior," and he began to hate his dad for the cruel abuse from his peers. Then, when Red was fourteen, his father was killed by a fifteen-hundred-pound Brahma bull in Cheyenne, Wyoming. To this day, Matt O'Brien remains the one and only rodeo clown to die from a gore injury directly to the anus.

His mother, on the other hand, was a lifeless woman with a taste for Irish whiskey. The small insurance settlement they received from his father's death disappeared into the smoky air of beer joints and honky-tonks. Sometimes she came home alone, sometimes she came home with a man, sometimes she didn't come home at all. For a while, she cleaned houses in and around their small hometown, but she spent most of her earnings on cigarettes and booze. When several of her customers began to suspect her of stealing, she and Red became outsiders in their community, living on food stamps and other government assistance. Finally, when Red was sixteen, his mother ran away with a welder. Red never told anybody she was gone, just continued to live in the old mobile home as if nothing had happened. He worked odd jobs, delivered newspapers before school, and forged her name to government checks. His mother's absence was actually an improvement in his life. He later heard that she ended up somewhere around Midland, but he never knew for sure.

Education was never Red's strong point. He hated science. He didn't understand math. History bored him. English seemed futile, since he already knew the damn language. The only class Red passed on a regular basis was PE. Most of the teachers had mercy on Red, though, and he managed to slip from one grade to the next. During his senior year, Red attended Career Day eagerly, hoping that the visiting representatives from various large corporations would see his potential. Hell, they might even offer him a job right now, without any college, Red thought. Deep in his heart, Red just knew that all this school bullshit didn't really matter in the real world. He knew that his intelligence and savvy would outshine his lackluster grades and prove that he was worthy of any career he might choose. But when he got the report back the next week, what they called a "Career Recommendation Summary," nobody seemed to understand that Red was a diamond in the rough. Right there under "Recommended Career Fields" it said: Truck driver. Construction worker. Custodial engineer. *Custodial engineer?* Red was smart enough to know what that meant: They thought he ought to be a fuckin' janitor. Red was so angry he left school two months before graduation and never returned.

His luck with women wasn't much better. He was painfully shy during high school and never dated. After dropping out, he found a woman he liked quite well. They met at a tractor pull, and she quickly accepted Red's offer for a date. She slept with him the first night, and Red had thought he was quite a charmer. Then, after a clumsy round of sex, she told him he could just leave the fifty bucks on the dresser. She smiled and said she could hold a spot for him every week if he wanted.

Finally, three years ago, Red thought he had found true love when he hit it off with a bleached-blonde woman at a dogfight. Red dated Loretta for three months, and then they made a road trip out to Vegas to tie the knot. Exactly one week after their wedding night, back in Johnson City, Red was finishing up his dinner of squirrel and Hamburger Helper when there was a knock on the trailer door. Loretta put down her cigar, answered the door, and then stepped outside to speak with the visitor. Probably Violet, Loretta's best friend who lived next door, Red thought. He went back to watching a rerun of *The Dukes of Hazzard* and was slugging down a sixteen-ounce beer when he noticed that the voices outside were getting loud. One was a male voice. Red stuck his head outside and saw Loretta arguing with a monstrously large man. He had a crew cut, huge yellow teeth, and hands the size of dinner plates. He wore overalls with no shirt underneath, and he clutched a bottle of cheap Mexican tequila in his dirty fist. Behind him, a worn Honda Civic clicked as it cooled down. Loretta and the stranger fell silent as Red stuck his head out the door.

"Everything all right out here?" Red asked, eyeing the stranger.

Loretta looked nervous. "Fine, Red," she barked. "I'll be back inside in a minute."

The stranger spoke up with a slur. "This yer brother you been tellin' me 'bout?"

"No, sir," Red said, doing his best to scowl as he came down the cinderblock steps. "I'm her husband."

If the chirping crickets had understood English, they would have immediately gone quiet. The big, drunk visitor looked from Red to Loretta and back to Red. "Tha' fuck you talkin' 'bout? Her husband?"

He went on to explain that Red couldn't be her husband, because, goddamn it, *he* was Loretta's husband. Red told the stranger to hold on, he'd fetch the marriage license, and the visitor said that he might as well fetch a roll of toilet paper, because Loretta was his own damn lawful wedded wife. They continued to argue and Red was thinking about slipping back inside for his twelve-gauge—but before he could make his move, the stranger popped Red upside the head with his tequila bottle. Red fell off the steps but rebounded nicely, picking up a loose brick from the deteriorating sidewalk and bouncing it off the man's chest. The man played possum, groping his ribs like they were broken, but then his eyes flashed and he moved with deceptive agility, getting Red in a headlock. The man began driving his knuckles into Red's scalp, and Red quickly decided he didn't like that at all. He managed to wriggle away, and dove for safety under the trailer. Once again the stranger was too quick; he grabbed Red by the cuffs of his pants and dragged him back out from under the trailer. Red came out grasping a square-nosed shovel and took a swing that would have made Mark McGwire proud. He caught the big man square in the forehead, and the impact made a sound like the buzzard that had hit Red's windshield the week before. Red was winding up for another piledriver when both men were distracted by the sounds of squealing tires and slinging gravel. Loretta was taking off in the stranger's Honda.

"Well, good goddamn," the stranger said.

"Fuck me nekkid," Red said. Both men stood silently for a few minutes, staring down the road after the long-departed sedan. Then Red went inside and returned with a six-pack of tallboys. He handed one to the stranger. "I'm Red O'Brien."

The stranger stuck out a beefy paw. "Billy Don Craddock."

Neither of the men ever heard from Loretta again. Billy Don had been Red's best friend ever since.

* * *

"Fuck you, Red," Billy Don said, sitting on Red's sofa. "Fuck you and the goat you rode in on."

Red O'Brien was used to setbacks. He'd faced them all his life. Actually, he didn't really face them as much as ignore them. "So all we gotta do is…"

"Didn't you hear what I just said? Fuck you. I ain't messing around with all that bullshit anymore. I been snake-bit, I been shot—in fact, the bandages on my gut are leaking again. Can't believe I let that horse doctor take care of me. Plus, I think I caught the clap from that damn stripper."

Red threw up his hands. "What in the world does that have to do with Roy Swank?"

Billy Don didn't respond, but just grabbed the remote and turned up the volume on *Buck Fever,* his favorite hunting show. Danny Jones was sitting in a tall tower blind, telling his viewers how to rattle up big bucks. *"Best way to do it,"* Danny said, *"is have one of your buddies under the blind with the antlers, while you're sitting up top keeping an eye out. You want to really smash the antlers together to simulate two bucks fighting."* A camera outside the blind showed a man in camouflage working two antlers.

"I'm tellin' ya, Billy Don, there's gotta be a way we can make some money offa all this."

Billy Don turned the volume up even louder. Back inside the blind, Danny Jones was whispering, because a large buck had just come into view of the camera.

Red tried another tack. "What the hell's your problem? You scared of that little spick?"

"Don't push me, Red."

"That's it, ain't it? You're scared. I wisht I'd knowed I was running around with a little girl." Red raised his voice about three octaves: " 'I'm Billy Don, and I'm scared a that mean ol' Meskin.' "

Billy Don turned to Red and emitted a low growl. Red had only heard it on two other occasions, and both times a guy had ended up in the hospital. So he quit prodding and decided to go get another beer. As if Red were psychic, the phone rang just as he rose off the couch.

Billy Don continued to watch the show. He acted as if he wasn't listening to Red's conversation, but he heard the words "Mr. Swank" and tried to catch what he could. Red was doing more listening than talking. A few minutes later, Red returned to the living area and smiled broadly at Billy Don. "Guess who that was. Swank wants to talk to us again, and he's ready to spit out some more cash."

Now Billy Don just nodded. Money had that effect on him.

On TV, Danny Jones was lining up his rifle sights now, getting ready to take a shot. *"You don't get many opportunities like this"* Danny whispered.

"You goddamn right you don't," Red agreed.

Marlin lay back in bed and watched Louise grooming herself in front of his bathroom mirror. She was wearing red thong panties and a matching lace bra, C cup. Definitely Victoria's Secret. God bless Victoria, whoever she was.

Louise ran a brush through her long blonde hair and looked in at Marlin. "You're quiet tonight."

He smiled back at her, trying not to appear lost in thought. "Sorry."

"What are you thinking about?"

Marlin ordinarily hated it when a woman asked that question. But when Louise asked it, it was different. He didn't have to be thinking about her or the sex they just had—and, in fact, she always knew he wasn't thinking about those things. She was just being a friend, wondering what was on his mind. "Oh, you know, the season coming up and everything," Marlin said. "Gonna be a busy one. Lots of rain this spring, so everyone's expecting a great year."

Louise walked into the room pulling on her floral skirt. The skirt fell to midthigh, showing off her great legs. She was an avid jogger, logging about twenty miles a week. Couple that with the hours she spent on her feet at the diner and her legs were as trim and sculpted as young pine trees.

"You met someone, didn't you?" She looked at him with affection in her eyes. Women had a way of knowing.

"Yeah." Marlin tried to smile, but he was a little uncomfortable. He expected Louise to ask, *Who is she?* But then he realized she wouldn't. Not her style.

She sat down on the bed next to him. "I think that's great, John. You deserve it. Lord knows I've had enough experience with this relationship business, so I know how important it is…to find the right one." She reached out and caressed his cheek.   .

Marlin nodded back at her, feeling awkward, a little embarrassed. Even though his relationship with Louise had always been casual, he still felt a sense of loss. Unspoken between them was the fact that this was their last night together. Marlin wondered if he'd miss the talks with Louise—the refreshing, open, honest discussions—more than he'd miss the sex. It was entirely possible.

At one-thirteen in the morning, a small rented sedan rolled west on Highway 290 through the quiet streets of Dripping Springs.

The driver, Julio Olivares, was a stout, squat man with a thick, droopy mustache, bushy eyebrows, and pockmarked skin. He was fifty-three years old and looked every day of it. He had yellow teeth from smoking, but it wasn't a problem because he never smiled.

Next to him was an expatriate American, Tyler Jackson. Former Marine, dishonorably discharged. Twenty-nine years old, six foot two, with a crew cut and a torso sculpted from iron. He was a monstrous man. If you looked closely, you could see needle marks in the crook of his arm. That's where the steroids went in. Jackson had a criminal record so profound he had been forced to flee the States three years ago.

Luis Ramiro, a tiny man in his mid-twenties, was in back, dozing. Luis was like that—laid-back—the kind of guy who could fall asleep with *federales* banging down his door. In fact, he had done exactly that on one occasion. Unlike Jackson, Luis didn't need brawn. He could shoot a fly off a horse's rump at a hundred meters.

They followed Highway 290 to the intersection of Highway 281, took a right, drove about two hundred yards, then crossed over to Miller Creek Loop. Six miles later, they saw the impressive granite entrance to the Circle S Ranch.

CHAPTER NINETEEN

"SO YOU WANT us to be, like, your bodyguards?" Red said. He and Billy Don were once again meeting with Roy Swank in the lobbyist's imposing den.

"Not bodyguards, exactly. More like my right-hand men…sorta look after things…be there if I need you."

Red didn't know what being a right-hand man entailed, but he was sure it involved a lot of cash. He looked around the sumptuous surroundings. Hell, the place practically reeked of crisp, new currency, especially small, untraceable bills that the IRS would never be privy to. Red hiked up his jeans and asked "What kinda money are you prepared to spend for our services?"

"Same as before," Swank said, sipping from a mug. "Ten thousand in cash. I'll need you for one week, max. You'll stay in one of my guest bedrooms."

Red looked over at Billy Don and noticed a gleam in his eye. The same kind of gleam Billy Don got when he sat down to eat a sixteen-ounce rib eye. No question, Billy Don was in. But Red was thinking he could get even more. "Well, it's not exactly the same as before. That time, it was for one night's work. And if I do say so myself, we performed splendiferously." Red thought he would impress Swank with that two-dollar word. Red had heard it just yesterday, uttered by a scientist on cable TV. Or maybe it was Martha Stewart. In any case, Swank just sat there, unimpressed. So Red pressed on: "The money part is good, but I sure could use a new set of wheels." Red was dreaming of chrome rims, complete with new Kelly tires. He got even luckier, because Swank thought he was angling for a whole new vehicle.

"I just bought three new Fords for the ranch," Swank said with an edge, like he was losing his patience. "Pick one out and I'll sign the pink slip over to you—one week from today. But that's all the slop that's in the trough, boys."

Red stood and grinned. "Mr. Swank, sir, you got yourself a deal. Now tell me a little more about that Meskin I seen runnin' around here."

"He's not Mexican, he's Colombian. And now there are four of them."

Bobby Garza had never been involved in a case—or cases, really—quite like this. One thing just kept leading to another, and that led to another. If what the bookie, Virgil Talkington, had told him was true, Garza was on to something that could nail a couple of the county's most highly regarded citizens.

As Garza pulled into the Exxon parking lot precisely at eight A.M. as planned, he saw Bo Talkington's large sport utility vehicle parked around the side. All of those new SUVs looked the same to Garza, but this one was easy to remember. It was green, the color of money, and it had a bumper sticker on the rear window that said, BANKERS DO IT WITH INTEREST.

Garza saw Bo inside the store, dressed in a lightweight suit, getting his regular morning cup of coffee and a bag of sweet rolls. Moments later, Bo walked out, proceeded to Garza's cruiser, and climbed in. After a handshake, Bo Talkington began telling Garza the details of the story his cousin Virgil had first relayed.

"I'm putting myself on the line, talking to you like this," the bank vice president said. "So you didn't hear it from me."

Garza nodded.

"You know Claude Rundell, my boss down at the bank?"

Garza nodded again.

"Then you probably know his wife Kelly."

Kelly was a redhead with runway-model looks, about twenty years younger than her husband. Garza had pulled her over on several occasions and always had to remain professional while handling her bold flirtations. One time, Kelly had commented that Garza looked "good enough to eat" in his uniform. He wrote her up for going sixty-five in a fifty zone, but had to laugh when she pulled away. "I've met her," Garza said.

"I'm telling you, her husband is a first-class horse's ass. Never pays her any attention, won't let her have the kids she wants, just a real all-'round S.O.B."

Bo paused to chase a wad of sweet roll down with steaming black coffee. When he finished smacking, he continued. "So you can't really fault a woman for wanting more of a man than that."

Garza knew precisely where this was headed, but he let Bo tell it in his own time.

"One time last year, she came into the bank to talk to Claude about something, and when she came outta his office we kinda made eye contact, and well…" Bo trailed off and let the silence explain the rest. "It don't really bother me telling you about me and her, 'cause she's fixin' to divorce him anyway. But as I's saying, Kelly told me something that Claude had told her a few years ago, right after they got married." Bo took another bite of sweet roll, then realized he was being selfish with the rest in the package. "Roll?" he said, offering one to Garza.

"No thanks, I had breakfast." Garza just gritted his teeth and wished Bo would hurry up with the story.

Bo gulped some coffee and then took a dramatic pause, as if he were about to tell Garza where to find the Holy Grail.

Skip Farrell, the widely read columnist and senior editor for *Texas Outdoors* magazine, was the ultimate schmoozer and wheeler-dealer, a man who had managed to turn his hunting hobby into a lucrative career. His columns highlighted premier hunting ranches and leases, innovative new hunting products, the latest weaponry, ammunition, camouflage, and outdoor gear, the most rugged sport utility vehicles and all-terrain vehicles, even the best restaurants and hotels in Texas' most popular small hunting towns, such as Llano, Mason, and Carrizo Springs.

Years ago, before his career in journalism, Farrell had had to pay for things like rifles, taxidermy, and butchering, just like any other hunter. Not anymore. A few kind words in his column could make product sales boom, lease fees skyrocket, and coffers in small towns overflow. So Farrell was indeed a popular man among the hunting community across Texas. Hunting invitations flowed to Farrell's mailbox like bucks to a doe in heat. Farrell had not been at all surprised when Roy Swank had called him the past summer and told him about an opening-weekend extravaganza he was having this year at the Circle S. *Wanna really show off what I'm doing with game management these days,* Swank had said. *Gonna be senators, congressmen, CEOs from around the state.* Farrell had gladly accepted. Swank had recommended that Farrell show up a couple of days early, plenty of time to see the ranch and take photos of Swank's prize bucks.

Now, as he drove up the winding dirt road to Roy Swank's house, Farrell was reflecting on how fortunate he was. In fact, he was so lost in his own good fortune, he almost didn't see the battered red Ford pickup careening around a curve on his side of the road. Farrell swerved onto the grass and cringed as the red truck barely missed the left front fender of his brand-new Chevy Suburban.

He looked in the side mirror and saw the redneck driver flip him off as he scooted down the road.

"Fuck you, too," Farrell said to himself.

"According to Kelly," Bo Talkington said, "Claude told her that he had taken a bribe from Roy Swank in exchange for turning Phil Colby down for a loan. 'Parently, Colby needed some cash to pay county taxes because they were right at the point of taking his ranch away. He went to Claude, Claude promised him a big loan, but then Swank approached Claude and gave him a hundred grand to turn Colby down. But the trick was to keep stringing Colby along, telling him he'd get the money, until the county was really banging on his door. Then, the day before Colby's very last deadline to pay up, Claude turned him down flat. Really fucked him over."

"So that left Colby with nowhere else to turn," Garza said, more of a statement than a question.

"Yeah, and I also heard rumors that Swank spread a little money around the county tax office, too, to prevent them from giving Colby another extension on his taxes. From what I heard, they had given him several extensions already.... He owed taxes from several years back, plus he was in hock with the big boys, too."

Garza raised his eyebrows.

"The IRS," Bo explained. "Man, it's like getting your nuts caught in a vise with those guys. You can put them off for a little while, but not nearly as long as the county. So Colby had to choose between losing the ranch to the county, or screwing up the rest of his life with the feds. I'd say he made the right choice."

CHAPTER TWENTY

"GRAB SOME A those pretzels, and those tater chips," Red said. Billy Don was pushing the shopping cart ahead of him, cruising the narrow, dimly lit aisles of the grocery store. So far they had six cases of beer, a box of Slim Jims, assorted snack cakes, a dozen cans of Vienna sausages, a bag of miniature chocolate donuts, and a large bottle of Pepto-Bismol.

They made their way to checkout, asking the teenage girl at the counter for an entire box of Red Man chewing tobacco. Twelve three-ounce packages. Enough for a week, Red thought. If they were going to be holed up for seven days at Swank's, better be prepared.

They left the grocery store and then swung by Red's trailer to grab a few sets of clothes and lock up tight for the week. On the way back to Swank's, Red bounced his thoughts off Billy Don. "The way I figger it," Red said, "we'll have plenty of time to sorta snoop around, see what Swank is up to. He can't keep an eye on both of us all the time, so we'll just see what we can come across."

Billy Don came forth with a chocolatey belch of approval. He had already broken open the donuts. He chased the loose crumbs in his cavernous mouth with a swig of Bud Light. It had been on sale.

Red looked over. "Don't be eatin' all a those at once. Save some for me."

Billy Don dug back into the box, grabbing two of the brown, waxy-looking rings this time.

Red looked back at the road. "Even if we don't find anything, we'll still be ahead ten grand each. Sounds like a sweet deal to me."

"Wat'choo think we might find?" Billy Don asked.

Red's mind had been knocking around that particular question for several days now, but he had been unable to come up with any plausible explanation. "Could be anything," he said, letting his imagination run. "They might be playing around with generics out there…you know, reengineering some kinda perfect deer. Or maybe doing something like those ol' boys over in Denmark who cloned that goat."

"I thought it was a sheep," Billy Don said around a mouthful of donut.

"Pretty sure it was a goat," Red said, not wanting Billy Don to be more up-to-date on current events than he was. "Named Dolly."

Billy Don tilted his head to the side as if the information was weighing his brain down.

"You know who they named her after, don'tcha?" Red asked.

"Dolly Madison?" Billy Don replied hopefully, pointing to the name on the donut bag.

Red shook his head. "Dolly Parton, on account a her big tits. You could make two tits out of each one of hers, and that's what they did with the goat… made two outta one." Red was always happy to share his insights with Billy Don on topics such as this.

Tim Gray had started operating on Wednesday, right after talking to Swank. He had set up shop in Swank's barn, which was actually clean, well-lit, and featured hot and cold running water—more inviting than many of the homes Gray had seen in Blanco County.

Even though Gray was dealing with tremors, chills, and the occasional feeling that he was being watched by little men in the hayloft, he felt like everything was going smoothly so far. The hardest part was rounding up the deer, which Swank kept in an adjacent five-acre pasture surrounded by a ten-foot fence. Gray had to chase them around with one of Swank's trucks until they tired out, then pop one with a tranquilizer gun. Fifteen minutes later the deer would lie down like an old man going to bed. After he finished with that deer, he'd tie a piece of surveyor's tape around its neck. Had to keep them sorted out. Didn't want to be scurrying around after deer he'd already worked on.

By Thursday at noon, Gray had operated on seven of the contraband-carrying white-tailed deer. It was a simple procedure really, less difficult than removing a benign abdominal tumor or spaying a bitch. All he had to do was put 'em under, open 'em up, remove the drugs, then stitch 'em back together. He didn't have to take quite as much care with these animals as he did with his customers' pets: If one of them died, that was Swank's problem. What did he expect, pushing Gray as hard as he was?

Staying awake wouldn't be a problem, either. Gray had a neat little system set up. Do a deer, do a line. Do a deer, do a line. That powder Swank had given him was damn good. He wasn't even sure if it was heroin or cocaine, but he didn't really care, as long as he kept buzzing along.

So far, all of the contraband was in good shape. The latex balloons were not corroded or cracked, not aging in any way. That made Gray feel a lot better after what he had found in that other deer, the one Swank wanted to give back to Phil Colby. Granted, the balloon had been in the deer much longer than with these animals. It had been the first deer they had worked with, sort of a test subject to see if the latex would hold. When Gray had gone in later to remove the drugs, he must have missed one balloon. But he had found it Tuesday evening, just the tattered remnants, no drugs left inside. At least now he knew why that deer had been behaving so strangely. Colby's precious deer would be fine.

Gray was sitting on a milking stool, just finishing up a line, when two Hispanic men and a large white guy in fatigues and combat boots walked into the barn. They stood just inside the entrance and surveyed the surroundings, as if they expected to find more than what they were seeing.

"*Hola,*" Gray said, trying to be friendly.

None of the men replied. Gray stood up and began to approach them, but thought better of it. Something about them made him nervous. He simply stood there fidgeting, feeling like a kid in the principal's office, as the men spoke to each other in hushed tones. Finally, the oldest guy, short, with a droopy mustache, approached Gray. The military-looking guy—a large weightlifter type—followed behind him.

"Tim Gray," the veterinarian said, sticking out his hand to the older man. He ignored it.

"How many deer have you operated on so far?" he asked in near-perfect English.

Gray wasn't sure who these guys were, but he figured they must be with Oscar. Probably best to answer him, he thought. "Seven."

The man looked at the ground and shook his head. The weightlifter next to him smiled broadly and laughed.

Gray smiled, too. Then Droopy Mustache nodded at the steroid junkie, who suddenly drove his right fist into Gray's solar plexus. Gray immediately doubled over and began gasping for air. His heartbeat was pounding so loudly in his ears, he barely heard Droopy Mustache say: "That is not good enough."

From the south-facing window in his den, Roy Swank could see three strangers approaching the barn where Tim Gray was working. One man—a big son of a bitch—was fair-complected, but the other two looked Colombian. *So Oscar really did it,* Swank thought. *Brought a trio of his assassins up here just like he said he would.* Swank crossed to his desk and opened the middle right-hand drawer. Sitting inside was his favorite pistol: a Colt Mustang Pocketlite .380. He eased the rack back a little to make sure there was a round in the chamber. The .380 wasn't a very powerful weapon, but it was compact and lightweight. This particular model fit neatly into his pants pocket, which is where Swank placed it. Like Swank always told his friends and colleagues: He had never been a Boy Scout—but he damn sure agreed with their motto.

"Hi, this is Marlin. I'm not here right now, so please leave a message at the tone."

"Marlin, it's Bobby Garza. Hey, I just wanted to say sorry that I couldn't give you more backup on that whole Swank deal. I believe you and everything, but without that powder, I didn't have a chance in hell of getting a search warrant. Anyway, if he's doing what we think he's doing out there, we'll catch up to him sooner or later. Just a matter of time. We'll talk more about it. But listen, I wanted to tell you about something else, too…about how Swank ended up getting the ranch from Phil Colby. You ready for this? Swank bribed Claude Rundell so that he wouldn't give Colby the loan he needed. Found out this morning. Anyway, I'll give you the full story. Give me a call."

The machine clicked off, the red light began flashing, and the room fell silent again.

The small man named Luis had been rustling around in Marlin's desk, but now he stopped, knowing what he needed to know. Not only was Marlin aware of what was going on, so was the cop. Luis had no idea what all that stuff was about a bribe, but he didn't care about that. He didn't know how to erase the message, so he simply turned the machine off. He let himself out the back door, leaving everything else just the way he had found it.

CHAPTER TWENTY-ONE

"DAMN," MARLIN SAID, as he watched the thin trail of blood meander down his chin. He always seemed to nick himself shaving when he was preoccupied. It was nearly eight o'clock and Becky—still "Nurse Cameron" in his mind—would be at his house shortly.

He splashed a little warm water on his face and that helped to stem the flow of blood. He had shaved and showered that morning, prior to his full day of Wildlife Commission meetings, but it always made him feel relaxed and comfortable to freshen up again before a long night. And poachers typically made the nights right before deer season busy ones. Rural residents would place calls reporting rifle fire, spotlights sweeping fields and hillsides, and vehicles trespassing onto their property. It wasn't unusual for Marlin to get home at four or five in the morning, just hours before first light and the official start of one of the most anticipated annual events in Texas. Sometimes Marlin would catch a few hours of sleep and then head out in the morning to check hunters' licenses, make the usual rounds to the butcher shops and taxidermists, and answer calls as they came in from the dispatcher. Other times, Marlin wouldn't even bother to sleep; he'd just load up on coffee, eat a light breakfast, change clothes, and get back to it. This schedule repeated itself Saturday night. It was grueling, but Marlin loved it. It was like deer season was a huge party and he was the bouncer. Behave yourself and you could come right in. But try to skirt the rules and you'd get tossed out on your ass.

Marlin was actually kind of glad he had the coming of opening day to distract him from his date with Becky. Date? Was that really what it was? Marlin looked in the bathroom mirror and said to himself, "I've got a date." He smiled and shook his head. It sounded kind of funny, and he couldn't even remember the last time he had used that word. Sure, he had been seeing Louise for a while. But that really wasn't what he'd call dating. It was just having sex with someone he felt comfortable spending time with. It wasn't butterfly-inducing, knee-wobbling, sweaty-palmed dating. He had forgotten what it was like.

Marlin hopped in the shower at fifteen minutes before eight, hoping that Becky wouldn't arrive early. As he lathered up, he took stock of his middle-aged body. His muscles weren't as defined as they once were, and he had some small love handles. But all in all, not too bad. Marlin's body was like that of a linebacker who hadn't played in nearly twenty years—which is exactly what he was. He had played Division II ball at Southwest Texas State University and had held the school record for unassisted tackles for a few years. His torso was still powerful, yet not as lean as it once was. His arms were in good shape, but not as bulky as in his college weight-lifting days. Marlin, like most men his age, found it easy to rationalize away the benefits of staying in top shape. What's the point of having a rock-hard physique when your job doesn't really call for it? Football's one thing, but you don't need to be able to bench 250 to write a poacher a ticket. That line of thinking always made it easier to have a second helping of chicken-fried venison and another cold beer. But maybe it was time to dust off the weights in the garage, Marlin thought. Start watching his diet a little. He was rinsing the shampoo out of his hair when he heard the doorbell.

"Am I early? Nice outfit," Becky said with a giggle, standing on the front porch. Marlin had answered the door wearing a cotton robe, a wet towel hanging around his shoulders.

"No, sorry," he said swinging the door open. "I was a little late getting back from Austin. The Commission meeting ran a little long. Come on in."

There was an awkward moment as Marlin went to shake Becky's hand. He wondered if he should have given her a quick hug. After all, they *had* gotten to know each a little over the past week. Marlin closed the door behind her and escorted her beyond the small entryway into the living area. "I'll be ready in just a sec. Would you like something to drink?"

"What ya got?" Becky asked.

Marlin noticed that even though she had been very friendly at the hospital, she seemed even more easygoing and casual now. He liked it. He also liked the way she was dressed: faded, well-fitting jeans, a lightweight red sweater, and white tennis shoes. She smelled great, too, Marlin noticed, like one of those scented magazine inserts. He didn't know any of the popular women's perfumes by name, but he knew he had smelled this one before.

"How about a Coke or a beer?" Marlin replied over his shoulder as he made his way into the kitchen.

"A beer would be great."

Marlin opened the refrigerator and said, "Miller Lite all right?"

"That's fine," Becky called from the other room. "I like your house. But there're a few things missing that I thought you'd have."

"Like what?" Marlin asked, returning with a beer in a frosty mug.

"Trophies on the wall. You know, big bucks with big antlers out to here."

Marlin smiled. "Hey, we're not all in it for the racks."

"You do hunt, don't you?"

"Oh, you bet I do. When I can find the time. It's kind of ironic: I became a game warden because I love the outdoors, and especially deer hunting. But it's my job that keeps me from hunting as much as I'd like. Here, have a seat." Marlin gestured toward the couch and they both sat down. But then Marlin suddenly felt very self-conscious in the robe and stood up again. "Why don't I go get dressed real quick and then we can head out?"

"No hurry," Becky said. "I don't have to work tomorrow."

Marlin looked at her and grinned. Her remark sounded kind of forward, but he knew she hadn't meant it that way.

Becky turned bright red. "What I meant was, I don't mind driving back home late tonight since I don't have to go in tomorrow."

"I know that's what you meant. I'll be right back."

Becky looked around the living room and thought: *Definite bachelor.* The house was neat and clean and everything, but it just didn't have a woman's touch. Functional but boring furniture. No art on the walls, no color anywhere. Nothing was there just for the sake of making the room more pleasant—like a bowl of potpourri or a vase of flowers. The glass-topped coffee table held a few plastic coasters and a stack of magazines. She glanced through them. *Texas Trophy Hunters, Texas Parks and Wildlife, Southern Outdoors, Esquire...* *Esquire*? That seemed as out-of-place as a refrigerator in an igloo. But maybe there was more to John Marlin than she thought. He definitely seemed intelligent, sensitive, and, since she could think of no other word to describe it, worldly. Before she met him, she would have guessed that your average game warden was a grade-A redneck—a tobacco-chewing, truck-driving, Confederate flag-waving member of the NRA. So much for stereotypes.

She rose from the couch and walked over to a wall that displayed a collection of framed photographs. She saw what were obviously old family portraits, including a few shots that showed John with his parents, she assumed, and another young man about his age. There were a few hunting, vacation, and party pictures, and she recognized Phil Colby in many of them. There were also a couple of John with a brunette woman. Very nice looking, Becky noticed. *Is that a little bit of jealousy?* she wondered. She passed it off as curiosity.

She took a sip of her beer and skimmed through his CD collection on the entertainment center next to the television. George Strait, Johnny Cash, Dwight Yoakam. Those, she expected, but she also found Fats Domino, ZZ Top, Frank Sinatra, and AC/DC. This was getting interesting. She was holding a copy of *Fandango* when Marlin walked back into the room wearing his warden's uniform.

"Sorry 'bout the duds, but I gotta wear 'em when I'm on patrol. You like ZZ Top?"

She looked down at the CD case she was holding. "Love 'em, but especially their older stuff. Like this." Marlin arched his eyebrows at her in surprise. "*Mexican Blackbird* is a classic," she said.

In a growling, bluesy voice, Marlin sung, "Aw, let's drive that ol' Chrysler to Mexico, boys." Becky laughed and Marlin joined in, both of them feeling a little silly.

"You want another beer?" Marlin asked, gesturing at her empty mug.

"No thanks."

"Well, why don't we head out, then? I'm not promising the most exciting night of your life," Marlin said as he opened the front door for her.

He'd remember making that statement much later, and realize how wrong he was.

CHAPTER TWENTY-TWO

"YOU NEVER TOLD me why you hunt," Becky said. They were at a rest stop on Highway 281 near Miller Creek Loop, finishing the picnic dinner Becky had brought along as promised. No calls from the dispatcher yet. It was a balmy evening, partly cloudy with just a trace of a southerly breeze. Crickets performed a buzzing symphony and frogs called urgently from the nearby creekbank.

Marlin pondered the question for several moments before responding. "You know, I've thought about that myself a lot, and I'm not exactly sure why I do it. It's just something that's part of me, I guess. I mean, I love venison, and that always seems to be my main reason. Gotta fill the freezer and get enough to last the year."

"So you eat it all?" Becky asked.

Marlin looked at her as if she had asked if he breathed oxygen on a daily basis. "Well, yeah, I wouldn't hunt anything I'm not planning on eating. For instance, I don't like dove meat, so I don't hunt dove. Same with fishing. I like a little catfish occasionally, just not enough to get me out on a boat to catch my own. But I do know plenty of hunters who just want to find the biggest buck in the county and don't really care about the meat. I think that's the perception most non-hunters have of us: just a bunch of trophy-driven killers."

Becky touched his arm lightly, "Oh, I hope you don't think that's what I was saying…."

"You don't mind hunting?"

"No, of course not. We're part of the food chain, aren't we?"

Marlin nodded.

"And as long as it's done humanely," Becky continued, "then I really don't see the problem with it."

"I'm glad you feel that way," Marlin replied. Then, without thinking: "Next time, I'll whip up some chicken-fried venison. Ever had it?"

"No, but that sounds great."

Marlin hadn't meant to be presumptuous about a next date, so he flushed a little and looked down at his plate. Then he continued with his train of thought. "There's more to hunting than just the venison, though. It's like feeling a kinship with the outdoors, a way of staking your spot in nature, being a part of it instead of just a spectator. Most people, all they ever see of nature is what they can see from their car windows."

Becky raised her hand. "Guilty as charged. Not that I've never been for a hike in the woods or a picnic in a state park or things like that. But I'm not exactly Calamity Jane, riding a horse and killing my own dinner."

"But you do appreciate the outdoors?"

"Love it. The problem is, when you live in the city, you can get everything you need at the grocery store, the mall…you can even watch wildlife twenty-four hours a day—on the Nature Channel. So most people don't have a lot of reasons to get out and explore. I'd say you're a lucky man. You seem to love what you do, and you get to do it away from all the turmoil of the city and the crowds, the road rage and the stress."

Marlin nodded. Sometimes he took it all for granted, and it was nice to hear someone reaffirm his choices in life. It was easy to wonder, at times, whether he should be off chasing the almighty dollar like everyone else. *Life's too short,* he always concluded.

"This is really good," Marlin said, taking a bite of his fried-chicken sandwich.

"I hope you don't mind it cold. When I was a kid, we used to always eat leftover fried chicken right out of the fridge."

"Excellent," Marlin said, just as a call came in over his cruiser's radio.

Marlin took Highway 290 north through Johnson City, then turned west on Sandy Road. Four minutes later, he pulled into a ranch entrance between two stone columns. The mailbox said BUSHONG. One of the Bushong's neighbors had called to report rifle shots. Marlin climbed out of the cruiser, opened the recessed gate, then continued on. He followed the winding driveway about a half-mile through a thick copse of tall first-growth cedars, then the cruiser broke back into open terrain. The headlights bounced off sluggish cattle standing on each side of the road. Marlin came to several forks, and each time he turned as if he had a mental compass. He came to two more gates, which he opened and closed behind him as he progressed onto the ranch.

Finally Marlin came to a large field and saw what he was looking for: Bobby Bushong's old Chevy pickup moving slowly in the low grass. Marlin steered the cruiser off the rutted road and pulled alongside the driver's side of the truck.

" 'Evening, Bobby," Marlin said to the shaggy middle-aged man inside. A curious young weimaraner whimpered from the bed of the truck.

"How you doing, John?" Bushong replied.

"Just out making the rounds. Got a report of some shots over here."

Bushong nodded. "Doing a little spotlighting, cleaning up some of the pigs out here before the hunters show up on Saturday. They never want to shoot 'em, and they don't believe me when I tell 'em they eat as good as the pork they buy in the store."

"Any luck?"

"Got two big ol' sows and a young boar over yonder."

"Anything else?" Marlin asked as he switched on the spotlight attached to the side of his cruiser.

Bushong grimaced. "Well, you know how it is."

Marlin played the spotlight over the field and came to rest on the three wild hogs. A large white-tailed doe lay next to them. "I guess that's all you need for tonight, huh? I mean, those should last you a while...."

Bushong brightened. "I reckon they will."

"And I imagine you remembered to buy a hunting license this year."

"Yes sir," Bushong said, reaching for his wallet.

Marlin waved him off. "That's all right, I don't need to see it."

The men made small talk about the prospects of the upcoming season, then Marlin turned around and left the ranch.

"Didn't you see the deer lying there?" Becky asked.

"Yeah, I saw it."

"Well, that was illegal, wasn't it? It's not hunting season until Saturday, right?"

Marlin was back on Sandy Road, just cruising, heading northwest to the edges of Blanco County. "Let me tell you something about Bobby Bushong," Marlin said. "His family has been on that ranch since the turn of the century. He somehow manages to make a living, selling fenceposts and firewood, raising cattle, leasing it out to hunters. He's a hardworking man, and he's not a cheater. But sometimes it can get a little rough, like with the bottom dropping out of the cattle market this year. There's a lot of families like his, people who would rather make do for themselves than turn to the government for food stamps. He'd never go out and shoot a deer just for the antlers or just for the sport of it. What he was doing was putting food on the table."

They rode on in silence for a few minutes. Then Becky said, "But how do you know he won't do it again?"

"Oh, he'll do it again. And they'll eat every last scrap of it." Marlin opened his mouth but couldn't find the right words. Finally he said, "The way I see it, part of my job is knowing who needs to get busted and who doesn't. Sometimes that's an awfully easy call."

Red was sitting on the plush leather sofa next to Billy Don. *Man, that soft leather sure cradles you,* Red thought, *like easing down onto a plump hooker.* Both men were drinking beer from longnecks and had been warned several times by Roy Swank not to spill it. "That's full-grain leather, you know, not split-grain," he'd say, as if expecting the two rednecks to nod their heads in appreciation. "And try not to get your goddamn donut crumbs all over everything," he added, glaring at Billy Don. Billy Don swept a clumsy hand over the sofa, flinging crumbs out onto the bearskin rug. Swank was half-drunk, from what Red could tell, and sat nearby in a matching leather recliner. He was nursing a big tumbler of scotch on the rocks, but he didn't seem too concerned about the possibility of his own spillage.

The living room was immense, larger than the entire square footage of Red's trailer, and it seemed to Red that it would cost a fortune to fill it up with furniture. He could think of other things he'd spend his money on, like a new Remington shotgun or a tricked-out exhaust system for his truck. But the one thing he wouldn't change would be the entertainment system. With that high-definition wide-screen TV, you could sit back, watch the Nashville Network, and damn, the Dixie Chicks were so lifelike you wanted to reach out and cop a feel. He could sit here for hours, which is exactly what the three of them had been doing. It was starting to get a little goddamned boring, to tell the truth.

There wasn't much conversation, and during the silences, Red had to remind himself why they were here. Actually, he still wasn't sure why they were here. They weren't really bodyguards, and Swank hadn't asked them to do much around the house or the ranch. "Just be ready to do whatever I tell ya," he had said. "And try to keep the newspaper columnist away from the small guest house." Red figured that's where the Meskins were. At one point, Red had bluntly asked Swank who the Meskins were. Swank wouldn't show his hand, though; he just said that they were "associates" who had "differing opinions" on matters of "great importance." They'd be gone in a few days. Instinct told Red to watch his ass.

Whiling away time, Red had noticed something about Swank. What he noticed was, this big, powerful businessman wasn't as different from everyone else as he'd like you to believe. He was just a man, with a line of bullshit as weak as the next guy's. He wasn't always calm and collected, like some big-shot who didn't get a little sweaty under the pits the same as everyone else. He got nervous, he paced the room, he worried about beer getting spilled. When he wasn't in a pissy mood, he told stories that were full of lies, just like every other ol' boy in Blanco County. The only real difference was that Swank had somehow managed to make a shitpile of money. Red figured Swank kept a large sum of cash tucked away somewhere in the ranch house; after all, Swank had already given him and Billy Don a pretty good amount. Red knew he'd never get his hands on any more of it as long as they all just kept sitting around watching the damn TV.

CHAPTER TWENTY-THREE

THE NEXT CALL came in from A. Robinson Road near Pedernales Falls State Park, east of Johnson City. Mrs. Beulah Byrd, a retired schoolbus driver and regular caller to the poacher hotline, had reported a vehicle sitting on the shoulder of the road using a spotlight. "They ain't got the brains God give a billy goat," she had told the dispatcher. "I walked out to the end of my driveway and they's just setting out there, squeezing off a round ever' now and then. They's drunker'n Cooter Brown, too, from all the hollering." Mrs. Byrd found it all highly amusing. "Only weird thing," she said, "is it sounds like they's shooting pistols, not rifles." She said it in a conspiratorial tone, as if she were trying to unravel the JFK assassination.

Marlin did a U-turn on Sandy Road and headed east back to Highway 281. He jumped the speedometer up to ninety and got to A. Robinson Road in about four minutes. Another six minutes and he was approaching the state park. Marlin glanced over at Becky and smiled. She was gazing intently up the road and seemed to be enjoying the excitement.

"There they are," Marlin said quietly as he spotted a late-model Ford pickup on the side of the road. Marlin shook his head in disbelief. The buffoons still had their portable spotlight sticking out the window, lighting up a pasture on the other side of the road.

Marlin slowed to about twenty and eased past the truck with his spotlight on. It was always best to get a complete picture of the situation before stopping. He glanced into the cab and saw two Hispanic men staring back at him. One held up a beer can in salute as Marlin rolled by.

Something is strange here, Marlin thought as he did a 180 and came up behind the Ford.

"I gotta piss like a mule," Billy Don announced, and then extracted his large frame from the downy comfort of the leather sofa.

Red and Roy Swank didn't respond. They were too busy watching *SportsCenter* on ESPN, where a reporter was saying that the Cowboys' star receiver was doubtful for this weekend's game against the Redskins. "Damned pantywaist," Red said with contempt. "Guy gets a quarter-million a game, the least he could do is play."

Swank nodded, but Red could tell his attention was elsewhere.

Red licked his lips and turned to his boss. "Notice your scotch is running a little low there, Mr. Swank. Want me to grab ya another bottle?"

Swank looked over at Red with glazed eyes. "In the cabinet under the wet bar," he said, pointing. "Chivas Regal, not that other crap."

Red rose and walked behind the bar. He emerged with a new bottle, cracked the seal, and poured four fingers in Swank's glass. "That oughta set ya up," he said with a smile. He placed the bottle on the end table within Swank's reach.

Red sat back down on the sofa and looked at Swank out of the corner of his eye. "Mr. Swank, I gotta tell ya, I'm still not real sure why we're out here. Not that I mind or anything. We could watch TV for a week, all I care. Just wanna make sure you're getting your money's worth."

Swank took a long pull from his glass but didn't say anything.

"These Meskins you got runnin' 'round here," Red continued, "now, something tells me you and them got some kinda deal going on that you don't wanna talk about. That's fine. But I hate to see a man like yourself get screwed around by a buncha south-of-the-border types. I'm just wondering if there was some way I could help out."

"You're helping out just by being here," Swank croaked, his voice rough from the whiskey. "More than that, you don't need to know."

Well, at least he's talking, Red thought. So he plowed forward. "I just don't think they're giving you the respect they oughta be giving you, Mr. Swank. They're out there skulking around like they own the place. You keep saying it'll all blow over soon, then they'll be gone. But in the meantime you're holed up in here like a rabbit." Red paused a moment to let that sink in. If he could just get Swank to loosen up, maybe he could find out what was going on. Then he could find a way to cut himself in on it.

Swank turned to Red and looked as if he might say something. Then he shook his head and looked back at the television. "Just drink your beer, son. And enjoy the free ride while you can."

For a few seconds, Marlin considered running a check on the license plates. *Play it safe,* a voice told him. But in twenty years, Marlin had never run into a situation he couldn't handle. Plus, he had to admit, he didn't want to look nervous in front of Becky. Vanity. So he put his spotlight on the Ford truck and used his PA. "Driver…step out of the car." He waited, but nobody emerged. He repeated the order, but the driver did not obey. He could hear one of the men responding in Spanish.

"He doesn't understand you, John," Becky said. "He just said he doesn't know English."

Marlin grinned to cover up the uneasiness he was feeling. "Guess you took a little Spanish in high school, too."

"Four years," Becky replied. "I use it all the time on the job."

Marlin pondered his next move. *Run the plates, you idiot,* the voice said again. He ignored it. "Well, I guess I gotta do this the old-fashioned way." He swung the cruiser door open and climbed out. He pulled his flashlight off his hip while his right hand remained on his holstered .357 revolver. Then he approached the truck on the passenger's side, a trick he had learned from a veteran warden. The poachers always expected you to approach from the driver's side, and if you could throw them off, even in a small way, it was to your benefit. Marlin only went as far as the middle of the truck bed and shined his light in through the rear window. He paused for a moment to get a good look at the two men staring back at him. One of them was older, with a droopy mustache. The other was young and slight.

"Pasajero: bajate del camión," Marlin said, using a phrase he had memorized.

The passenger grinned at Marlin through the window. Then he shrugged as if he didn't understand.

"No comprende?" Marlin asked.

The man rattled something off in Spanish that was too quick for Marlin to understand. But both men were laughing and smiling, just as they had been doing since Marlin first saw them. *Probably just a couple of illegals who've had a little too much too drink,* Marlin thought. *Saw a deer on the roadside and just couldn't resist taking a shot, and now they've brought the law down on themselves.* Marlin didn't see a deer carcass in the truck bed or anywhere on the roadside. Probably best just to take the weapon away from them, tell them to sober up for a while, and then go on their merry way.

That's exactly the way Marlin had it figured—until he heard Becky scream.

To Marlin, the next few moments seemed to happen in slow motion. His entire body felt sluggish, his mind addled, his reactions dulled. When he looked back, he saw a massive figure grabbing at Becky through the window of the cruiser. In the millisecond that transpired before he reacted, Marlin could see Becky was trying to get away, trying to scramble to the driver's side, but her seat belt was holding her back. The gargantuan man had her by both wrists and was leaning into the window. Becky shrieked again. By then, Marlin had begun moving back toward the cruiser, his gun drawn. He wasn't running, because panic was your worst enemy in a situation like this. He positioned himself about ten feet away from the man and aimed the revolver at the center of the man's back. Marlin was vaguely aware of some movement behind him.

Marlin, still facing the cruiser, yelled, "Freeze! Let her go and get down on the ground!"

That's when a tremendous force jolted Marlin's brain and his world went dark.

CHAPTER TWENTY-FOUR

THURSDAY NIGHT, PHIL Colby lay in the hospital feeling fidgety, on edge. He had tried to call John Marlin at about eight, but got no answer. The answering machine didn't even pick up. Colby hadn't expected to reach Marlin; it was, after all, just two days before the deer season. But still, it would have been nice to talk to him. Colby had a lot of questions for him.

The hospital was quiet, with only the occasional nurse wandering by Colby's open door. At ten o'clock, he rang Marlin again, still with no answer.

I've had enough of this place, Colby thought, and climbed out of the bed. He was still feeling a little woozy, but his strength was coming back quickly. "Hell, I've been kicked by a horse and felt worse than this," Colby said to himself, to bolster his shaky legs.

He went to the institutional-looking nightstand and quickly found the clothes he had been wearing when he was admitted. He pulled on his pants and sat down for a minute. *Funny how the vertigo can creep up on you.* Just then, a heavyset, middle-aged night nurse came into his room. She started to say something, then eyed his blue jeans. "Going somewhere, Mr. Colby?" she asked with a stern expression.

"Yeah. Home," Colby replied coolly.

"I don't think so. Dr. Hansen wants you in here for at least a few more days for observation."

Colby shrugged. "Tell you what…I'll observe myself. If I notice anything unusual, I'll be sure to let you know."

"This really isn't a good idea, Mr. Colby. Please lie back down and let me check your vital signs." She stepped forward while removing the stethoscope from around her neck.

Colby put a hand in the air. "Nurse. I know you're only trying to help me out. And you don't want to get in trouble with the doctors. But until you've met me, you don't even know the meaning of the word 'hardheaded.' " Colby checked her name tag. "Marilyn, here's the deal. I'm going home tonight, with or without the doctor's permission."

Nurse Marilyn paused for moment, biting her lip. Then she knelt down in front of Colby and checked his pupils. In a soft voice, she said, "Fine. But please—let me check your vitals before you go."

"It's a deal," Colby smiled.

His pulse was a little high, but everything else checked out fine. Colby continued to dress while Nurse Marilyn proceeded down the hall to find some forms for him to fill out. She had said something about liability and insurance and asked him to please wait for five minutes. He waited ten, and then he put on his shoes and walked to the nearest elevator.

He followed the signs to the front exit and walked out into the cool night. Then he realized, in his semifogged state, that he didn't have a car. Maybe this leaving wasn't such a good idea after all.

When Marlin came to, his head was pounding, his vision was blurred, and he felt nauseous—yet he knew exactly where he was. Lying on the floor of the old rock cabin on the lower pasture of the Circle S Ranch. When Marlin and Phil Colby were kids, the dilapidated structure had served as their fortresslike headquarters. They'd ride horses down from the main house, bringing along their .22s to do a little plinking. Or they'd haul out the fishing rods they stored inside the house and wet a line in the nearby Pedernales River. It had been two decades since Marlin had set foot in the house, yet he immediately recognized the barn-wood interior and the rusted woodstove in the corner.

"John…how are you feeling?" The voice seemed to come from the end of a tunnel. It sounded familiar…and yet…

Marlin felt a warm hand on his cheek. He blinked several times to clear his vision, and finally focused on the face of Becky Cameron. She was kneeling on the dirt floor beside him, holding a flashlight. Marlin struggled with confusion for a moment, and then his whole body tensed as he remembered what had happened. Marlin attempted to sit up, but Becky held him down. "It's best that you stay still for a while," she said in a reassuring tone. "John, can you tell me your last name?"

What kind of stupid question is that? Marlin wondered. "Marlin," he croaked through an arid throat.

"What day is it?"

"It was Thursday night. I don't know if it still is."

"Good. I was worried that you might have a concussion."

"What the hell happened?" Marlin asked, knowing that Becky wouldn't have an answer. "Who were those guys?" He already had a pretty good idea.

"I don't know. They put us in the backseat of your truck and brought us out here. They blindfolded me. I don't know where we are. They wouldn't let me ask any questions, and neither of them said a word the whole time."

"Neither of them? I thought there were more than two."

"There were three, but only two in your truck. The other drove the truck they were in. I think he came out here, too."

Marlin took a moment to soak all this in. His brain was swimming, and he couldn't seem to manage a sensible train of thought. All the facts were in his head...he just couldn't put them in any kind of logical order. He reached around gingerly and felt the wound on the back of his head. He had a lump about the size of a golf ball, topped with a pretty good gash. Dried blood matted his hair. He'd probably need stitches, but that was the least of his worries at the moment.

"Where are they now?" Marlin asked, propping himself on one elbow. It was the only thing he could think to ask.

"Outside. Or at least one of them is. I heard the truck drive away earlier, and I heard two doors closing when they left. I think one guy stayed behind with your truck. I hear him moving around every now and then, and I can smell a campfire. They nailed the door shut when they left, and the windows are boarded up. The only thing they said was for us to stay put or we'd be sorry."

Of course, no matter how muddled Marlin's synapses were, no matter how hampered his cerebral abilities, he knew Roy Swank was behind all this. "Becky, I'm sorry," he said softly.

"What for? It's not your fault. How could you know poachers would react like that?"

"They weren't poachers," he said, watching her face closely. He didn't see fear, only confusion. So far, she seemed unshaken by the abduction, unwilling to cringe in fear. He wondered if that would change as she learned the truth. "I think they're drug dealers. Working with a guy named Roy Swank. We're on his ranch right now."

Marlin took a deep breath and told her the entire story…the shooting of Trey Sweeney in his deer suit, Buck's abnormal behavior, the white powder found by Thomas Stovall, every detail. He had to pause at times and gather his strength, but Becky sat by patiently each time and waited for him to continue. When he was done, she didn't cry or tremble or yell at him for dragging her into this mess. She just asked if he wanted some water. "Yes, please," he said.

She handed him a jug from somewhere and he took a long drink. It was icy-cold and felt fantastic, reaching the parched recesses in his throat. He hadn't realized until then how thirsty he was.

Meanwhile, Becky rose to her feet and walked over to the door. Then she surprised Marlin by banging on it like a narc on a drug raid.

Seconds later a thickly accented voice came through the door: *"Que pasa?"*

She answered back, sounding just as peeved. "I need some aspirin, some peroxide, and some towels in here. Plus some more water—sanitary. To clean his wound."

"I no speak Englees," the man responded in a taunting voice. Marlin could hear faint laughter.

"Like hell you don't," Becky replied. She waited, but the man said nothing further. So she repeated her demand, this time in Spanish, and more forcefully than before. She seemed to go on for quite some time, but Marlin couldn't keep up with her fluent Spanish.

Marlin heard the man grunt and then say a few words back.

Becky turned to him and said, "He's bringing us a few things so I can clean you up."

Marlin had to laugh, even though it hurt.

An hour later, Becky and Marlin heard a vehicle pull up, followed by a single slamming car door and then a muffled conversation in Spanish between two men. These were the first voices Marlin had heard outside the cabin, leading Marlin to believe that Becky was right: Only one man was guarding the cabin. That information might prove useful in the future. One of the men sounded quite agitated.

"Any idea what they're saying?" Marlin asked.

"The loud guy—he sounds like an American to me—is pissed that the other guy asked for our supplies. Said he has better things to do than run errands."

Moments later, Marlin heard a scraping noise on the outside of the door. He speculated that the kidnappers had simply installed brackets on either side of the outward-swinging door (which accounted for the hammering Becky had heard), and then placed a two-by-four in each bracket to hold the door closed. It was the only door to the one-room house. Outside, the man they had spoken with an hour ago called out, "Move away from the door. Remember, I have a *pistola.*"

Marlin and Becky did as they were told, and a few seconds later the door swung open. From the sliver of moon Marlin could see rising in the horizon, he knew that it was about midnight. Two dark forms entered, shining a powerful spotlight at Marlin and Becky huddled in the corner.

A stern voice, clearly American, spoke from behind the spotlight: "Listen up, Marlin. If you want these supplies, you've gotta do something for me. I've got a cell phone here. I'm gonna dial a number and you're gonna leave a message for your pal Bobby Garza. You're gonna tell him that everything is just fine at the Circle S Ranch, that everything you told him earlier was a big misunderstanding."

Marlin wondered how they knew about his conversation with the deputy. "Now, why in the hell would I do that?"

There was a pause, then the voice said harshly, "Because if you don't, I'll kill him. And his family. And right before I do it, I'll tell 'em you sent me."

Marlin winced. He knew that Garza was one of the few advantages he and Becky had. Once Garza learned Marlin was missing, he'd come straight to the Circle S. But now, his captors were taking that advantage away. Marlin heard the beeping of a phone being dialed, then an enormous man stepped from behind the spotlight. "No fuckin' around, ya hear, or I'll make the little lady there understand the true meaning of pain."

Marlin nodded and the phone was thrust into his hands. He held it to his ear and heard Garza's voice-mail greeting at the sheriff's office. Marlin wanted to shout a warning into the phone, let Garza know what was happening and where they were. But he wasn't about to put Becky into that kind of danger.

"You'd better make it damn good," the big man growled.

Marlin could faintly see the second man, the one who was in the truck earlier. The man smiled and shrugged—a strange gesture, Marlin thought.

At the tone, Marlin said, "Hey, Bobby, it's John Marlin. You're not going to believe this, but I talked to Thomas Stovall earlier this evening and he said that business with the white powder was all a practical joke. Friends put him up to it. Real funny, right? Wish I could write the guy up for being an idiot. Anyway,

I just wanted you to know what was happening. Talk to you later."

Marlin hung up, feeling more defeated than ever, and the big man grabbed the phone out of his hands.

The two captors backed out of the cabin, leaving a paper grocery bag inside the doorway. Marlin heard the two-by-four slide back in place. Seconds later, he heard an engine start and a vehicle drive off into the night.

Marlin was feeling a little woozy. It was his first time standing since he had regained consciousness—and he was fooling himself if he thought he would get over the blow to the head easily. He felt a wave of nausea and his knees began to weaken. Becky recognized the look on his face and helped him back to the threadbare blanket on the floor. She handed him the jug of water again, and he drank deeply.

Becky had hung the flashlight from a nail on the wall and it cast a pale glow around the room. The batteries were dying quickly. "I need to get your head cleaned up before the light fades," Becky said as she grabbed the grocery bag the man had left. She began pulling items out: "Gauze. Band-Aids. Rubbing alcohol...that'll sting bad. Peroxide...that's better. Hey, they even got some Advil in here. They must be humanitarians."

Marlin managed a weak smile.

"The problem is, you need stitches. But I'm not about to try to stitch you up in this...place."

Marlin shrugged weakly. "I'll get 'em done later."

"If we don't get...If we wait too long, stitches won't work. You'll just have to let it heal as is. You could end up with a nasty lump there."

"No problem. I'll wear a hat." Marlin was doing his best to appear unrattled.

Becky kneeled down on the blanket next to him and asked him to lie on his stomach. Marlin flipped over, crossed his arms and rested his forehead on his wrists.

"This is a pretty bad cut, and I don't want it to get infected," Becky said. "I'm going to pour some hydrogen peroxide on it, but it shouldn't sting." She unscrewed the cap on the plastic bottle, poured a little into the cap, and gently poured the peroxide onto the wound. After a minute, she dabbed at the wound with a gauze pad. "I'm not going to try to put a bandage on you. It needs air anyway. Sorry I can't do more."

Marlin rolled onto his side and looked her in the eyes. "You're doing plenty," he said. "Thanks."

Marlin listened: There were no noises from outside the house except the gentle wind. Marlin propped himself on one elbow, then reached up and cupped a hand around Becky's neck. She leaned toward him…and they kissed. Marlin instantly felt his trousers tighten, and his pain seemed to evaporate.

Becky placed a few more gentle kisses on his lips and smiled. "We'd better take it easy, buster. You need to save your strength."

CHAPTER TWENTY-FIVE

PHIL COLBY HAD chanced upon a cab driver just ending his shift and had offered him fifty bucks, flat, for a ride to Johnson City. A good deal for the cabbie, but more than Colby could really afford to pay. *Screw it,* he thought. He was tired and just wanted to get home.

His house was dark when he arrived and there were no messages on the machine. Not a very welcoming return home. Of course, everybody thought he was still in the hospital. He tried to call Marlin again but got no answer. Colby figured he was out looking for poachers.

Colby undressed and took a long, hot shower, trying to keep his stitches dry. It was nice to be back in his own surroundings. Tomorrow he would hook up with Marlin, and then he'd find out the latest on Buck. Last he knew, Swank still had the deer but was planning to return him. That was a strange deal. It almost seemed like a dream, Marlin telling Colby in the hospital that Swank wanted to "do the right thing." Swank doing the right thing was about as likely as George Foreman turning down a hamburger.

Colby finished showering, then went to the kitchen and dug some cold pizza and a longneck out of the refrigerator. *Can't get a meal like that in the hospital,* he reflected. He sank into the living-room sofa and aimlessly flipped through the channels, exhausted, but not yet ready for bed.

Finally, Colby drifted into a deep sleep on the sofa.

* * *

Tim Gray, the veterinarian, is floating, scooting, flying, billowing under a starry, starry, oh-so-starry Texas sky, heart pounding but feeling mellow, mellow, mellow, trees swaying, reaching toward him, talking to him as friends, sometimes as strangers, tall strangers, cattle lowing, eyeing him with confusion, marvel, admiration, this sentient being who has it all in front of him, has it all figured out, whose life is so much more complete with this altered consciousness, this supreme clarity, revelations of universal secrets descending on him like asteroids as the tall grass strokes his bare calves, his knobby knees, his naked thighs, the soles of his feet melting into the earth with each step, unseen birds with long, monstrous beaks watching him from shadowed limbs, moonlight bouncing off flagstone, piercing his skin with welcome warmth, making him drowsy and suddenly he is on his back feeling the ground spin, vague memories of grotesque antlered deer, grinning, morphing into dark-skinned men clutching at his arms his legs his soul, laughing, spitting, and then they're gone and everything feels right as he slips under, to wake, he now knows, never again…

"I've gotta pee really bad," Becky said. She looked at Marlin as if he would know what to do about that particular situation. Now that he thought about it, he had a pretty urgent need himself. At least his head was starting to feel better, he thought.

Marlin glanced around the small room, which was a little more well-lit now, the morning sun beginning to sneak in where it could. Other than the blanket, the flashlight, and the water jug, the room was bare. Not even an old coffee can. "I guess you could go over in a corner," Marlin offered. "Maybe we should designate a spot…in case we're…we're in here for a while."

Marlin and Becky had not discussed their situation at length. He kept expecting her to ask him what they should do, what the men would do with them, but she didn't. Either she was scared to ask or she realized that Marlin's guesses were as good as hers. In any case, he didn't want to say anything that might frighten or dishearten her. Marlin actually felt fairly safe; if somebody wanted them dead, they'd be dead already.

Becky shook her head at his suggestion. "Don't think so. Maybe I'll just hold it for a while longer."

Earlier, Becky had been the one to stamp her foot and demand medical supplies. Now, Marlin felt, it was his turn to do a little negotiating. He walked to the door and hollered, "Anybody out there? Hey, amigo!"

Seconds later, Marlin heard a muffled voice just inches from the other side of the door. *"Que pasa?"*

"The lady needs to go to the bathroom," Marlin answered. *"El baño."*

"Use the floor. It ees dirt."

"Aw, come on now…be a sport. Let her out for a minute to take a leak. Would you want your mother treated this way?" Marlin knew that traditional Latin American men treated their mothers with great respect. Maybe that fact would work to his advantage.

Marlin smiled at Becky as he heard the board slide from its brackets. Then the interior of the room was bathed in sunlight.

Their captor, the smaller man from earlier, stood in the doorway. He smiled and said, "Juss couldn't hold it any longer?" An onlooker never would have guessed he was a kidnapper—except for the nine-millimeter handgun dangling loosely in his right hand. He waved it in Marlin's direction. "You…move to the back." Marlin did as he was told. Now the man spoke to Becky. "Come on out…don' be shy."

Becky exited and stood to the man's right. He tossed an empty milk jug into the room. "That is for your needs," he said as he shut the door. Marlin heard the board slide back into place. While she was gone, Marlin searched the room once again—every shadow, every corner. There was absolutely nothing that could be used as a weapon. He kicked at the dirt floor. They could try digging under, but chances were good that the small man was circling the cabin regularly, keeping an eye out for just such an attempt. He looked up. The sloped ceiling was built with solid pine laths under heavy-duty sheet metal. Couldn't get through all that without alerting the entire county. Plus, there was no way to even reach the ceiling without a ladder. So, basically, there was no way out. At least not quietly.

Becky was ushered back through the door a few minutes later, looking relieved. "He let me go behind a bush, down by the river. We were right, he's the only one out there. And your cruiser is parked just a few yards from the door. No other vehicles. If you can believe this, we made small talk about the weather. He's kind of a funny guy."

Suddenly Marlin had an idea…or at least the beginnings of one. "Could he see you, what you were doing?"

"Not really. It was a small bush, though. I couldn't have slipped away."

"No, I wouldn't want you to try that. But I've got something else in mind."

* * *

Skip Farrell, the columnist, thought it would be an excellent photo for his article: the main house at the Circle S Ranch, a sprawling wood-and-stone affair surrounded by hundred-year-old oaks, early-morning dew sparkling on the native grasses in the foreground.

To the left of the main house was the large guest house, a hunting lodge, really, with rows of bunk beds, a full kitchen and four bathrooms. Plenty of room for at least thirty people. He snapped a few shots and then turned to the small guest house on the other side of the main house. He saw a dark face in one of the windows and waved, but the man didn't wave back. A moment later, a huge man with a buzz haircut, muscles bulging beneath a tight, black T-shirt, emerged from the house. "'Mornin'," Farrell called out.

The man walked straight toward him and stuck out his monstrous hand, palm upward. Farrell reached to shake the extended hand, but the man shook his head. "The camera," he said.

Farrell was starting to get nervous. He didn't like the dull look in the man's eyes. "Uh, yeah, it's my Nikon. Just taking a couple pictures for the article. You here for the big hunt this weekend?" The man certainly didn't look like a hunter, at least not the type that went after deer.

In reply, the behemoth grabbed Farrell's twelve-hundred-dollar camera and yanked it from his grasp, snapping the strap that was looped around Farrell's neck.

Farrell backed up a few steps, rubbing his neck, and watched in astonishment as the man fumbled with various controls on the camera. He finally popped the back of the camera open and exposed the film. A few strange sounds came out of Farrell's mouth as he struggled for words. He truly had no idea what to say, and he quickly realized it would probably be best not to say anything at all.

The big man yanked the film from its spool, dropped it on the ground, and then casually tossed the camera back to Farrell, who barely had the presence of mind to catch it.

Marlin and Becky sat on the dirt floor with their backs against the wall as Marlin outlined his plan in hushed tones. He knew it would take both of them to carry it off—and if Becky showed even the slightest trace of hesitation, he wouldn't risk it. When he finished, he waited for her reaction. But instead of speaking, she leaned over and kissed him once again.

"How's your head?" she asked.

"Better by the minute," Marlin said, and returned the kiss.

They made love with no regard to their surroundings or their circumstances. For the little attention they paid it, the crummy blanket on the dirt floor could have been a satin-sheeted bed in the Waldorf-Astoria. The flashlight hanging on the wall could have been a fading candle flickering its last sensuous light. For Marlin, the pain was gone, replaced by a joy, a sense of completeness he hadn't felt in years.

Afterward, they lay in each other's arms as the flashlight finally went dark. The room was dark, until their eyes adjusted and the sunlight sneaking through the old building's cracks and crevices cloaked everything in gray. Neither spoke for quite some time, both wanting to postpone the inevitable return to reality. Becky was the first to break the silence. "This has been quite an interesting first date," she said.

"I do my best to generate a little excitement," Marlin replied. Then he added, "But it's really our second date, isn't it?"

"Oh, so you were counting that lunch we had as a date? I wasn't sure. I thought you were just wanting to talk to me about Phil Colby's condition."

The mention of Phil's name brought Marlin's mood back to earth, reminded him of people, places, events outside of this twenty-by-twenty shack. Whatever this abduction crap was, he didn't have time for it. He had a best friend to check up on—and a new relationship with Becky that he couldn't wait to explore. Despite his wounded head and sapped strength, he felt a burning resolve to escape.

CHAPTER TWENTY-SIX

PHIL COLBY AWOKE at eight-thirty feeling pretty good, considering. He grabbed a quick shower then started the coffeepot. While the coffee was brewing, he called Marlin again. Still no answer. And still no answering machine. Colby was starting to get a little concerned.

He hung up and called Junior Barstow, his boss at the Snake Farm and Indian Artifact Showplace. Junior was pleasantly surprised to hear his voice, asked about his health, and said no, it was no big deal if Colby didn't want to work for a few days. "Hell, take a week if you need it," Junior said. "Rest up. Lord knows you deserve it. Just be ready for some serious butchering when you come in. You know how backlogged we get at the beginning of the season."

Colby poured the coffee into a traveler's mug and headed out for John Marlin's house, five minutes away. When he pulled into the long gravel driveway, he saw a strange car, but Marlin's cruiser was gone. *Ah,* thought Colby...*maybe Marlin's made a new lady friend.* It wasn't Louise's car, and besides, she never stayed the night.

Colby climbed the front steps and rang the doorbell. Then he rang it again. Finally he pounded on the door, but still nobody answered. *Maybe they went into town for breakfast,* Colby speculated.

He peered into the house through a living-room window, but everything looked normal.

He turned and started to leave, but then he decided to have a better look. After all, he had a key to the place. Might as well stick his head in and double-check on everything.

"Your veterinarian, he ees gone," Oscar said, exasperation evident in his voice. He was calling Swank from the small guest house.

Swank was a little surprised to hear from the Colombian because they hadn't talked in two days. And no news was good news as far as Swank was concerned. But now they apparently had a problem. "What are you talking about, gone? That's ridiculous. Maybe he's just grabbing some breakfast somewhere." Swank had checked on Tim Gray just last night, and everything seemed fine. Sure, he was flying high, packing both nostrils on a regular basis, but that was typical.

"You think I am focking stupid? Hees truck ees still here, but he ees not. What does that tell you?"

Swank pondered it for a minute. "He could be asleep in the barn, or passed out somewhere. Did y'all look around real good?"

"He ees not in the barn, he ees not in hees truck, he ees not in your house. Did he not agree to work until the job was complete?"

"Well, yeah, but your men put quite a scare into him....Maybe he's just taking a break."

"It don' matter to me," Oscar said. "Juss as long as everything is ready to go by midnight. And if it ees not ready, I will do it my way."

"What are you saying, Oscar?" Swank asked, trying his best to keep his courage up.

Oscar screamed into the phone. "I don' care about your beeg hunting party or the value of your animals. Those drugs will be out of those deers by midnight...one way or another!" He slammed the phone down.

Great, just great, Swank thought. Where the hell was Gray, anyway? You couldn't count on anybody to do a damn thing right. He glanced out the window toward the small guest house. Somehow Swank had managed to let a small army of crazed drug lords invade his property like a cancer. Only, there wasn't any treatment available...except time. There was still a chance this could all blow over. Even if Oscar made good on his threat and killed all the remaining deer, Swank could come out of all this okay. Might even still make a bundle.

Then he noticed the buzzards circling a couple hundred yards behind the barn.

Could be a dead rabbit, raccoon, or some other varmint. But Gray was missing—and that gave Swank an uneasy feeling.

Oscar's man Julio Olivares, the one with the droopy mustache, had no real concerns about a possible confrontation with Deputy Bobby Garza. If the deputy had not believed the message Marlin had left for him last night, then it was up to Julio to resolve the situation. Oscar hated loose ends.

Julio had killed several men in his lifetime; in Colombia, men in the drug business died all the time. A body would be found in a ravine or in the trunk of a car, a single shot to the head. More often than not, authorities hardly even investigated such matters. They might do a quick background check on the deceased, discover a history of drug-related criminal behavior, and let it go at that. Why bother with more?

Of course, Julio would prefer not to kill the American deputy. Not because of any deep-seated respect for life, but because it created so many more headaches. In the United States, he couldn't afford to just abandon the body, especially a lawman's body. Better to take him hostage like the other two, hold him until Oscar said everything was okay, then return to Colombia. Julio and his men could probably be back across the border before the hostages even realized they were no longer being guarded.

But…the deputy could be a problem, and Julio could kill him if he needed to, without even the slightest tug on his conscience. That was a nice thing to know, that he could murder someone without the slightest compunction.

It was also nice to do this task on his own. Oscar had considered sending Tyler along with Julio, but that muscle-bound freak generally created more problems than he solved.

Julio pulled the rental car to a stop in front of the lawman's house, then unfolded a Texas map and puzzled over it for a few minutes. To anyone watching, he looked like another lost tourist who had wandered off Highway 290. He climbed out of the car with his sport coat over his arm, concealing the revolver in his right hand.

He glanced casually down the street, cocked the hammer on his pistol, and rang the doorbell. He'd have to do this just right. If the deputy gave him even a moment's trouble, if he hesitated to obey for even just a second, Julio would have to resort to violence.

He rang the doorbell again, hoping that the lawman was home; Julio wanted to complete this chore and get back to the ranch. He rang the bell a third time and began to think the house was empty. Suddenly the door was jerked open and Julio's finger involuntarily tightened on the trigger.

"What I want you to do is grab a couple shovels and bury his body....I don't care where."

"But Mr. Swank, don't we need to call the law in on this?" Red replied.

"Son, you gotta understand...he died from his own hand...a drug overdose. The man had a problem, and I was his friend, just trying to help him. Brought him out here to try and dry him out. I don't see how bringing the law into it is gonna do anyone any good. Think of how his family will feel. It'll just be a lot of embarrassment all around. Plus, they won't be able to collect any life insurance. You wouldn't want that, would you?"

Red glanced at Billy Don, who was preoccupied with a wart on his elbow. Red looked back at Swank. "Just bury him anywhere? Without no funeral? Now, I'm willing to bet that's almost illegal."

Swank puckered his lips. "You can have his truck."

"That new Chevy?"

Swank nodded his head. "Betcha could sell it for some good cash down in Mexico. After I'm done with you here."

Red thought it over for a few seconds. "Where're the shovels?"

Colby swung the door open and called, "Marlin? Hey, buddy, you here?" He'd hate to walk in on John with a woman. Maybe they were just shacked up and not answering the door or the phone. That wasn't exactly Marlin's style, but you never know.

No answer, so he walked through the house. Empty. No clue as to where Marlin was or who owned the car outside. Colby scribbled a note—*Call me*—and placed it beside the telephone. Then he remembered that the answering machine was off. Probably a slipup on Marlin's part, so Colby decided to turn it on. When he did, the light began blinking, indicating a recorded call. It was the same as Colby's machine: If it was turned off by accident or by a power outage, the machine saved any calls that hadn't been reviewed. Curiosity got the best of Colby and he pressed the PLAY button.

"Marlin, it's Bobby Garza. Hey, I just wanted to say sorry that I couldn't give you more backup on that whole Swank deal. I believe you and everything,

but without that powder, I didn't have a chance in hell of getting a search warrant. Anyway, if he's doing what we think he's doing out there, we'll catch up to him sooner or later. Just a matter of time. We'll talk more about it...."

Now, what the hell was that all about? Colby wondered.

"...But listen, I wanted to tell you about something else, too...about how Swank ended up getting the ranch from Phil Colby. You ready for this? Swank bribed Claude Rundell so that he wouldn't give Colby the loan he needed. Found out this morning. Anyway, I'll give you the full story. Give me a call."

Colby listened back to the message several times, just to make sure he heard it correctly. Then he felt the familiar hatred for Roy Swank blossoming deep in his belly. Colby wanted to grab the answering machine from the bar, hurl it across the room, slam his fist into the nearest wall...anything to quell this festering rage.

But then Colby realized something: If Marlin was missing—and he seemed to be—then it likely had something to do with this message from Deputy Garza. Something to do with Roy Swank. Colby's anger evaporated, replaced by concern for Marlin.

CHAPTER TWENTY-SEVEN

COLBY THOROUGHLY SEARCHED Marlin's house but found no more clues, nothing that told him where Marlin was or what had happened with Roy Swank. Then his eyes came to rest on the computer. Worth a shot.

He booted it up and was immediately faced with a control panel asking for a password. He tried all the obvious words—names of Marlin's relatives, past pets and girlfriends, favorite songs—but had no success. Then a thought occurred to him and he typed in BUCK. Damn, it worked! Just like the movies.

Colby quickly found a bunch of word-processing folders and began to scan through them. Mostly files related to Marlin's work...minutes from Wildlife Commission meetings...letters to landowners regarding wildlife management...memos from higher-ups about changes in game laws.

Then he spotted a file titled ATTORNEY GENERAL. He opened it.

Julio's finger twitched on the trigger, but he managed to refrain from firing. A pregnant woman had answered the door. She wore a faded blue bathrobe and had curlers in her hair. No makeup. Dark circles under her eyes. In her arms was a toddler who took one look at Julio and began to wail. In spite of all this, the woman smiled.

Julio was momentarily taken aback. Oscar had said nothing about a wife or family. Just a deputy. Grab him or kill him, Oscar had said, it didn't matter. Just make sure he is not a threat. Julio had never killed a woman or child before, but he was always willing to try something new.

"May I help you?" the woman asked, looking a little surprised to have an unexpected visitor on her doorstep.

"Yes, I am looking for Bobby Garza," Julio replied, eyeing the toddler with discomfort. Screaming children tended to attract attention from passersby. He glanced back over his shoulder to see if any of the neighbors were watching. When Garza came to the door, Julio would force his way into the house at gunpoint and then figure things out from there.

"I'm sorry, hon, he's not here," the woman said in a cozy Central Texas drawl. "Something I can help you with?"

Julio smiled his best smile, which looked more like a constipated grimace. "That is very kind, but I really need to speak with Señor…uh, Mr. Garza. Where might I find him?"

The woman produced a pacifier from somewhere within her bathrobe and stuck it into the toddler's mouth. The child immediately began sucking, but kept both eyes on the intriguing stranger. "You don't know Bobby very well, do ya?" the woman asked, laughing, as if there were some joke that Julio was not privy to.

Why must everything be so difficult? Julio wondered. Why couldn't she just answer the question instead of asking her own? Perhaps she would be willing to answer if she had a loaded pistol pointed between her eyes. "No, I am just in town for a few days. I am with the Mexico City police," Julio said, making a story up on the fly. "We are here studying the law enforcement techniques of rural police officers. I was supposed to speak to your husband…."

She shook her head. "Bobby never said anything to me about that."

Julio was losing patience. He caressed the pistol grip with his thumb. "Perhaps, I can find him…go speak to him. Where did you say he was?"

The deputy's wife seemed to be losing a little of her friendly demeanor. She studied Julio through squinted eyes, still shaking her head. Julio was about to raise his sport coat, jam the pistol in her face, or better yet, aim it at her child. But she answered first. "Everybody knows, this time of year, he's out fishing at Lake Buchanan. He almost didn't go this year, though. Some emergency at work. But this morning he said it had been taken care of and he took off. He musta forgot all about ya."

Fishing? To Julio, it certainly sounded like the phone call from Marlin had worked. Julio nodded at the woman. "Well, then…I am sorry to bother you."

"How's your sandwich?" Marlin asked.

"Not bad. And yours?"

"Pretty good."

Marlin watched Becky eat. She was proper without being stuffy, gently holding her sandwich in a napkin. Marlin had already managed to get mustard all over himself, not to mention the grime and dirt he had collected in the last twelve hours, but she still looked like she could have just stepped out of the shower. Amazing. *How do women do that?* he wondered.

"I have to say, you've been pretty amazing through all this," Marlin said. "Most gals would be freaking out right now."

"Working at a hospital kind of teaches you to keep your cool. Sometimes you can't worry about what's going to happen in an hour or in the next ten minutes, all you can do is concentrate on what's happening right now. I'd say we're in pretty good shape at the moment." She took another small nibble.

Marlin liked her sense of confidence.

"For one thing," she continued, "I don't think Luis would have given us these sandwiches if he were planning on doing anything to us. And he definitely wouldn't have told me his name."

"Oh, I see I have a regular criminal psychologist in my presence. What makes you think that?"

"Once you relate to a victim on a personal level, you feel more empathy for them. Something I've learned through nursing, because it's also true of patients. You can't help but become attached to some of your patients, especially the kids. But it makes it that much harder to take if something happens to them. Sometimes, to keep your distance, you find yourself calling them 'Mrs. Whoever' or 'Mr. So-and-so' instead of calling them by their first names. It's a strange thing in the hospital…if you hear a nurse getting chummy with someone, you can be pretty sure that person is going to be okay. Kind of sad, when you think about it."

Marlin knew exactly what she was talking about. He tried not to get too friendly with local poachers, even though many of them were very likable, because it made it tougher to write citations. Marlin already thought he was too much of a pushover at times. "I think you're right," he said. "Seems like these guys are just holding us…waiting for something…or someone. My guess is that they somehow figured out how much I knew, so they want me out of the way for a while. Maybe until they can cover everything up."

"Did you tell anyone about your suspicions?"

"Just Bobby Garza," Marlin said.

"Bobby sure is popular this weekend, Phil, but he's not here. He went fishing. It's his day off, you know," Vera Garza said. Colby was on her doorstep, a copy of Marlin's letter to the state attorney general in his pocket.

Colby was surprised. Judging from Marlin's letter, Garza knew as much about the situation at the Circle S Ranch as Marlin did. "Wha...When did he leave? Where did he go?" Colby finally managed to respond.

"You sure you don't want to come in for some iced tea?" Vera asked again.

Colby shook his head, looking a little worried.

Vera eyed him with concern, but decided not to pry. "He took off this morning. He was headed up to Lake Buchanan, meeting a friend from Burnet up there."

"When's he coming back?"

"Sunday evening. You know, he always likes the lake on opening weekend of deer season 'cause it's so quiet. Then he hunts deer later in the season—after all the amateurs are outta the way, he says."

Colby was momentarily at a loss. He was hoping to pump Garza for information, tell him that he couldn't find Marlin. He wanted a cop on his side...and not Sheriff Herbert Mackey. That guy was as a crooked as a pig's tail.

"Sweetheart, is something wrong?" Vera asked in her comforting Texas way.

Colby forced a weak smile. "Nothing I can't handle. Is there any way I can reach Bobby? Is he staying at one of the cabins up there?"

"No, they always camp out. You can try his cell phone, but you probably won't have much luck. Just like I told the other guy."

"What other guy?"

"There was a Mexican cop 'round here earlier, saying something about needing to talk to Bobby. Seemed kinda weird to me."

"What do you mean?"

"He said he was from Mexico City and he was suppose to talk to Bobby about how country cops do their jobs. What would a Mexican cop care about how we do it here in Blanco County?"

Colby sat in his truck for a long time and thought things over. He knew that his best friend appeared to be missing, but he was having a tough time believing it. Speaking of unbelievable, the letter Marlin had written to the attorney general seemed outrageous. Deer acting as carrying cases for drugs? On the other hand, Colby knew Marlin wasn't one to go off on wild tangents or to jump to conclusions. The letter didn't offer up any firm proof, but Colby figured that Marlin must have some. And if anybody was capable of participating in such a ballsy scheme, it was Roy Swank. Swank also had the connections to get as many deer across the border as he wanted, without the usual quarantining procedure. He probably had friends at all levels, guys who could sail the deer through with a minimum of paperwork and without a proper inspection.

But what did this Mexican cop have to do with everything? Could he be a Mexican drug agent, also working to shut Swank down? That seemed unlikely, considering the drugs were leaving Mexico rather than coming in. Colby figured that Mexican cops—like their American counterparts—would be far more concerned about imports rather than exports. No, it was entirely likely that the guy wasn't even a cop.

Colby had tried Bobby Garza's cellular phone several times with no luck. Either he was out of range on the middle of massive Lake Buchanan, or he had turned his phone off for the weekend. That left Colby with limited options. What if Marlin's letter was all speculation and he had no evidence against Swank? In the letter, Marlin had said he was in the process of putting together some evidence. That didn't sound like he had anything solid at the moment. If Colby went to the DEA, Marlin could end up looking like an idiot. Might even cost him his job. On the other hand, what if he was in trouble and Colby did nothing?

The more Colby thought about it, the more he realized he really had only one alternative: As much as he hated to do it, he'd have to talk to Sheriff Herbert Mackey. He dreaded the thought of it, but even Mackey wouldn't be dumb or dishonest enough to just dismiss Colby. In his wildest imagination, regardless of the sheriff's other moral shortcomings, Colby couldn't picture Mackey being involved with drug smuggling. The man was about as backcountry conservative as they come, always spouting on hypocritically about God and country, preaching eye-for-an-eye justice to anyone who would listen. Of course—according to local rumor—that never stopped Mackey from squeezing money out of the criminals unfortunate enough to find themselves under his meaty thumb. Colby knew this particular type of redneck well, the kind of person who thinks criminals are no better than stray dogs...dogs who need a well-placed kick on occasion to keep them in line. But to protect a drug smuggler? Colby didn't think there would be a bribe big enough to sway even a greedy opportunist like Mackey—and Marlin's letter hadn't mentioned Mackey being involved. If Colby approached Mackey on a professional level, right in his own office, he'd have to do something. Wouldn't he? And hell, Mackey might surprise Colby and know exactly where Marlin was.

On the other hand, if Mackey *was* working with Swank, this would be a good way to rattle Swank's cage a little, make him realize that people were becoming suspicious of him. That might help Marlin in the long run.

So that was the plan. Go speak to Mackey. Keep it local. Try to track down Marlin…at least give it another day…before calling in the feds.

CHAPTER TWENTY-EIGHT

THE FIRST OF the hunters began showing up at the Circle S Ranch at one o'clock on Friday. A cold front had come through and now it was a crisp, partly cloudy afternoon, temperature in the high fifties, a light northerly breeze... ideal weather for deer hunting. But Roy Swank's thoughts were miles away from the big hunting extravaganza he was hosting over the weekend. He was eleven hours away from a gruesome deadline. Oscar and his men were bound to come calling at midnight, just as Oscar had promised, and the deer situation would be no different than it was now. Tim Gray was dead, there was no getting around it. And without him, there was absolutely no hope of getting the drugs out of the deer...at least not while they were alive. Swank had already resigned himself to the fact that he was going to lose some big money on the remaining deer. Oscar and his men would simply kill them, splay them open and get the goods. They had no concern for Swank's hunting operation, no respect for a herd of bucks that would make the average hunter's eyes bulge and heart race.

Roy Swank remained isolated in his den, watching the hunters arrive, from behind the large, leaded-glass windows. At the moment, Swank wasn't concerned about being a good host, rushing out to greet his visitors. He was worried about keeping these two separate worlds—the Colombians and the hunters—from colliding. My god, there were senators and congressmen coming! What would they think if they saw these dark-skinned thugs lurking around the property? Swank couldn't dismiss them as ranch hands because they were all dressed like Cubanos out for an evening on Miami Beach.

Then, inevitably, Swank came to grips with what he had to do. Go to Oscar…tell him the truth. The veterinarian was dead, the drugs were still in most of the deer. Ask Oscar to leave, come back late, when his guests were asleep, and take the drugs out of the deer however he needed to do it. But please, do it quietly. Swank would even give him a couple of tranquilizer guns. That way, at least, Swank could walk out of this thing with his dignity, not to mention his freedom. He'd take a big hit on the lost deer, but there simply was no other choice. Frankly, Swank had been surprised that Oscar had waited as long as he had. He couldn't see why Oscar wouldn't go for it. That was it, then. Finally, a plan that would end this fiasco. Not with the greatest results, but the best that could be hoped for.

Swank was feeling better, reaching for the phone to call the small guest house, when he was interrupted by a knock at the door. Skip Farrell, the columnist.

"Mr. Swank?"

The ex-lobbyist put on his biggest smile. "Skip! Come in, come in. Would you like something to drink?"

Farrell accepted a bourbon and Swank's apologies for being a poor host. "I'm really sorry I've been so tied up with some other matters the last day or so. I wanted to show you around the ranch a little bit."

"No problem. Beautiful place you have here. Cletus gave me a tour, like you asked." Cletus Hobbs was the current foreman of the Circle S, a loyal, hardworking man. He knew every detail of Swank's deer-importing operation… except the most important part. The drugs. Swank never saw any reason to clue Cletus in, and he wasn't sure he could trust him with that kind of knowledge anyway. No, it was just Tim Gray and Swank himself who knew how valuable the deer really were.

Farrell said, "Listen, I ran into a guy down by the small guest house who exposed the film in my camera. Kind of rude, really."

Swank gave him a concerned look. "What'd he look like?"

"Big guy, like a Marine."

Swank pulled a lie out of the air. "Oh yeah, that guy works for me. Doesn't like to have his picture taken—some kind of religious deal. To tell the truth, he's a little strange. Best to keep your distance."

"I got no problem with that," Farrell replied.

"All right, then, let me tell you about this weekend." Swank ran down the guest list with Farrell, along with the daily agenda. Big welcoming dinner tonight. Hunting all day Saturday and Sunday morning. Then a celebration barbecue Sunday afternoon, when Swank would award a trophy to the hunter with the biggest buck. There might even be a few TV crews here for that. Plenty of photo ops for Farrell's article. "I can set you up in a blind with one of the hunters, if you'd like," Swank said.

Farrell beamed. "That'd be great. I could get some nice shots of deer coming to the feeders."

"How 'bout I put you with Tony Morales tomorrow morning?"

"The Speaker of the Texas House?"

"That's him."

Farrell smiled and raised his bourbon glass. "I can drink to that."

Phil Colby walked into the cramped Blanco County Sheriff's Department at lunchtime, when things would be quiet. The "department" consisted of a small windowless room with fluorescent lighting, and one drab office at the back of the room. Mackey's office.

Colby recognized a young deputy poring over paperwork at a small metal desk against one wall. He saw Darrell Bridges, one of the dispatchers, on the phone at a switchboard against the other wall. Three other desks sat empty in the middle of the room. Pretty quiet. But then, law enforcement in a county with fewer than seven thousand residents did not require much manpower.

Colby stood just inside the front door, waiting, wondering what, exactly, he was going to say when he found the sheriff. Then he took a few steps to the right and saw Mackey sitting at a massive wooden desk inside the single office. He was stuffing his face with what appeared to be a ham sandwich. Colby meandered through the desks and file cabinets and rapped on Mackey's open door.

Mackey glanced up from a magazine but didn't say anything. A real people person.

"Sheriff Mackey, you got a minute?" Colby asked, hating to be in the same room with this man.

"Just finishing up my lunch," Mackey said, popping one last humongous bite into his mouth. "Hab a seed," he said with his mouth full.

Colby walked in front of Mackey's desk but didn't sit in the ugly, armless chair worn shabby by the posteriors of burglars, thieves, poachers, speeders, and other assorted lawbreakers.

Mackey drained the last of a Mountain Dew, stuffed a wad of chewing tobacco into his cheek, then looked up at Colby.

"You seen John Marlin lately?" Colby asked.

"Nobody has. We haven't been able to reach him on his radio since late last night. Jean told me about it this morning."

"You got men out looking for him?"

"Naw, not yet. More'n likely he's just out hound-dogging some poachers. Could be his radio's busted. Or maybe he's spending some time with a lady friend."

"I think it's more serious than that. I think John's in trouble of some sort."

"Well, now, I wouldn't worry about him too much just yet. Marlin's a big boy, he knows how to handle himself. I'm sure he's just keeping busy, what with deer season coming up."

"Yeah, I know he's not exactly gonna be hanging around the Dairy Queen," Colby said, putting a little attitude in it. "But I've been trying to reach him since yesterday evening. He's not at home, nobody at Parks and Wildlife has talked to him since the meetings yesterday." Colby was reluctant to jump right into the heart of the matter, the whole issue with Swank, the drugs, Marlin's letter to the attorney general. He wasn't sure if he should even bring that stuff up at all. That was the whole problem with this situation: He didn't know if Mackey could be trusted. "In any case," Colby continued, "I want to file a missing-persons report."

The sheriff looked at Colby with indifferent eyes for a moment, then spat a stream of brown tobacco juice into the empty Mountain Dew can. "Oh, come on now. Just give it a little time. Marlin will show up."

Colby could tell that Mackey truly didn't care if Marlin was missing or not. So he dove in headfirst. "There's something else you need to know. Something weird is going on out at the Circle S Ranch and Marlin knew about it." Colby then laid out the facts as he knew them, most of which he'd learned from Marlin's letter. He told Mackey about Marlin finding the white powder on Thomas Stovall's ranch, about the powder getting stolen from Marlin's cruiser. The deeper he got into the story, the more foolish he felt. It all sounded pretty ridiculous. The only good thing—as he told the story, Mackey's face seemed to be getting a little flushed, the smug look was slowly evaporating. Colby finished the tale and laid the copy of the letter on the desk in front of Mackey. "It's all right there, in a letter Marlin wrote to the attorney general. And, of course, you already know about the guys that busted into my shop and put me in the hospital. They were after Buck...one of Swank's deer. The one that was acting so crazy that night when Marlin tranquilized it. Marlin—and I—think that deer still had drugs in it. That's why it was acting so wild."

Mackey shook his head, but without much enthusiasm. "How do you know they were after the deer? I thought you didn't remember anything about that night. That's what you told my deputy after you woke up."

Colby clenched his teeth. "I just know. What else would they have been there for? They didn't steal anything."

Mackey picked the letter up and looked at it like it was a dog turd. He read through it quickly. Then he stood, shut the office door, and sat back down.

"Did Marlin send this letter yet?" he asked.

"Hell, yes! I found it in his e-mail out-box," Colby lied. Now Mackey had to act.

Mackey leaned back in his chair and looked like he was trying to regain some of his composure. "Well, I'd say Marlin's really fucked himself this time. See, son, in my line of work you got to have a little something called evidence. Don't sound to me like Marlin has any evidence at all. If he'd been able to hang on to that powder—assuming it was drugs, and that's a big 'if'—then maybe we'd have something. But without it, all you got is a lot of suspicions. And Roy Swank of all people? Come on! The man is a leader in this community. Hell, he does more for this county than most of the rest of the citizens combined. What in the world would he be doing with drugs? Sounds like a goddamn fairy tale to me."

Colby felt his heart pounding, his forehead beginning to bead with sweat. He battled an incredible urge to lean across the desk, grab Mackey by the collar, and drive a fist into his face. He slowly grabbed the letter from the desktop where Mackey had placed it. "So, what's your plan, then? You're just gonna sit on your fat ass and do nothing? Not even look for Marlin?"

"You'd best watch your mouth, son. You're speaking to a man that can have you picking cotton for a year."

Colby decided it was time to leave…before he did something stupid.

Mackey spoke to his back: "Whyn't you leave that letter with me? I'd like a copy for my files."

Colby looked him in the eye. "Fuck you. This stays with me."

Mackey stood abruptly, one hand on his holstered handgun. "I'm warning you, boy. Don't talk to me that way unless you want to spend some time in lockup."

But Colby was boiling over now and couldn't help himself. He gave in to the sweet temptation that lures a man to lose control. "Know what I think,

Mackey? Swank paid you off to keep your mouth shut. You're just a lowlife yes-man who would do anything for a buck. You can take that tin star off your chest and cram it up your ass."

Mackey moved quickly despite his size. He came around the desk and popped Colby in the jaw before Colby could even prepare himself. Colby saw Mackey's big right fist arching back for another shot…but Colby beat him to it. He drove a left hand straight into Mackey's throat, feeling the windpipe give under the blow. Colby's father had always told him that nothing ends a fistfight like a punch to the balls or the throat…and he was right. Mackey staggered back and sat roughly on his desk, a confused expression on his face. His breath wheezed in and out like a fireplace bellows.

Colby didn't know whether he should run for help—or just plain run. He yanked the door open and saw that the young deputy, Ernie Turpin, was already standing outside the office door, obviously concerned by the sounds of the skirmish.

"Mackey's having a heart attack," Colby blurted, just to buy some time, and then hurried out of the building.

CHAPTER TWENTY-NINE

DIGGING A HOLE in Central Texas is never an easy undertaking. Typically, you go through about six easy inches of topsoil before hearing the shovel bite into a stubborn layer of limestone. From then on, it's a sweaty, bone-jarring nightmare. It's best left to professionals equipped with power augers and dynamite.

Red and Billy Don finally finished their gruesome task at five o'clock.

Both men had dug their share of holes before, for fence-posts, underground power lines, and the like, but digging a grave…that was an entirely different proposition. Swank had told them to go at least six feet deep. But as the afternoon wore on and each inch of earth seemed incrementally more difficult to excavate, the men quickly agreed that four feet—well, maybe it was really more like three—was just fine.

They lowered the tailgate, removed the tarp, and stared at the corpse underneath. Red looked at Billy Don. Billy Don looked at Red.

"Go ahead and grab hold," Red said.

"Why do I always get the nasty jobs?" Billy Don fumed.

"All righty, we'll do it together."

Both men reached slowly for Tim Gray's body, stealing glances at each other like men looking over their shoulders during a duel. Then they each grabbed a leg.

"Fuckin' gross, man," Billy Don said. "He's even stiffer than before. Stinks, too."

"Just think of him as a big white-tail buck," Red advised.

They dragged the corpse from the truck bed, keeping their heads leaned back as far as possible. Then they plopped the ex-veterinarian unceremoniously into the shallow pit and slowly shoveled the dirt and rock on top.

Afterward, they stepped back and took a look at the small mound of rubble.

"Don't exactly look like the graves out at Miller Creek Cemetery, does it?" Red said.

Billy Don leaned on his shovel, out of breath. "I don't even know the guy, Red, but this don't seem right."

Red grabbed two cold beers from a cooler in the truck and handed one to Billy Don. After a long silence, Red said, "Maybe we should say a few words. Ya know…Bible kinda stuff."

"I ain't read much of the Bible," Billy Don replied.

So Red stepped tentatively up to the grave, removed his cap, and held it over his heart. "O Lord…we're gathered here today to unite…No, wait, that's the marriage deal. Uh, O Lord…please accept this good man into your divine flock up there. Grant him forgiveness for his sins and treat him good, please, and even though he walks through the valley of the Sodomites, he fears no evil. He's walking tall, Lord…and carrying a big stick. Please embrace him, in the name of Jesus and the holy smokes. Amen."

"Amen," Billy Don echoed.

Red glanced around furtively, as if to make sure nobody had seen the little religious ceremony. Then he poured the remainder of his beer onto the grave. "Drink up, Bubba. It's the last one you're gonna git."

At six o'clock, with the sun slipping behind the Central Texas hills, Roy Swank climbed up into the back of a pickup to give a quick speech. He looked out at the crowd—all the guests had now arrived—and was awed by the collection of powerful men surrounding him. He counted four members of the Texas legislature, both of Texas' U.S. senators, the state attorney general, half a dozen judges, and many captains of private industry. Most of them were sitting at picnic tables in the shade under the towering oak trees next to the large guest house. Some were standing, drinking beer, chatting with old friends, meeting new ones. But the murmur came to a halt when Swank rose to address the crowd.

"Good evening, and thank you for coming," Swank began, beaming his best smile. "I think I know most of you personally…and most of you know each other. If you don't, I'm sure everyone will get a chance to get acquainted over the weekend. And what a weekend it's going to be."

Red was beside himself. He and Billy Don were finally getting the chance they had been waiting for. When they had gotten back from burying the vet, Swank had given them strict instructions to stay in the house and keep away from all of his guests. With the welcoming dinner and the socializing and bullshitting that would follow, Red figured they had at least a good couple of hours to rummage through the house.

To be honest, though, Red had kind of lost hope that they would find anything worthwhile. Sure, maybe some cash. But whatever was going on with the Mexicans…well, he had no clue about that. The daydream he had had earlier about Swank fiddlin' with the genes of big deer? No way. That kind of stuff was accomplished by people over in Germany and Russia and Houston.

But still, it would be good to look around. You never knew what you might find.

As Swank continued with his speech, he began to feel the adrenaline kick in. He was a smooth talker, at his best in the spotlight, and he had used his natural advantage for years in social settings such as this. As a lobbyist, he had gotten more accomplished over toasts and informal addresses than most congressmen did in years of House debates and committee meetings. Up in the truck bed, it felt great to have all eyes on him, and this sense of control yielded the first traces of optimism that he had felt in weeks.

"I've managed, through some kind input from state biologists and God's good grace, to grow some wonderful bucks on this humble ranch of mine," Swank said, making a sweeping gesture with his arm. "And I've got a feeling several of you will be seeing them through a rifle scope real soon."

Many of the men nodded and smiled, no doubt picturing a Boone & Crockett deer in the crosshairs. Swank was buoyed even further by their enthusiasm. Yes, he thought, things were finally getting back on track. Oscar and his men had agreed to Swank's proposition. They had left just minutes ago, and Swank thought he could still see the dust lingering in the air from their departure. They would come back at midnight, take the deer with tranquilizer guns, and be gone—all while his guests slept. His worst troubles were almost behind him.

"You find anything yet?" Red was in Swank's master bedroom, peering into dresser drawers, while Billy Don was investigating the gigantic walk-in closet. Red had read somewhere that most people hide their most valuable possessions in the master bedroom.

"Just a shitload of boots," Billy Don hollered back. "Must be fifty pair of Tony Lamas in here. Gen-yoo-wine ostrich and lizard, too."

Red appeared in the closet doorway and saw that Billy Don was on the floor pulling on a pair of alligator skins. "Forget the damn boots, wouldya. We ain't got time for that shit. Keep looking."

Red went back into the bedroom and looked under the oak-frame king-sized bed. Nothing but luggage. He jostled a few of the bags. Empty.

Swank was ten minutes into his speech, rambling on about the three key factors that dictate the growth of a whitetail—genetics, environment, and age. His audience didn't seem too fidgety yet, so he pressed on.

"I've got some beautiful four-and-a-half-year-olds out here, but those deer still have some growing to do. So try to hold out if you can. Wait for the big boys." Swank made eye contact with an old friend. "And Senator Thomas: Try not to shoot a cow this year." The crowd chuckled in delight.

"Hey, Red, take a look at this." Billy Don emerged from the closet holding a cardboard box, a big smile on his face.

Red was on his knees going through a cedar trunk at the foot of the bed. "What is it?"

Billy Don reached in and held up a videotape cassette. "Skin flicks. There's gotta be twenty or thirty in here. This one here is called *Blow White and the Seven Dwarves*. Looks like a real freak show."

Red considered it for a minute. "Old man don't have no wife. Gotta get his rocks off somehow."

Billy Don grinned like a schoolboy. "Let's take a look-see."

Red stood, grabbed the tape from Billy Don's hand and tossed it back in the box. "Goddamn, how many times I gotta tell ya? We ain't got time for that. We're looking for cash or paperwork or something that tells us what's going on out here. Forget the porno movies."

Billy Don walked glumly back into the closet and stuck the box back on the top shelf where he had found it. Then he had second thoughts and grabbed one of the tapes for later that evening.

CHAPTER THIRTY

AT NINE THAT evening, Sheriff Herbert Mackey fixed himself a stiff drink. The cool liquid would feel good on his aching throat. That Phil Colby was one mean bastard. Talk about a cheap shot…Mackey himself had never even punched a prisoner in the throat. But it was damn sure effective.

All evening, Mackey had considered calling Roy Swank and telling him about Marlin's suspicions and Colby's accusations. But then Mackey realized something he had known all along: For his own well-being, he had to remain completely ignorant about what was going on at the Circle S. Swank made generous contributions to the Sheriff's Department—and some of that money went straight into Mackey's pocket. The unspoken understanding was that Mackey would let Swank run his ranch however he wanted. That meant Mackey had to turn a blind eye to all the importing violations Swank committed with his trophy deer. But Mackey had been stunned by everything Colby had said. No, it was best to remain out of the loop as far as Roy Swank was concerned. Then, if the shit hit the fan, Mackey could honestly say that he had no idea what Swank was up to. Sure, Colby would tell everyone about his visit to Mackey's office…but Mackey could dismiss it as wild speculation. Unless John Marlin showed up with some solid proof. Then Mackey would have to act. Then he'd have to nail Swank to the wall.

Mackey wondered whether he had made the right decision about Phil Colby.

He could have had one of the deputies pick Colby up on an assault charge. But Mackey had decided to let it go. His instinct had told him that arresting Colby would be a mistake…it would look like Mackey was protecting Swank in any way that he could. So he had let it pass. But he had vowed silently to get revenge on Colby when the opportunity presented itself. And it always did.

Colby hung out at Marlin's house until ten o'clock. He had been there all day, since his run-in with Sheriff Mackey. He knew that he couldn't go back to his own house…that would be the first place the deputies would look. And Colby was certain they would be looking for him. You can't just assault a police officer and get away with it. Worse yet, Colby had no witnesses to the fact that Mackey threw the first punch.

So he had parked his truck behind a grove of cedars, slipped into Marlin's house through the back door, and tried fruitlessly to figure out his next move.

The house was eerily silent. He kept hoping the phone would ring and he would hear Marlin's familiar voice. But as each hour passed, Colby became more and more convinced that Marlin had gotten himself into some serious trouble. Colby didn't like to think about it, but he knew that Marlin might not even be alive. If Swank was really running drugs, then he was mixed up with some serious scum—men who would do just about anything to protect their business.

Colby felt trapped. Regardless of his suspicions, he still didn't feel confident enough to call the DEA or the FBI or whoever the hell you're supposed to call in a situation like this. What would he tell them, anyway? They weren't likely to raid Swank's home based on Marlin's letter alone. They would want to talk to Marlin first, see what kind of evidence he had.

And in the back of Colby's mind, there was still the smallest trace of a chance that Marlin was just fine. If Marlin reappeared and Colby had called the authorities in on Marlin's behalf, it could be a real disaster for Marlin.

No matter how Colby looked at it, he couldn't come up with a good solution. He couldn't trust Mackey. The one cop he could trust, Bobby Garza, couldn't be reached. It wasn't time to call in federal agents yet. So that left just one option.

He'd go out to the Circle S and figure things out for himself.

* * *

Swank staggered out of the massive guest house at eleven o'clock. He had mingled with his guests all evening, drinking scotch, smoking cigars, playing poker...but most of them had turned in by now. A few diehards were finishing one last drink—which they would regret in the morning—out on the front porch under the stars.

By the time Oscar arrived, Swank figured, all the lights would be out, all the hunters snoring in their bunks. The Colombians would take their goods and Swank could quietly put all this nasty business behind him.

He entered the ranch house, locked the door, ambled down the main hall, and heard the wide screen television playing in the billiards room. He poked his head in and saw Billy Don on the leather sofa and Red in Swank's favorite recliner. Swank shook his head. The imbeciles were watching an infomercial about a male potency drug. Swank had always been amazed at the power of television...you could sell a ten-pound bag of dog shit if you put it in the right package. Maybe that was something he should look into.

Swank started to tell the rednecks to turn the TV off and go to bed...but he decided it would be worthwhile to have them awake at midnight. He didn't expect to see Oscar, but the crazy Colombian was unpredictable. So he left them where they were and groggily continued down the hall to his bedroom.

"D'you hear that?"

"What?" Red replied.

"A door closin' or sumpin'."

"Probably just Swank hitting the hay. Don't be so jumpy. The Meskins are all gone. You saw 'em leave, same as me."

"Sorry we couldn't find nothin', Red. Maybe they was just here to buy a horse or sumpin'. Maybe that's all it was."

Red stifled a yawn. He'd had too many beers and was fading fast. The whole evening had been a letdown. They hadn't even been able to find any cash. "You seen any horses out here?"

Billy Don shook his head.

"Well, then...how the hell they gonna buy one?"

"Maybe they done bought 'em all."

Red started to reply but realized it was futile. His heart just wasn't in it. So he swigged his beer and sat in silence.

"Hey, Red?" Billy Don called to him.

Red didn't reply.

"Red?"

"What?" Red said, like he was talking to a pesky younger brother.

"Know what I wanna do?"

"Does it involve Wesson oil?" Red asked, "'cause I've always told you I'm not into that."

"Very funny," Billy Don said, sitting up straight on the leather sofa. "I wanna watch one of them skin flicks."

Red started to make a smart-ass remark but, frankly, it sounded pretty good to him, too. "You're too late. Swank's back and they're all in his bedroom closet."

Billy Don grinned and held up the black videocassette. "All exceptin' this one."

"You awake?" Marlin asked.

"Yes," Becky murmured. "And a little scared."

Marlin was reclining with his back against a wall and Becky had her head in his lap. Looking down, he could see her gorgeous features in the glow of the Coleman camping lantern. Luis, their captor, had been kind enough to give them a few provisions…the lantern, a couple more blankets, more water…he had even given Marlin his wristwatch and wallet back. But regardless of Luis' friendly demeanor, Marlin knew that a criminal was a criminal. You could never be sure of what he might do next. So Marlin had decided it was time to do something about their situation. A few hours ago, they had agreed to wait until Luis had gone to sleep—judging by when the campfire had burned down—and then put their plan into action. Catch him when he was groggy.

Marlin stroked Becky's hair and his heart fluttered with mixed emotions… the thrill of having discovered this wonderful creature versus the fear of losing her. "I want to tell you again how sorry I am about all this. If I had had any idea…"

"Hush," she said, rolling onto her back, placing a finger on his lips. "It's not your fault."

He leaned down and they kissed. It was heaven—and he wondered if it would be the last time.

Marlin slipped out from underneath Becky and peered through the slender crack around the door. "Looks like the fire is fading." He tried to sound confident. He glanced at his watch. "Let's give it another half hour…till midnight. Then we'll get the hell outta here."

* * *

It was eleven-forty. Oscar and his men had driven aimlessly around the Central Texas countryside for more than five hours, making one stop for dinner at a barbecue joint outside of Fredericksburg. Now Oscar had heartburn to go along with his increasingly foul mood.

Oscar was becoming more and more anxious as they approached the main entrance to the Circle S Ranch. He knew he had already wasted far too much time. The time to act had come. He would take what was his…and show no mercy to anyone who tried to stand in his way.

The ranch gates were open and Julio pulled Oscar's rented Cadillac onto the dirt road. Even the suspension system of the big luxury car was not immune to the rugged terrain, and it bounced and rocked in the ruts of the road. Oscar cursed at Julio in Spanish, telling him to slow down. Julio simply stared at his dark form in the rearview mirror as he eased off the gas pedal.

At a fork in the road, Julio turned toward the ranch house. "You fool!" Oscar barked. "We mus' get Luis first. He is the bes' marksman. Go to the cabin." Julio swung off the road into some weeds and found his way onto the alternate path.

Oscar knew this whole thing with tranquilizer darts would be frustrating and time-consuming. He had contemplated not even bothering with tranquilizers— just open fire with the deer rifles and a spotlight. But he simply couldn't risk that much noise, even with Swank's connections to the sheriff. They would need to use the tranquilizer gun and Luis was the best man for the job.

"What about the game warden and the woman?" Tyler Jackson asked with interest. "Who's gonna watch 'em?" He had been hoping to draw a little guard duty himself. The woman was a knockout…all he had to do was tie the game warden up for a few minutes and…

"We will do what must be done," Oscar said sharply, as if he knew what Tyler was thinking.

Oscar berated Julio again as the Cadillac bottomed out on limestone. The lesser-used road would be no problem for a truck or SUV, but it was slow progress in a car.

"*Que hora es?*" Oscar asked to nobody in particular.

Julio glanced at his watch. "Eleven-fifty."

CHAPTER THIRTY-ONE

PHIL COLDY, BREATHING heavily, watched the Cadillac's receding taillights from his hiding spot. He hadn't expected any traffic on the ranch at this hour, but he figured it could be a hunter arriving late. Not likely, though, the more he thought about it. Especially in a Cadillac. And now they weren't even going to the ranch house, they were changing course and taking the road that led down to the lower pasture by the river. He wished he could have seen inside the car, but it was too dark.

If Marlin was actually being held captive somewhere on the ranch, Colby knew he still had the element of surprise on his side. The occupants of the Cadillac apparently had not spotted him hiding in the tall grass, and his truck was parked safely two hundred yards past the ranch entrance in Thomas Stovall's driveway.

Under the cloak of darkness, Colby slowly approached the ranch house. As the guest house came into view, Colby saw twenty or thirty vehicles parked neatly along the driveway. So the hunters were all here, after all, ready for opening day. That made Colby somewhat anxious. Would Swank really invite the state's top power brokers to his ranch while he was holding a man hostage? That would be outrageous, even for Swank. The hunters would be swarming over every square inch of the ranch in the morning, and Swank was too smart to think that Marlin wouldn't be found. Colby's doubts started to get the best of him and he began to turn around. But, in his mind, he replayed Bobby Garza's message on Marlin's answering machine. He remembered Marlin's letter to the attorney general. And he pressed forward.

Colby stopped a hundred yards away from the main house and listened. All was quiet. He could see the front wraparound porch of the guest house. It was unoccupied except for the moths flittering around the porch light. Colby felt safe moving among the trees around the house toward the barn. He knew that Swank owned no dogs. He also knew which floodlights, mounted on posts at random around the house, were triggered by motion, so he was able to carefully avoid them.

The metal barn loomed in the darkness several hundred yards behind the house. Colby decided it was as good a place as any to look for Marlin. He followed the curving road to the barn, walking quietly in the limestone dust.

The barn was well built, but not completely weatherproof, and Colby could tell from the dark seams that no lights were on inside. He put his ear against the cool sheet metal of the barn door and listened. Nothing. Colby took a deep breath and began to roll the large, heavy door open. To Colby, the noise equaled that of a freight train chugging along the tracks. So much for stealth. He opened the door wide enough to slip through and switched the lights on. The interior was just as he remembered…large, gated stalls, hay stacked against one wall, various ranching implements hanging from roof joists. And nobody to be seen. Staring into the wide expanse of the barn made Colby suddenly self-conscious, and he switched the light off. He pulled a small flashlight from his back pocket and quickly checked each stall. Empty, just as he expected.

"John?" he whispered into the darkness. He waited a moment and then retreated from the barn, leaving the door open.

Colby circled the barn and walked over to a nearby fence-line. A ten-foot fence. Colby knew this was the five-acre pasture where Swank kept his newest prize bucks. He scanned the sparsely treed pasture and saw nothing. The deer were probably huddled on the back side of the pasture, as far away from human activity as they could get.

Colby squatted on his heels for a few minutes, dejected. He cursed himself for not having a better plan.…Hell, he didn't have any plan at all. What was he supposed to do, just walk right up to Swank's front door and knock? Demand to see Marlin? Right about now, that seemed to be his only option, and it was a lousy one.

Then Phil Colby had one of those glorious moments—one of his college professors used to refer to it as "an epiphany"—when the truth suddenly presents itself of its own accord. But this wasn't just one epiphany, it was two.

First, if Swank was keeping drug-packing deer on his property, they were likely contained in a small area…a pasture just like the one in front of him. The deer couldn't be allowed to roam the ranch freely because they might never be seen again. Big bucks are the most elusive animals in the woods. Colby recalled one wildlife study where a hunter was turned loose on a high-fenced hundred-acre pasture with one lone buck. Over an entire hunting season, the hunter managed to get one fleeting glimpse of the buck. He never got a shot. If there were deer in this pasture, their bellies probably contained a lot more than corn.

Second, there were at least a dozen feed shacks and other assorted outbuildings within two hundred yards of the barn. But keeping a man hostage in any of those would be just plain stupid. As Colby knew intimately, there was only one building on the ranch remote enough to serve as a makeshift prison. The old rock cabin down by the river. Where the Cadillac was headed.

Marlin peered through the crack of the door frame again and saw that the fire was almost out. Surely Luis was dozing by now, otherwise he would have stoked the fire. After all, it was getting cooler, now down in the low fifties.

He turned to Becky. "You up for this? We don't have to try it if you don't want to."

She shook her head. "Let's bust out of this dump."

He smiled and walked over to her, put his arms around her. "Remember… when he opens the door, just stand there and look gorgeous."

She gave him a coy look, an expression that would have been arousing under any other circumstances. "I think I can handle that."

Marlin tilted his head, thinking, for a second, that he heard an engine…far away, on the bluffs above the river. But the rushing water made too much noise and he couldn't be sure.

He looked back at Becky. "Well, then…"

Julio was almost as mad at himself as he was at Oscar. He'd had about enough of his boss, who was really nothing more than a foul-mouthed young punk. Over the years, Oscar had never shown Julio the proper respect. All he ever did was criticize, like now. Was it Julio's fault that the Cadillac was a *pedaso de mierda* and couldn't make it out of the mud?

Julio gunned the engine again to drown out Oscar's latest string of obscenities…but the Cadillac remained firmly entrenched.

"Perro malparido! Wha' the fock were you theenking?" Oscar asked. "I

tole you to go around the focking mod!"

Julio gritted his teeth. "There are large rocks on either side. This was our only path." He revved the engine again to no avail.

"*Coño de tu madre!*" Oscar turned and looked at the hulking figure in the backseat. "Tyler! Geet us out of this focking mod."

Tyler nodded and climbed out of the car. Julio watched in the mirror as Tyler walked to the rear, leaned down, and placed both hands firmly on the vertical slope of the trunk. Julio floored it and a rooster tail of thick brown sludge machine-gunned up Tyler's body. Oscar and Julio could hear him cussing as he stepped away from the vehicle. "Keep pushing!" Oscar yelled. "You are already feelthy, so what does it matter?"

Tyler got back into position, Julio floored the pedal, and they could feel the bulky car slowly creep back onto solid ground.

Tyler hopped back into the car, still wiping mud from his torso, and they proceeded toward the winding hillside road that led down to the cabin.

Becky rapped firmly on the door. "Luis! Hey, Luis! I gotta go again." Thirty seconds passed, then a full minute.

"He must be sleeping," Marlin said. He pounded on the door with the ball of his fist. "Wake up, Luis! The lady needs a little privacy again."

They heard Marlin's truck door open and shut, less than five yards from the cabin door. Marlin looked over at Becky again, reaffirming that she was well lit by the lantern she was holding. Glowing like the Statue of Liberty at night.

Marlin pressed against the wall to the left of the door frame. Moments earlier, Marlin had felt the weight of the tube-sock filled with rocks. Plenty heavy to do the job. Amazing how many stones Becky had managed to gather on each bathroom trip. They heard the familiar sound of the board lifting out of the brackets on either side of the door…then the door swung open.

At first, Red and Billy Don sat in stunned silence, sure that the videotape they were watching was some kind of joke or illusion. Finally Red said, "Good God Almighty."

"I ain't never seen such," Billy Don said, eyes glued to the set.

Then, a mere nanosecond later, Red realized he was staring directly at the goose that laid the golden egg! Roy Swank would pay a small fortune to get this tape back. It was the one delicious, wonderful, oh-so-fantastic opportunity Red had been waiting for all his life. Damn, here it was, right under his nose… and when he wasn't even expecting it! Yes, life was fixing to change bigtime for Red O'Brien. There would be no more Milwaukee's Best when he could afford Budweiser. No more Hamburger Helper when he could afford prime rib. Hell, he'd burn his old mobile home to the ground and replace it with a shiny new double-wide! Get all new furniture, including a dinette set. Drop a new engine into the Trans Am sitting on his front lawn.

Red was overwhelmed by it all. "Turn it off, Billy Don! Turn it off!"

"Wha…?"

Red jumped to his feet and pushed the EJECT button on the VCR. He slid the videotape out and clutched it to his chest. This was his winning lottery ticket, and it wasn't leaving his grasp. "Go grab our things and meet me at the truck!"

"But, Red, we're supposed to stay here and…"

"Goddamn it, just do it! Hurry!"

CHAPTER THIRTY-TWO

THE DOOR OPENED all the way…and Marlin knew that Luis' next few moves would determine whether the plan was a resounding success or a dismal failure. There was Becky, standing in the warm halo of the Coleman lantern… in her red panties, hair hanging seductively over her shoulders, breasts pushing against the confines of her recently tightened Wonderbra.

As most men would, Luis automatically took a step forward, eyes focused hungrily on the woman in front of him, the pistol all but forgotten in his hand. Then, just as Marlin had anticipated, Luis decided it was a trap and Becky was simply a decoy. So he turned quickly to face Marlin.

The game warden simply smiled at him.

That's when Becky stepped forward and swung the weighted sock from ankle height, bringing it down squarely on the crown of the Colombian's head. Luis' knees buckled momentarily, but he didn't fall.

He did fall, however, when Marlin drove him to the ground like a tackling dummy.

Both men lay prone on the dirt floor. Marlin tried to pull himself on top of the wiry man, but Luis writhed and kicked and flailed. Marlin threw a hard right and felt the man's nose collapse under his fist. Luis squealed in anguish and seemed to find renewed strength from his pain. He managed to pull his upper body free from Marlin's grasp and started clawing at the earth. Marlin was on his knees now, arms wrapped around Luis' thighs, as the Colombian, lying on the ground, grabbed the door frame and tried to pull himself away. He was amazingly strong. Luis freed one leg and kicked Marlin on the side of the head. Marlin slammed a big fist into the smaller man's abdomen and heard the air rush out of his lungs. Luis kicked again, catching Marlin hard on the bridge of his nose. Marlin tried to shake the dizziness he felt in his head, and Luis took advantage of this brief moment to wriggle free, jump up, and lunge for the exit.

Then, the whole room danced crazily as Becky swung the Coleman lantern and hit Luis on the shoulder. Glass shattered and the small man's shoulder was suddenly aflame. He swatted at the flames and screamed in agony, as Marlin and Becky were too astonished to do anything but watch. The fire began to crawl down the man's torso and Becky turned away in revulsion.

Marlin moved forward to help smother the flames, but Luis had something else in mind. He streaked out the door and ran downhill toward the Pedernales River.

In sparse moonlight now, Marlin felt around on the dirt floor for the gun and finally found the cool metal grip. "Grab your clothes, Becky!" he said. She was already pulling on her jeans.

He took her by the arm and they ran out the door of the cabin, only to see a big white Cadillac lurking in the moonlight twenty yards away, pointing directly at them. An instant later the headlights of the Cadillac bathed them in light.

Marlin's mind raced. The occupants of the Cadillac, by any stretch of the imagination, couldn't be anything but enemies. Marlin's cruiser was a mere twenty feet to his left, but he had no idea whether the keys were even in it. Worst of all, the cabin sat in an open clearing; the nearest woods were fifty yards away, precluding a run for cover. In this brief pause, while Marlin was trying to decide what to do next, his decision was made for him. Marlin, struggling to see past the powerful headlights, heard a car door open. And then he heard the familiar sound of a shotgun being racked. A voice—that of the beefy American—said, "Drop the gun and stay where you are."

Bitter disappointment flooded every nook and cranny of Marlin's brain. They had been so close to freedom...and to lose it again so quickly was almost more than he could stand. He glanced over at Becky, who was now holding her blouse self-consciously over her breasts.

Marlin let the gun fall to the ground and stepped in front of Becky, shielding her from the light. "Pull your blouse on. And hold on. I promise I'll get you out of this yet." Marlin knew it was a shallow promise. He had no idea what he was going to do. But if he had to sacrifice himself to gain her freedom, that's what he would do. "Listen, I have an idea…I'm going to make a run at the car, try to distract them…and when I do, I want you to run to your left. There's a dam over there that leads…"

"Forget it, John," she said. "No way. They'll shoot you for sure."

"It's the only way—"

"I won't do it." She looked him hard in the eyes. "We'll get out of this together."

Inside the Cadillac, Oscar was livid. Once again he had been failed by incompetent help. Oh, how he wished everyone in this world could be as trustworthy as himself!

As they had approached the cabin moments earlier, they were surprised to see the door standing open, with light emerging from the inside. Oscar had ordered Julio to coast quietly to a stop with the lights off. Seconds later, they were dumbfounded to see Luis dashing out of the cabin with his upper torso on fire. How he had managed to get himself into that kind of predicament, Oscar had no idea. Luis was nowhere to be seen now. Probably floating facedown in the river, if he had made it that far.

Tyler held the game warden and the woman at bay with the shotgun while Oscar tried to figure out his next move.

Julio, still in the driver's seat, broke his usual silence and offered his grim opinion. "We must kill them."

"Quiet!" Oscar ordered. He needed time to think. Killing a civilian, like the man who had snapped Oscar's photo from the hedges, was one thing, but killing an American officer of the law…well, that was bound to cause serious complications. On the other hand, there was really no way around it. They had to make a clean getaway, and they couldn't allow the lawman to give them any more trouble. The girl, she would be an unfortunate bystander.

In the silence, frogs on the riverbank began a shrill chorus. It almost seemed to Oscar as if they were mocking him, urging him to make a decision.

The deer were waiting. Oscar could have the drugs back in his hands in a matter of hours. Then he could simply fade into the background, find another buyer among his extensive network of contacts, and return home. Perhaps Julio was right this time. Oscar himself acknowledged that he didn't always make the wisest decisions under pressure. Trusting that idiot Roy Swank, for instance. He should have dealt with that man much more firmly several days earlier. Should have made him pay cash for the drugs and figure out the distribution on his own. The man was a novice and a fool. However, Swank knew nothing of the hostages. Killing them here, with Swank's own shotgun, would likely put Swank in prison for years. That appealed to Oscar at this point. It was also the quickest, easiest way out. "Shoot them!" he called out to Tyler.

Waiting in the beam of the headlights, Marlin had an uneasy feeling that a decision was being made. He knew that now was the time to act if he was going to act at all. Maybe he should grab Becky and take off toward the dam. It would be tricky in the dark, but what other choice did he have? The dam was very narrow and probably under a foot or so of water, with so much rain lately, but he knew he could find it by sheer instinct. The teenager in him would take over and find it. His pursuers would probably think the entire river was at the same depth and just plunge in at a closer point on the bank. They'd find themselves in five feet of water while Marlin and Becky ran for safety.

He could see the silhouette of the man with the shotgun, but he couldn't make out any features. Marlin could tell that the shotgun was aimed at him, not Becky.

"Get ready to run," he whispered to Becky. "We'll both go."

"You sure?"

Before Marlin could respond, he heard a horrifying command from the interior of the Cadillac: "Shoot them!"

The man with the shotgun immediately fired a blast.

CHAPTER THIRTY-THREE

MARLIN INSTINCTIVELY LEAPT sideways to the ground, dragging Becky with him. He was aware of a severe burning in his left arm. He felt defeated, cowardly, waiting to hear a second blast that would silence all sound forever. Then he heard something much sweeter. The shouting of a familiar voice, with a smooth-as-honey Central Texas accent.

"Freeze, you son of a bitch, or I'll cut you in two where you stand!"

Phil Colby was out there somewhere in the darkness.

Marlin looked over at the shotgunner and saw him nervously pacing in front of the Cadillac, peering into the darkness, trying to get a fix on Colby's location.

"Put the gun down!" Colby yelled. With the babbling river's noise, even Marlin couldn't tell how far away Colby was.

Marlin realized that the large American was now focusing on Colby, not him and Becky. He glanced over at the gun he had dropped moments earlier.

A string of insistent Spanish came from the Cadillac.

In response, the shotgun kicked again as the man fired a volley of buckshot in the direction of Colby's voice.

In one fluid motion, Marlin dove to the ground, grabbed the pistol, and came up on one knee, firing.

The man with the shotgun dropped his weapon and looked down at a rapidly darkening patch on his muddy shirt. He placed his palm flat on his chest as if to stem the flow. Then he crumpled to his knees.

"Get out of there, John!" Colby yelled.

Marlin grabbed Becky's arm and immediately ran toward the sound of Colby's voice. He heard another shot and glanced back at the Cadillac. Two more men had jumped out and the one on the driver's side, a guy with a droopy mustache, was firing a handgun. Out of the glare of the headlights now, Marlin could see Colby crouched on one knee in the darkness, returning fire at the Cadillac. Marlin and Becky ran to him.

"I'm out of bullets," Colby said as Marlin and Becky squatted beside him. They all flinched as a round whistled over their heads.

Marlin looked at Becky. "You okay?"

She nodded.

"Take her to the trees," Marlin whispered to Colby. Then he turned and fired from instinct, without even checking the sights. The armed man flinched and ducked behind the fender of the car.

Marlin couldn't see the other remaining man, but then he heard the engine turn over in the Cadillac. The car immediately lurched forward, spun a 180 in the dirt and silt, and headed back the way it had come, back up the hill. The entire time, the armed man tried fruitlessly to climb back into the car—but the driver was leaving him behind! Marlin watched in disbelief as the man fired two shots at the departing vehicle. The car roared away, leaving nothing but darkness.

Aiming at a memory of the man's location, Marlin unleashed four rounds, emptying the gun. He moved to his right in case the man returned fire at Marlin's muzzle flash, but there was no response. Ten seconds later, Marlin heard frantic splashing as the man plunged into the river fifty yards away. Then the hills became silent once again.

In the moonlight, under the big Texas sky, Marlin hugged his best friend. "Damn, am I glad to see you."

"Jesus, that was spooky, John! You nailed that guy with the shotgun! Who the hell were they?"

"I'll tell you the whole story later, but right now, let's just get out of here."

"Wait a second. At least tell me who this young lady is." In the darkness, and with Becky out of her nurse's uniform, Colby hadn't yet recognized her.

Marlin was at a loss for words. His best friend had just saved his hide and here Marlin was with the woman Colby intended to pursue.

"You already know me, Phil. Nurse Cameron." She stepped forward and hugged Colby. "Thank you. Thanks to both of you. That was unbelievable."

Colby remained silent for a moment. Then he turned to Marlin and said, "Well, hell…you beat me to the punch, pardner. I don't blame you."

Even in the dim light, Marlin could see Becky give him an inquisitive glance. Marlin deflected it by changing the subject. "Let me go see if the keys are in the cruiser. Y'all wait right here. If nothing else, I can radio for help."

Marlin returned a minute later in the cruiser. "Hop in. Let's get out of here while we can."

"Let me look at your arm first," Becky said.

Marlin felt the warm, sticky blood on his bicep. "I think I took a piece of buckshot, but it's fine."

Becky objected, but Marlin convinced her that his wound could wait. They began the long drive up to the ranch house. Along the way, Marlin told Colby about being abducted by the Colombians, who, they both agreed, had to be Swank's suppliers. Colby told Marlin about finding his letter to the attorney general, coming to the ranch, and then deciding to check out the old rock cabin. He also told Marlin his theory about the deer in the five-acre pen. "Those have to be the drug deer, John. He couldn't just let 'em roam the property or he'd never figure out which was which."

Marlin agreed, clapping his hands together. "The DEA will nail him, then The deer will be just waiting there. All they gotta do is open one up."

Colby cleared his throat. "Well, we may have a little problem there, old buddy."

"What are you talking about?"

"I kinda let them go."

"You *what?* Are you out of your mind?"

"Calm down for a minute and think about it, would you? It's better this way. First of all, I had no idea what was going to happen down here. It might not have turned out as well as it did. Then what would have happened? Those deer could have stayed in that pen for years and nobody would have been the wiser. So I had to let 'em go just in case. Remember, the hunters are going to be in the blinds bright and early tomorrow morning. With all those trophy deer running around, what do you think's going to happen?" Colby gave Marlin a sly smile.

Marlin was warming to the idea. "Damn, you're right. We just need to make sure they have the right audience when it all comes down. I'll need to make a few calls."

"There's something we need to do first, though."

"What's that?"

"It's Buck, John. I saw him. He's still up in the pen."

Deputy Bobby Garza had been disappointed to cut his annual fishing trip short, but there was no way around it. Three hours earlier, when he had checked in with his wife, she told him about the two visitors she had had: First, some guy identifying himself as a Mexican cop, and then Phil Colby. She said that they both had seemed nervous and both were asking for him. Instinct told him it had something to do with Marlin's theory about Roy Swank's deer. Sure, Marlin had left that message about Thomas Stovall's practical joke. But for some reason, Marlin's voice-mail just didn't sit right. He had sounded a little peculiar.

On the drive home, Garza had used his cellular phone several times to call Marlin, but got no answer. Same thing with Phil Colby. He called Herbert Mackey to check in, but the sheriff said that everything was quiet. Garza played it cool and told Mackey the fish weren't biting so he was heading home.

Garza knew all he could do at this point was wait. It was past midnight now, and he was on Miller Creek Loop nearing his house. On a straightaway, he saw headlights from an approaching vehicle. *Damn,* Garza thought, *they are really moving. Probably teenagers out with their daddy's pickup.* Garza's unmarked cruiser was equipped with radar, so he flipped it on. Ninety-seven miles per hour. Garza pulled onto the shoulder and waited. In a flash, the vehicle roared past him…a battered red Ford truck that looked just like Red O'Brien's.

Garza cursed silently. He was tired and just wanted to hit the hay. At eighty, eighty-five, he would have let them go. But ninety-seven, that was just too much. He wheeled his Crown Victoria around and headed after them.

"Shit, Red, that was Bobby Garza!" Billy Don whined, bracing himself against the dashboard. "Slow the fuck down!"

Red glanced in his rearview mirror, seeing nothing but darkness now. His old truck still had plenty of life left in her. Let the cop try and catch up. "Can't do it, man. I'll take the old Kerrville highway. He'll never find us on that old road."

Red banked clumsily around a curve, then began to brake hard to make the turn just ahead.

But the turn was coming up much too quickly. The brakes wouldn't bite and the truck began to fishtail. Red oversteered and the truck straightened again, but they were off the road now, bouncing over the bar-ditch. Red covered his face as one particularly large oak tree rushed toward the windshield.

When Garza came around the curve, dust was still floating in the air. He saw plowed earth leading to taillights at the base of an oak tree, so he braked gently, knowing the chase was over.

After pulling to the side of the road, Garza grabbed his portable radio. "Jean, you there?"

"Ten-four."

"We've got a ten-fifty on Miller Creek Loop. About three miles east of the Circle S. Need an ambulance, over."

"Ten-four. On the way. Over."

Garza grabbed his flashlight, jumped out of the cruiser, and trotted over to the red truck. Just as he had suspected, it was those two local rednecks, Red O'Brien and Billy Don Craddock. Garza had dealt with them plenty of times in the past, mostly for minor offenses, and he actually kind of got a chuckle out of them. They were like Andy Griffith's Otis.

Billy Don appeared to be unconscious and Red was moaning gently. Both men were bleeding from the head. *That's what you yokels get for not wearing seat belts,* Garza thought. How many times had he written them up for that one?

Neither of the men was bleeding profusely, so Garza decided it was best to let them remain in the truck until the medics arrived.

"Red, you okay?" Garza asked.

"Aw, man," he moaned softly. "My fuckin' truck."

At that point, Billy Don stirred, looked over at Red and said, "Gimme a beer."

Garza had to smile. Both men seemed to be okay.

"Screw your beer, man!" Red said, clawing for the door handle. "I just wrecked my truck!"

Red pushed on the door, but it wouldn't give.

"Red, why don't you just stay in the truck?" Garza said gently. "The ambulance will be here soon."

"I want out," Red said, slurring. He either had a mild concussion or had had a few too many, Garza decided. Red tried again, this time using his shoulder, and popped the door open.

A videocassette clattered to the ground at Garza's feet. Garza picked it up and looked at the label. "Looks like you boys been havin' an interesting evening."

CHAPTER THIRTY-FOUR

JUST AT SUNRISE, Clyde Webster pulled on his overalls and headed out to his barn to collect eggs like he did every morning. He wasn't sure if the rooster had begun crowing yet, because Clyde was getting on in years—nearly eighty-five now—so he couldn't hear quite as well as he used to.

A significant portion of his hearing loss had occurred during World War Two. "The Big One," that's the only thing he and his friends would call it. *If you'd been there,* Clyde would tell people, *you'd call it the Big One, too.* He'd been in the middle of some damn nasty maneuvers, where mortars lit up the night like the Fourth of July…fights where you'd have to pile the bodies up like cordwood the next day, or even worse, you'd have to pick up pieces and put them in a canvas bag.

Despite all the bombing, the gunfire, and the near-constant screams of anguish, there was one sound Clyde remembered more grimly than all the others. The sound of a round hitting an infantryman's helmet. It was almost the same sound as a raindrop falling into an empty bucket. *You hear that sound, brother, you know right off someone's dead.* He still shuddered when he heard anything like it.

Whenever Clyde thought about the war, which wasn't too often anymore, he considered himself pretty lucky. Sure, he had seen some horrific things—once saw a man cut clean in two by a mortar—but all Clyde got was some damage to his eardrums, thanks to a Jap land mine. He was almost too embarrassed to explain his injury to anyone who asked about his Purple Heart. Didn't seem right that some guys had to lose an arm or a leg or maybe go blind to get theirs.

It was the damnedest thing with the hearing loss, though…he could hear low notes and high ones, it was just a few mid-level tones he lost. There was one Marty Robbins song where Clyde couldn't hear about half the lyrics. That made him sad in a nostalgic kind of way, but he always shook it off.

Veterans of the Big One came home heroes, unlike those poor Vietnam veterans. In the 1960's and 1970's, many Americans seemed to forget that everything they enjoyed—from big, comfortable homes and nice cars, all the way up to the ability to walk down the street as free men—came at the expense of the casualties of war. Right there on television you'd see people burning American flags, for Chrissakes. Clyde had seen a young long-haired fellow doing that same damn thing down at the Capitol in Austin one Memorial Day. Clyde had walked right up to the fellow and, despite the bursitis in his shoulder, knocked that young punk cold. He'd do it again, too, if he had to. *Nobody's going to burn the ol' Stars and Stripes around Clyde Webster.*

But this morning, Clyde wasn't thinking about his old war buddies as he sometimes did. He was just thinking about collecting eggs, going back to the house, and waiting for the omelet Helen made him every morning. So when Clyde entered the barn, he wasn't expecting to see a man standing there with a gun. A Mexican man at that, with a big, droopy mustache. Before Clyde could react, the man grabbed him by the straps of his overalls and yanked him completely into the barn. The Mexican began to shout at Clyde, saying that he needed a car.

The gun really didn't scare Clyde that much, or the shouting, or even the thought that the man might actually shoot him. But he was concerned for his wife in the house. This gunman had crazy eyes, a frenzied look that Clyde had seen too many times on the battlefield. As soon as he got the man a car, Clyde knew, he and his wife would both be dead.

The man had released Clyde and was blocking the door now, yelling at him some more. Clyde heard some of it, but not much. He calmly reached over and grabbed a pitchfork that was hanging on the wall. Now the man would have to shoot him, he knew, but that would alert Helen. At least she'd be safe. She knew where the shotgun was.

But the man didn't shoot Clyde right away like Clyde expected. He just yelled some more and waved his arms around. He seemed to want to approach Clyde to strike him, but the pitchfork kept him at bay.

So, for a moment, they were at a standstill. Clyde then realized that the man might simply leave him here and go into the house to find the car keys. Then he'd find Helen, too, and who knows what would happen?

Sunlight was beginning to stream though the rafters of the barn, and now Clyde did hear the rooster crowing. It was loud and strong, probably just a few feet outside the barn door. For just an instant, the Mexican man turned his head toward the sound in surprise. But it was long enough. Without hesitation, Clyde stepped forward, gave it all his strength, and ran the man through with the pitchfork. For a moment, they were locked in a grisly face-to-face stare. Then the gun fell to the ground and the man followed. With blood spilling out of his mouth, he tried to say a few last words to Clyde. But Clyde wasn't listening. He had already gone to make sure his wife was all right.

Thirty minutes after sunrise, with all the hunters fed and sent off to their deer blinds, Roy Swank sat around one of the tables in the large guest house. He was sipping coffee, fighting a nasty hangover, but feeling pretty good overall. Hadn't heard a peep out of Oscar last night, and that was a blessing. He knew he'd probably been in tighter spots over the years, but he couldn't think of any right off. Now it was all over and done with.

"Cletus, bring me some more coffee, wouldya?" he called out to the ranch foreman, who was washing the breakfast dishes.

Cletus came over with the pot and filled Swank's mug to the top, then had a seat at the table.

"So what do you think?" Swank asked. "Gonna be a good morning?"

Cletus nodded. "Weather's perfect, and I think the rut is in full swing. We should hear some shots any minute now, once the big boys start to show themselves."

Swank rose and headed for the door. "I'll be in the house. Come and get me when the hunters start coming back."

"Will do."

Swank walked out into the brisk morning air and turned toward the barn. Now that the sun was up, he could see that the gate to the adjacent five-acre pen was open. That cinched it, then. Oscar had been here—and now Swank's troubles were over.

Swank walked over to the pen and began wandering through the thickly wooded areas. He had told Oscar to stack the carcasses in a secluded spot, so the hunters wouldn't see them. If Cletus or anyone else found them, Swank already had a story made up: He had received a call from Mexico informing him that the deer were diseased and needed to be destroyed.

But as Swank continued to roam the pen, he became a little nervous. He hadn't seen a single carcass, much less a drop of blood. By the time Swank had covered the entire five acres, his heart was palpitating. The deer were gone. That meant one of two things. Either Oscar had taken the carcasses with him, which was highly unlikely...or—Swank didn't even want to think about the alternative—the deer were loose on the Circle S Ranch.

Cletus put the newspaper down and stood to answer the phone in the guest house. "Circle S."

"Hey, Cletus, it's Marlin." The men knew each other well.

"What are you doing, you old buzzard?"

"Well, you know, opening day. Gotta start making some rounds, keep all you old poachers in line," Marlin said, falling into his hunting-camp drawl.

Cletus laughed. "Hell, you won't be writing me up for anything this weekend. I'm not about to go out to the blind with all the city boys out here. Liable to get myself shot."

"I've heard about the big shindig over there. Big-time senators and the like. Heard any shots yet?"

"Just a couple, so far. But it's early yet."

Marlin tried to keep his tone from sounding serious. "Listen, I'm gonna head over there later and see what kind of bucks y'all are growing nowadays. How late you imagine they're all gonna be hunting?"

"Swank told 'em all to keep with it till about ten. Told 'em to stay out there even if they get one, so they won't disturb the other hunters by driving through the ranch."

"All right, then. I'll see you about ten o'clock."

"Wanna rub elbows with the big wheels, don't you?" Cletus said, giving him a hard time.

"You got me, Cletus. You got me."

CHAPTER THIRTY-FIVE

ON SATURDAY, NOVEMBER 6, some of the biggest bucks in Blanco County history were harvested on the Circle S Ranch. The highlight was a twelve-point with eight-inch drop tines and a twenty-four-inch spread. By ten-thirty, all the hunters had returned and were now gathered at the butchering shed, exchanging excited handshakes, comparing deer and swapping tales from the morning hunt. Skip Farrell, the journalist, was making the rounds, asking the men to pose for publicity shots with their trophies. They were all happy to oblige. Many of the men were already enjoying the day's first Bloody Mary or cold beer.

Off to one side, apart from the hunters, stood John Marlin, Phil Colby, Becky Cameron, and another man who, from his dress, was obviously not a local. His name was Art Collison, Marlin's roommate from Southwest Texas State University, now an agent with the DEA.

"Seen Swank yet?" Marlin asked Colby.

He shook his head, eyeing the crowd.

Marlin turned to Collison. "I appreciate you coming up from Laredo on such short notice."

"No problem, John. It was good to hear from you."

"And thanks for not bringing the entire cavalry with you."

"I thought about it, but I agreed with something you said on the phone."

"What's that?"

"That you might be wrong."

Marlin started to reply, but the crowd suddenly broke into applause.

Roy Swank was approaching from the main house, accompanied by a slender man in dark slacks and a golf shirt.

Several of the hunters called out to Swank in appreciation, telling Swank what a great hunt it had been. Swank raised his hands in a gracious gesture, as if he were receiving the Nobel Prize...but his smirk was nowhere as self-satisfied as Marlin would have normally expected. In fact, the man looked flat-out worried. He even shot a glare over at Marlin and his group.

As the hunters finished clapping, Swank said, "It's you gentlemen who deserve the applause. Just look at all the fine trophies you took this morning. I'm impressed. I want to talk to each one of you personally, to hear your thoughts about the herd I'm raising out here, but what say we head back to the bunkhouse so everyone can clean up and get ready for lunch?"

Before the crowd could start to dissipate, Marlin spoke up. "But Roy, don't you want to get some of these deer field-dressed...see what kind of weights we're talking about?"

Swank acted as if he had just noticed Marlin. "Well, hello there, John. Our local game warden, folks," he said to the crowd. Several of the hunters turned to look. Swank continued, a small nervous tic now apparent on his face: "There will be plenty of time for that, John. I bet these men are tired and would like to grab a hot shower."

But Marlin knew that the time was now. "I don't know, Roy. From my estimation, it looks like we could be looking at some county records here, if not state records. I know I'm curious. What about you?" Marlin said, addressing everyone but Swank.

Several of the men spoke up.

"Let's go ahead and dress 'em out, Roy!"

"I know I'd like to know."

"Let's do it! Hell, we got a game warden right here to verify it all!"

Without waiting for Swank to answer, Cletus Hobbs stepped forward, unfolded his hunting knife, and walked over to the heaviest deer. He looked over at the hunter who had shot it. "Want me to do the honors?" he asked, knowing that most of these men had never gutted a deer in their lives. The hunter told him to go ahead.

The big buck was hanging spread-eagled by its hind legs. Cletus made the first incision, beginning at the pelvic bone, and expertly opened the deer up all the way to its sternum. As Cletus spread the abdomen open, preparing to split the sternum, a condomlike package fell to the ground. It was about the size of a golf ball and appeared to be filled with white powder.

"What the hell?" one of the hunters murmured.

Cletus, as intrigued as everyone else, opened the abdomen all the way. Dozens more packages cascaded to the ground.

Skip Farrell stepped closer and took a quick series of photographs.

"What in Christ's name is going on here?" Swank said, red-faced, as the crowd turned to look at him.

Marlin's old roommate stepped forward, flipping open his wallet. "I'm Art Collison, Mr. Swank. With the DEA. I think we need to have a little talk."

"So you're telling us that you knew absolutely nothing about the drugs?" Marlin asked incredulously. It was an hour later and he was in Swank's den now with Collison, Swank, and the man in the golf shirt.

"That's what Mr. Swank is saying," said the golfer. He had introduced himself as Buddy Geis, Roy Swank's attorney, right after Collison had approached Swank at the butchering shed. Geis had agreed to talk to Marlin and Collison—providing that Swank would not be arrested and booked at this point. Nothing but a bunch of misleading circumstances, Geis had insisted, things they could clear up in no time. "We're not refuting the existence of the drugs...or of the other men involved...or the fact that they kept you and Miss Cameron hostage. We truly regret the ordeal you went through."

Marlin shot him a *Fuck you* look.

"But these men," Geis continued, "had identified themselves as Mexican nationals—wealthy landowners with trophy white-tailed deer for sale. Mr. Swank had invited them up here to see his hunting operation, but he knew nothing about the drugs; he thought he was purchasing and importing nothing more than some valuable wild game. Granted, he may have called in a few favors to get as many deer imported as he did, but there's no way he could have possibly known what was in those deer. As far as the men who kept you hostage...to be frank, we're not even sure they are who they said they were. You may never be able to track them down."

Marlin looked at Collison, who shook his head. "It was up to Swank to sell the deer," Collison said to Geis. "The foreigners couldn't have known who he was selling them to, so how would they have gotten their drugs to their dealers in the States?"

"We're not certain about that," Geis said. "All we can figure is that they had men working in the U.S. who tracked the deer down and removed the goods… maybe after the deer were sold, or maybe even while they were right here on this ranch, without Mr. Swank knowing. It really makes perfect sense, if you think about it. That way, they had an accomplice who didn't even know what he was in on. So they didn't have to cut him in."

It was all an obvious pack of lies…but Marlin knew that a jury would probably buy it. It certainly sounded no crazier than smuggling drugs inside live animals.

Marlin glared at Swank, who leered smugly back at him.

"If you're so innocent, then why was your lawyer already here?" Marlin shot at him.

"I'm an avid hunter myself," Geis said. "I simply came out because I wanted to see if the other hunters got any Bowie and Crockett deer this weekend."

"It's *Boone* and Crockett," Marlin growled. He could hear Collison stifling a laugh behind him.

"Uh, right," Geis said. "That's what I meant."

Marlin's anger was beginning to reach a boiling point. He stepped up close to Swank, towering over the shorter man. "This is the biggest bunch of bullshit I've ever heard."

"Careful, Mr. Marlin," Geis said. "You're coming awfully close to violating my client's rights."

Marlin turned to leave, but decided to deliver one last shot. "We're gonna get you on this, Roy. Plus the bullshit you had going at the bank."

Swank's eyes showed a trace of surprise.

"That's right," Marlin went on. "I know all about your bribe to Claude Rundell. So you better enjoy this ranch while you can, because it won't be yours for long."

Swank let out a long sigh and looked away from Marlin as if he were bored. "I have no idea what you're talking about, Marlin…now please go away."

Collison had his hand on Marlin's shoulder, gently holding him, sensing that he was about to go after Swank.

Colby, who had been waiting outside at the lawyer's insistence, entered though the den door. "Hey, John…come out here for a minute. There's someone here to see you."

"Who is it?" Marlin asked, not wanting to walk out without getting some satisfaction.

Colby locked eyes with Marlin and winked at him. "Come on out, John.

These guys'll still be here in ten minutes."

Marlin walked out with Colby into the hallway, closing the door behind him. Waiting for him was Deputy Bobby Garza.

"Where in the hell have you been?" Garza asked Marlin. "I was calling you all last night."

Marlin wanted to fill Garza in on everything that had happened, but there wasn't time. He wanted to get to Swank now, while the lawyer was still talking. Get them to slip up on something they would have to contradict later. "We stayed at Chuck's Motel last night because we didn't feel safe at my place or Phil's," Marlin told him. "It's a long story, Bobby, but everything I told you the other day seems to be true. I called in the DEA. Sorry, I didn't mean to go around you or the Sheriff's Department on this one, but you know how Mackey is, and…"

Garza shook his head. "Are you kidding? Don't worry about it. Those DEA guys will nail his nuts to the wall."

"Don't be so sure. Swank's lawyer is in there slinging lies all over place. And with Swank's connections…you know how those scumbags cover each other's asses. Dammit! If he manages to slip out of this…"

"Relax, Marlin," Garza smiled. "How would you like a confession?"

Marlin looked at Garza like, *Well, duh, I'd love one.*

Garza held up a videotape and said, "Marlin, ol' buddy. Don't say I never gave you nothin'."

CHAPTER THIRTY-SIX

MARLIN WALKED BACK into the room, accompanied by Bobby Garza and Phil Colby. Swank looked a little surprised that Garza had appeared—probably wondering why Mackey wasn't here instead, Marlin thought—but Swank didn't say anything. Geis was finishing a call on his cell phone—confirming a tee time for later this afternoon, apparently. Marlin waited until he had both men's complete attention.

Geis hung up and Marlin waited for just a moment, savoring what was about to happen.

"Roy, I think Deputy Garza here needs to talk to you about an unrelated matter."

"What are you talking about?" Swank demanded, glancing nervously over at his lawyer.

Geis started to speak, but Garza cut him off. "Nothing to be concerned about. But I do need to inform you that I think I've recovered some property that was stolen from you. Have you been burglarized recently?"

"No! This is ridiculous. This...this..." Swank stammered, unsure what Garza and Marlin were up to.

Marlin held up the videotape without exposing the label. "Deputy Garza made an arrest last night, and the two suspects confessed to stealing this from your residence. You might know them—Red O'Brien and Billy Don Craddock?"

Swank shook his head and shrunk in his seat. "No, I don't think…Wait, maybe I do know them.…I'm not sure."

Covering all the bases, Marlin thought. *Because he doesn't know what the hell we have.*

"Why don't we take a look at this tape, Mr. Swank, then you can confirm whether it is your property or not."

Without waiting for an answer, Marlin walked over to the entertainment center and plugged the tape into the VCR.

Geis looked at Swank, wondering what the hell was going on, but Swank just shrugged.

Marlin hit the PLAY button, and the men waited in silence for the tape to begin.

Then the first images came on the screen. A blonde porn star eating a banana in a very suggestive manner. Then the picture jumped and the quality changed. It looked like home video and the frame showed a slain doe, lying in the grass among some cedar trees.

"Oh my god," Swank gasped. "Turn it off."

"Hold on there, Roy," Marlin answered, with a huge smile. "We're not even sure it's yours yet."

On the screen, Roy Swank entered the frame—and began to dress the deer carcass in women's lingerie.

Geis looked over at Swank like the fat lobbyist had just farted. "Jesus, Roy, what the hell is this all about?"

"Turn it off!" Swank shouted, and rose to approach the VCR.

Garza stepped in his way.

Marlin said, with plenty of sarcasm, "Oh, so it *is* your property. Glad we got that cleared up."

"Always nice to help out a victim such as yourself," Garza said.

"Do something!" Swank yelled at Geis, who just shook his head.

Onscreen, Swank was beginning to strip off his clothes.

"Of course," Marlin said, "this is evidence in a case, so Deputy Garza can't return it right away."

Swank began to cry now, huge sobs that made the other men turn away in embarrassment. "For the love of Christ, stop it!" Swank bawled. "Just tell me what you want! What do you want?"

Marlin hit the PAUSE button, freezing the image of Swank with his pants down to his knees. "Let's see…Where do I begin?"

* * *

An hour later, a well-dressed Hispanic gentleman approached the main bridge in Laredo, intending to cross over into Mexico. He was driving a late-model Cadillac with a rental sticker on the bumper. Larry Blackwell, a border guard for seventeen years, decided to check it out. Too many stolen cars were crossing the border nowadays.

He motioned the driver over to the side and rapped on the driver's window.

The window came down and the driver gave Blackwell a big smile. "Yes sir, Officer?" he said with a thick accent.

"May I see some identification, please?"

The man handed him a passport. Humberto Moises Rivera, it said, and it appeared legitimate. A naturalized American citizen.

"Mr. Rivera, may I see your rental papers for this automobile?"

"Oh, yes sir," Rivera said eagerly, handing the guard some additional papers.

Everything looked to be in order, Blackwell thought, but you could never tell, with computers and printers as advanced as they were these days.

Blackwell handed the documents back to the Hispanic man. "Where are you traveling today?" he asked.

"Going to see my family in Monterrey. Beeg family reunion."

"Reunion, huh? That sounds nice. What are their names?" Blackwell asked.

"Perdóneme?"

"Your family members…what are their names."

"Well, there ees my brothers, Javier, Rafael, and Raul. My sisters, Isadora and Maria…" The man noticed the guard had a pad out and was writing the names down.

"Any aunts and uncles there? Maybe some cousins?"

"Sure," Rivera replied, and continued to list names. After he had provided a dozen or so, Blackwell motioned that he could stop.

"Please wait here for a moment, Mr. Rivera," he said, and returned to the small guard station.

Blackwell simply sat for five minutes, drinking coffee. It was one of the oldest tricks in the book. Ask some questions, wait a while, then ask 'em again, see if the answers matched up.

Blackwell exited the guard station and approached the car again.

"Okay, Mr. Rivera, we're almost done here and then you can be on your way. Just tell me again…what are your brothers' names?"

The man's smile evaporated. "Why for you ask this again? I have already given you those names."

"The names, sir."

The man looked through the windshield at the bridge ahead of him. "There is Javier...and..."

"Who else?"

"And...I am a busy man! I must be on my way!"

Blackwell placed his palm on the butt of his gun. Then he said, with an edge in his voice, "Step out of the car, sir. Right now."

Moments later, Oscar stood to the side and watched in amusement as several men searched the interior of his car. *These fools,* he thought, *they will find nothing. There is nothing to find.* He had tossed his handgun out on the road many miles back. As far as his fictitious family, so what if he could not remember names on a list? In the U.S., they could not hold him for that. In Colombia, yes, but not here.

He watched as the one named Blackwell removed the keys from the ignition, walked to the rear of the car and popped the trunk.

In an instant, Oscar's world came crashing down. From ten feet away, Oscar could clearly see the contents of the trunk—and he realized with great despair that he had fallen victim once again to another man's incompetence. Tyler had not done what Oscar had asked. He had not disposed of the body of Barney Weaver, whose corpse grinned lifelessly up at the border guards.

EPILOGUE

PHIL COLBY STOOD on the bed of his truck and drove the last in a long line of eight-foot T-posts, then looked back at his work. Large rolls of horse-fence were waiting in a nearby trailer. He'd have the fence finished tomorrow, then he could let Buck out of the barn, free to wander. Colby sat down on the tailgate just as Marlin came bouncing up the driveway in his truck. Becky Cameron was in the passenger seat.

"Fence is looking good, Phil," Marlin said as he climbed out of the vehicle.

"You really think five acres is enough?" Colby asked, surveying the area to be enclosed by the deerproof fence.

"Aw, yeah, don't worry. Maybe we can leave a gate open, let a couple of good-looking does in."

"A couple?" Becky said with a grin. "What does he need more than one for?" Before either man could reply, Becky said, "You look worn out, Phil. I'll go grab us all some iced tea if you've got any."

"How 'bout a cold beer instead? There's a six-pack in the fridge," Colby replied.

"Be right back," she said.

Both men watched her walk away in her khaki shorts.

Marlin figured it was as good a time as any. "Listen, Phil, I wanted to talk to you about Becky...."

Colby held up his hands, palms out. "Hey, don't worry about it."

Marlin shook his head. "I just want you to know that I didn't plan it this way. I know you were interested in her, but…"

Colby cut in. "You think if I was the one holed up in the cabin with her, I wouldn'ta done the same thing?"

Marlin didn't know what to say.

"She's a great gal, John," Colby said. "Quit moping around about it and just enjoy yourself."

Just like that, Marlin knew why he had been friends with Colby for so long.

"But about this fence." Colby changed the subject. "It just doesn't feel right, to keep him in a pen this small."

"He'll be fine."

"Yeah, but what about next season? And even in between seasons, there are always poachers around. I imagine Buck will hang around the house here for the most part, but you know he's gonna wander off sometimes."

"What if he had four thousand acres to roam around on?" Marlin said, barely able to contain himself.

Colby gave him a sidelong glance. "What are you talking about?"

"I'm talking about your ranch, Phil. It's gonna be yours again."

Colby's lips moved, but nothing came out.

"I just came from a meeting with Roy Swank," Marlin continued. "Just me and him. No lawyers. We made a little trade—a rather disgusting videotape, for the ranch. I told him it was a funny thing, tapes like that had a way of ending up on the Internet. He was all too happy to make a deal."

Colby started laughing, the kind of laughter accompanied by tears of joy. He came over to shake Marlin's hand, and the handshake turned into a hug.

"Jesus, John. You don't know what that means to me."

"I know. You got Bobby Garza to thank, too. He bent the rules a little bit. As soon as Swank deeds the property back to you, Garza is gonna give him the tape, no questions asked. Red and Billy Don gave Garza that tape so he wouldn't nail 'em for theft and DWI and speeding and…"

"Gaw-damn, I'm gonna have to buy those rednecks a beer sometime," Colby said. "On second thought, maybe I'll hire 'em to work the ranch."

"Are you out of your mind?" Marlin couldn't tell if Colby was serious.

"Hey, what better way to keep 'em from poaching the property?"

Marlin smiled. "You know, you may be right."

Marlin and Colby sat down on the tailgate and watched the sun begin to dip behind the oak trees.

"What about the smuggling, John? Isn't Swank gonna get nailed for that?"

"Man, I hope so. He's still gotta deal with those charges, but I don't know what kind of case the feds can put together. Tim Gray and two of the Colombians are dead. The leader, this guy Oscar, is in jail and hasn't said a word yet. I doubt he ever will. Mackey has admitted to taking some bribes from Swank, but it sounds like he didn't really know what was going on out there. In any case, Mackey's gonna be out of a job, and I know a fine young deputy named Garza who's just dying to take his place. So, to be honest, I figure if Swank hires enough Austin lawyers, they can get a jury to believe just about anything. Swank could walk away with probation, or maybe even get off scot-free."

Colby sighed. "That just ain't right."

"On the other hand," Marlin said, "if Luis gets out of the burn unit and decides to save his own skin—no pun intended—he could put Swank away for a long time."

Colby nodded. "John, you said something yesterday that I meant to ask you about. When we were still at Swank's, you were talking to that lawyer, Geis, and you said something about finding another tape..."

Marlin nodded. "Several years back, Cletus called in about some shots fired on the Circle S. I went over there and found a doe all prettied up like the one on the tape we saw. There was a video camera set up, but the poacher had taken off. Now, looking back, I realize it wasn't a poacher, it was Swank."

"Did you look at the tape?"

"Hell, yes. Nothing on it, though."

Colby shook his head. "That guy is one sick puppy."

The men heard Colby's screen door slam and Becky returned with three longneck bottles.

They drank in silence for a moment, enjoying the last light of the evening.

Just as the sun dipped beneath the horizon, they heard a deer snort beyond the fenceline. A large buck emerged from behind a grove of trees and stared at the trio.

"It's gonna be a great season, John," Colby said, as the graceful animal snorted again and bounded off into the brush.

ABOUT THE AUTHOR

Ben Rehder lives with his wife near Austin, Texas, where he was born and raised. His Blanco County mysteries have made best-of-the-year lists in *Publishers Weekly, Library Journal, Kirkus Reviews*, and *Field & Stream. Buck Fever*, the first in the series, was nominated for the Edgar Award.

KEEP READING FOR AN EXCERPT FROM BEN REHDER'S

BONE DRY

On the morning of Saturday, November 5—opening day of deer season—a statuesque blonde beauty strolled out of the trees, pulled down her khaki shorts, and peed beneath Cecil Pritchard's deer feeder.

"Well, suck a nut," Cecil said to himself, sitting in his deer blind a hundred yards away. He looked down at his coffee mug, blinking dumbly. Maybe he'd added a little too much Wild Turkey. And this *was* his fourth cup. But when he looked up again, the Nordic goddess was still there, hiking up her shorts. His brother-in-law would never believe it.

The day had started normally enough. Cecil climbed out of bed at four A.M. sharp, pulled on his camo coveralls, and brewed a pot of Folgers. *Nothing gets you going like the smell of fresh coffee,* Cecil thought, whistling happily. He would have loved a big plate of scrambled eggs, bacon on the side, and a basketful of biscuits, but Cecil wasn't much of a cook, and his wife, Beth, was still drowsing in bed. Goddamn woman was as useless as a negligee on a nun. On weekdays, when he'd come home from the machine shop at lunchtime, he'd usually find Beth staring at the soap operas or Jerry Springer on TV, and Cecil would be left to make his own lunch. The way Cecil saw it, that was a serious infraction of the marriage vows. So, as he had prepared for the morning hunt, Cecil made sure to stomp around the mobile home as heavily as possible, kind of get the whole floor vibrating. It'd serve her right if she couldn't get back to sleep after he left.

He met up with Beth's brother Howard at the ranch gate at five in the A.M., just as planned—plenty of time to reach the blinds before first light. Seeing as how they had a few minutes to spare, Cecil took the opportunity to remind Howard what a lazy, good-for-nothing sister he had. Howard heartily agreed while munching a breakfast taco his own wife had prepared for him. *Sorry, I ain't got but one,* Howard said around a mouthful.

The men split up and Cecil proceeded to his elevated tower blind, a beauty he had ordered from the Cabela's catalog last spring. Once inside, Cecil readied himself for a long, relaxing morning hunt. He loaded his Winchester .270, double-checked the safety and leaned the rifle in the corner. He pulled out his binoculars and gave the lenses a good cleaning. Then he poured a hot mug of java, added a generous dose of bourbon, and waited for sunrise.

The black night slowly gave way to gray, and then the rolling hills of central Texas started to take shape. The birds began chirping tentatively and then went into full chorus. Cecil leaned backed and soaked it all in. He was sitting twelve feet up with a view that God himself would appreciate. Man, this was living. Cecil waited all year for this morning, and he just knew there was a big buck somewhere in the woods with his name all over it.

That's when Cecil heard a car rambling along the gravel county road that paralleled the ranch's eastern fence line. Weeks ago, Cecil had considered relocating his blind, but the road saw such little traffic, he had decided to leave everything as is.

Looking through his binoculars, Cecil saw a rusty mustard-yellow Volvo easing down the road. It disappeared behind some trees and then the motor faded away. Cecil had thought the occupants were gone for good. But apparently, he was wrong.

Now, Cecil was staring slack-jawed at the blonde trespasser, knowing that all his pre-season plans and preparations were wasted. He was furious. The woman might as well have erected a flashing neon warning sign—DEER BEWARE!—because no self-respecting buck would come within a thousand yards of so much human scent.

Finally, Cecil managed to get over his astonishment and do something. He stuck his head out the small window of the deer blind and yelled, "Hey, lady! What the hell are you doing? Get your ass away from there!"

The tall blonde casually buttoned her shorts, smiled, and flipped Cecil the bird.

Cecil decided enough was enough, and rose to go give the woman a serious tongue lashing, maybe escort her back to her damn rattle-trap of a car. But as he stood, he spilled his coffee, dropped his binoculars to the floor, and—goddamn it all!—banged his riflescope against the side of the blind. Cussing loudly now, Cecil opened the blind door and began to climb down the ladder—only to hear a car door closing and the Volvo gently puttering off into a fine Texas morning.

At nine A.M. on Saturday, November 5, a thick-chested man with crow's feet, jowls, and graying hair was throwing a hump into his live-in Guatemalan housekeeper—but his mind was elsewhere and his erection was starting to droop. The distraction was laying right there on her nightstand: the Travel section of the newspaper. He could see an ad that said: *Barbados, from $549! Call your travel agent today!*

Shit, if it were only that easy. But Salvatore Mameli—formerly known as Roberto "The Clipper" Ragusa—couldn't just pick up and go like normal people. His life was way too fucked up for that.

A few months back—maybe it was more like a year now—Sal had forced himself to take stock, to figure out how he wanted to spend his golden years. After all, he probably still had a couple of good decades left. He was only fifty-seven—knock wood—way past the average age of most men in his former line of work. *So what is it,* he had asked himself, *that I really want out of life?* It boiled down to this: He wanted to live his life in peace, away from the Feds, in some distant country where he wouldn't have to worry who was waiting around the next corner. He wasn't asking much, really, but it would require a lot of dough.

The irritating thing was, Sal still had plenty of money from the old days—a small fortune that the government couldn't seize because Sal had actually earned those particular assets through legitimate businesses. But those accounts were eye-balled like a stripper at a bachelor party. If Sal tried to make a sizeable withdrawal—especially in cash—red flags would go up and he'd be surrounded before he made it to the airport.

No, what Sal needed was fresh money that could be easily concealed. Lots of it. Then he could make his break.

He could picture the location in his mind: definitely someplace tropical, like this Barbados place. Maybe a small island that had no extradition treaty with the U.S. Better yet, no rednecks, pickup trucks, or country music. He'd had his fill of that shit.

Sal had lived in Blanco County, Texas, for three years now, which was about thirty-five months more than he could handle. And Johnson City, the county seat? Forget about it. You couldn't find decent Italian food anywhere. You had to own a satellite dish to catch most of the Yankee games. And everyone was so damn friendly, it made his asshole pucker.

For two and a half years, Sal had simply laid low, trying to figure out his next move. Unfortunately, the U.S. Marshals Service always had its eyes on him so closely he could barely take a crap without a marshal there to offer him toilet paper. Just a few more trials, they kept saying, and then you'll be free to do what you want. Leave the country, we don't care. But for now, you owe us. With your life. And Sal had to admit that was true. He knew he could be rotting in federal prison right now—assuming some wiseguy didn't shank him in the ribs out in the yard. All of Sal's pull from the old days wouldn't mean shit. Some greaseball would waste him without batting an eye. That's the way it was nowadays, no respect for men like Sal anymore.

So three years ago, as much as he hated to do it, Sal had chosen the only alternative. The problem was, the trials could take years to wind their way through the judicial system. After all, the Feds were in no hurry. They were going after some heavy hitters, so they wanted to dot every *i* and cross every *t*. And, of course, there could be mistrials, appeals, and all kinds of delaying tactics that could keep Sal Mameli squarely under the U.S. District Attorney's thumb for years to come. With each day that passed, Sal couldn't help worrying that his former associates were closer to tracking him down.

And he knew the kind of justice they would exact if they found him.

After all, Sal used to be one of the guys in charge of dealing out punishment. That's where he had gotten his nickname, the Clipper. He had done some nasty things to some nasty men, left bodies in the kind of condition that would make the most hardened medical examiner shudder. Sal knew what the horrifying possibilities were, and that's why he kept a loaded .38 in his nightstand and a sawed-off twelve-gauge under the front seat of his Lincoln. Every noise in the hallway at two A.M. could be a goon with a garrote, instead of his son, Vinnie, making a trip to the john, or his wife, Angela, sitting like a zombie in front of late-night TV, a bottle of vodka by her side.

But then, just six months ago, things had begun to look brighter. Opportunity had pounded firmly on Sal's door, as it had so many times in the past. For some reason—a drought, a low aquifer, or who the hell knows why—residents all over Blanco County had begun clearing their lands of cedar trees and other brush. At first, Sal had barely glanced at the newspaper articles addressing the situation. Then, on a drive through the country with Angela, Sal noticed the tractor-like machines that were used to clear brush. They seemed to be everywhere, rumbling over ranchland like so many Sherman tanks. *This,* Sal thought, *could be exactly what I've been looking for.* After doing a little research, finding out precisely what this land clearing was all about, Sal realized there was an enormous amount of money to be made in the brush-removal business. Hell, he had run a successful concrete company back in Jersey, and had even taken on several juicy projects here, before the water issue brought new construction to a screeching halt. And this brush-removal business, how hard could it be? The concrete business required large machines, cedar clearing required large machines. All you needed was some operating capital and some big, dumb guys to run the equipment. Piece of cake.

So Sal had jumped right into the brush-removal business with only two things in mind. Number one: Stashing away some serious cash. Number two: Buying a one-way ticket to some off-the-map Caribbean island where nobody asked questions, checked for proper papers, or cared who the hell you were in a past life. Sal could almost smell the salty breeze and the coconut oil. He could picture a tanned, nubile body—definitely not his wife's—lounging in the chair next to him.

Sal had noticed something else in the last few months: The Feds seemed to be loosening their grip a little. He no longer had a team of deputies on his tail every time he left the house, no longer heard strange clicks on the line during every phone call. There was still a plain-vanilla sedan outside his home on occasion, with government plates, but the fat putz inside was easy to handle.

It made Sal laugh to think they actually trusted him.

On the other hand, he *had* been their star witness half a dozen times already, and they seemed to think he was a man of his word, that he'd stick around to the end. With more freedom than he had had in three years, now was the time to make a break for it. Or at least get the plan in the works.

With his new business in full swing, the money starting to pour in, Sal was consumed around the clock by thoughts of flight. That's why, on this particular morning, as Sal was getting a piece of tail, his heart really wasn't in it. He had too much to think about, including tomorrow's meeting. Sal was getting together with a rich old bastard named Emmett Slaton, Sal's largest brush-removal competitor. Sal was going to offer Slaton twice what his business was worth. *Hell of a deal,* most people would say. Of course, the "deal" consisted of a reasonable down payment now and a balloon payment next year that, in reality, poor old Emmett would never see. It was the same arrangement Sal had with several other area business owners. Better yet, Sal had secured the down payments via a small-business loan at a local bank, another obligation he had no intention of fulfilling. The idea was to have as much money as possible coming in, and as little as possible going out. Then, when the time was right, he'd skip the country, leaving his creditors holding the bag.

If he tried the same stunt back home, he'd wind up with his throat cut and his body tossed in the Hudson River. But down here? Shit, who was gonna stop him?

At ten o'clock Saturday morning, Susannah Branson, senior reporter for the Blanco County News, wheeled her Toyota into Big Joe's Restaurant in Johnson City. There was a scattering of vehicles in the parking lot, including John Marlin's green Dodge Ram pickup, issued by the state.

She checked her makeup in the rearview mirror and fluffed her wavy brunette hair. Susannah had been looking forward to the interview with the county game warden for several days. Rumor had it that John Marlin would soon be back on the singles market, and Susannah had had her eye on him for a long time. Ever since high school, actually. He was just her type: a big, strapping guy, with broad shoulders, dark hair, and dark eyes. *No sense in wasting time,* Susannah thought, and unsnapped one more button on her blouse.

She entered the small café and spotted Marlin at a booth, sipping coffee. He rose to greet her. "Morning, Susannah."

"John, thanks so much for meeting me," she said with a smile. She gave him an appraising look. "Have you lost weight?"

"Tapeworm," Marlin replied.

"Oh, uh, well," Susannah stammered, unsure whether to laugh. After all, the man was a game warden. Who knew what he might pick up out in the woods? "I know you're busy today, with opening day and everything, so I won't take up much of your time."

"I appreciate that, but this is important stuff. Don't rush on my account." Marlin gestured toward the booth and they took a seat.

A waitress quickly took Susannah's order—coffee only—and scooted away.

Susannah ran her hands through her hair and said, "What we're working on is a piece that addresses the environmental effects of clearing brush. Any possible effects on wildlife, livestock, etcetera. I figured you'd be the best man to talk to—especially with Trey Sweeney in the shape he's in."

Trey Sweeney was the county wildlife biologist—an ace in his field, but somewhat eccentric. Sweeney had recently returned from a vacation in Brazil, where he had contracted a mean case of dengue fever. His health was much better now, but Trey had been acting a little more strangely than usual lately. The previous Saturday night, a deputy had found Trey at the high school football stadium, rooting wildly for the home team. Unfortunately, the football game had been played the night before.

Marlin nodded at Susannah. "I'm glad you called. I think it's important that the ranchers and other landowners hear the other side of the brush-clearing story." Six months ago, with Blanco County in the midst of a severe drought, county commissioners had recommended that residents remove as much brush from their land as possible. After all, brush—chiefly small scrub cedar trees—consumed an enormous amount of surface and ground water. By removing it, residents hoped to replenish the aquifer and pump life back into sluggish wells.

Residents had responded by conducting a full-out assault on cedar trees.

Across the countryside, the buzz of chainsaws became as persistent as the droning of summertime cicadas. Huge mounds of cut cedar waited to be burned on every ranch, deer lease, and rural homesite in the county. To date, officials estimated that ten percent of the cedar had been removed. To John Marlin and other wildlife officials, this was cause for alarm. They knew that a drastic change to the ecosystem—like clearing every cedar in the county—could have less-visible long-term implications.

Susannah removed a small tape recorder from her satchel. "You mind if I tape this?" she asked. "Helps me get all the quotes right."

"Sure. No problem."

"Well, Mr. Marlin," Susannah said with false formality, something she herself found rather charming, "tell me what you think about all this cedar clearing."

Marlin paused for a moment and took a sip of coffee. "Let me start by saying that it's not necessarily a bad idea. But it might not be a good idea either. We obviously have a water problem, as we've all known for some time. Seems like every year we hear about how it's getting worse. Wells run dry, springs and creeks quit flowing, and Pedernales Reservoir is at a record low, even though we haven't opened a floodgate since the dam was built. And just looking at the face of it, clearing cedar seems like a good way to attack the problem."

"But…" Susannah prompted him.

Marlin shrugged. "I think we're all kind of rushing things. We need to step back, take a look at the bigger picture and think about how our actions could effect the wildlife. Animals have four basic biological requirements—food, water, space, and cover. Whenever man interferes with any one of those, it can have major consequences. For instance, white-tailed deer need brush cover to survive."

"But the deer don't eat cedar trees, do they?"

"No, but they usually bed down in thick brush. And they use it to move around without being seen. Without all the cedars, they'd be a lot more vulnerable to predators like coyotes, cougars, and bobcats. Especially the fawns."

"I never thought about that."

Marlin shook his head. "Most people don't. But for all the ranch owners who are making good money with deer leases, it's something they should consider. They should be wondering what the deer population will be like in five or ten years.

"It's not just the deer," Marlin continued, speaking with obvious heartfelt intensity. "Wild turkey, rabbits, raccoons—they all need a fair amount of brushy habitat. And people should keep in mind that if you fool around with one link in the food chain, it can cause a domino effect. Let's say—just as an example—we remove all the brush and the rabbits become easy prey. Coyotes will have a field day for a while and their population will explode. Pretty soon, we've got coyotes all over the place, but they've eaten all the rabbits. So what do they go after next? Livestock. Goats, sheep, calves. I *know* the ranchers don't want that.

"Or here's another good example: the beaver. Five hundred years ago, before the Europeans came over, there were maybe three-hundred million beavers in North America. Place was crawling with them, from Mexico all the way up to Alaska. But then one of the English kings ruled that only beaver fur could be used to make hats. So beaver fur became big business, and it almost wiped 'em out. Fewer beavers meant fewer beaver dams, and that had a horrible impact on the natural habitat. Suddenly, all the ponds and watering holes that the beavers created were disappearing, which had an effect on waterfowl, songbirds, deer and elk, raccoons, the list goes on. Hell, those dams even helped keep the aquifers full back then by slowing down runoff. They limited soil erosion, even helped ease flooding."

Marlin shook his head and smiled thinly. "I know I'm rambling on a little. We're here to talk about cedar clearing, right?"

"No, that's all right," Susannah said, leaning forward, trying to make eye contact. "Like you say, it all ties together. I can tell this issue means a lot to you. You're a very passionate man, John. I can see that in you."

The game warden held her gaze for a few seconds, smiling, playing the game with her. Then he glanced down at his cup. "I need a little more coffee. You want some?"

Susannah nodded, and Marlin gestured at the waitress. "Okay, next question," she said. "What about the red-necked sapsucker?"

"I was afraid you were going to ask me that." He thought for a moment. "Yes, it's an endangered species and yes, it nests almost exclusively in cedar trees in Central Texas. So the official Parks and Wildlife Department position is that we are against most brush clearing in sapsucker habitat."

"And what's your personal *position*, John?" Susannah asked.

He gave her an appreciative smile, acknowledging the double entendre. Just as he was about to respond, the waitress appeared to refill their coffee cups. After she left, Marlin's face was serious again. Back to business.

"Can we talk off the record?" he asked.

"Sure."

"I think, sometimes, when a species becomes endangered, that's the way nature wants it. Think about it: More than ninety-nine percent of all species that ever existed are now extinct. And man has had little to do with the decline of the majority of them. Hell, with most of them, we couldn't have kept them around if we wanted to. They just weren't in Mother Nature's plan anymore, and when that happens, there's not a damn thing we can do about it."

"That's an interesting point." Susannah paused, stirring her coffee, unsure what to ask next.

"You're looking good, Susannah," Marlin said, out of the blue. "Beautiful as ever."

Susannah could feel her face getting warm. She was used to a little back-and-forth flirting, but nothing so direct and sincere. "Why, thank you, John. That's…that's very sweet."

He nodded, drank the last of his coffee, then said, "So…we all done here?"

"One more question." Susannah reached down and switched off the tape recorder. "Would you like to have coffee with me sometime?"

The game warden grinned and held up his cup. "We are having coffee."

"No," Susannah said. "I mean…well, you know what I mean."

For the longest time, Susannah thought he wasn't going to answer.

The Complete Series of Blanco County Mysteries

Available now, or coming soon, in ebook, print, or both.

Buck Fever
Bone Dry
Flat Crazy
Guilt Trip
Gun Shy
Holy Moly

For more information, visit www.benrehder.com.

Made in the USA
Columbia, SC
15 September 2023

22868758R00128